OUTSIDE
THE LIGHT

Ags Connolly

© 2024

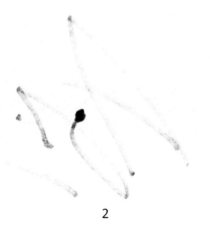

2

PART ONE

1

AS MIKE ROWE OPENED his eyes, something flitted across his vision in the darkness. He first thought it might have been an animal, or a person. Or that it might also have been nothing. Rowe was in his car, parked on a grass verge on a rural back road in the pitch black. It wasn't an unfamiliar environment to him, and he knew things moved in the dark all the time.

The confluence of thoughts appeared as his brain stirred and finally registered that it was the ringing of his phone that had woken him up.

Rowe reached over and picked up the handset from the passenger seat. The caller's name appeared as Stanwell, as in Assistant Chief Constable Nicholas Stanwell. At a more reasonable time of day, Rowe would likely have let the call ring out, possibly even considered blocking the contact altogether. But the timing of the call and the nagging urgency of its ringing in the silent blackness struck him differently. He answered.

'Rowe.'

'Mike? It's Nick Stanwell.'

'I know, Nick. What's the problem?'

He was working on the assumption that any call at 4:30am was unlikely to be good news.

'Sorry to disturb you at this hour, Mike. No problem exactly. Something has come up overnight that, while not ideal by any means, may present an opportunity for a satisfactory conclusion to, er, the current situation for us all.'

Rowe was quiet for a moment before he responded.

'Nick, I just want my papers signed now. I'm not looking for a solution or a compromise.'

'Understood. This is rather unique however, and I wouldn't be bringing it to you if I thought it was a waste of time.'

Rowe was quiet again. It wasn't the call he had been waiting for. In truth, he had only answered it because Stanwell was one of the few work-related figures he could still tolerate. He was regretting having done so and starting to consider how rude it might be to simply hang up. Stanwell broke the silence.

'A few hours ago, someone died in a custody cell at Fenwood of what appears to be natural causes. An unfortunate event certainly but relatively straightforward from our point of view. The deceased was not local but was a British citizen. As I'm sure you know, we will need to complete the basics before handing it over to the inquest.'

Rowe remained silent.

'Chief Superintendent Carne would like you to take charge of our end, liaise with the coroner and hand things over when you deem it appropriate. Once that's done, she will sign off on your resignation.'

Rowe was gazing through his windscreen, just able to discern the silhouette of either a bird or a bat skipping between trees. He realised that whichever it was, it had probably been what caught his eye when he awoke, and the abruptness of the phone call out of the silence had allowed his mind to play tricks on him. He knew that could happen too.

'Mike,' Stanwell went on, 'I know you're not her biggest fan presently, but DCS Carne sees this as a chance to resolve things after the sad business with Hannah Crockett. A positive note for your policing career to end on whilst she appears benevolent to the wider world, of course. I must say I don't think it's the worst idea I've heard. In the circumstances, I can't conceive of a more favourable end to the stand-off between you two.'

A few more seconds of silence passed before Rowe spoke.

'Okay, Nick. I only answered because it was you. I'm not interested, but thanks I suppo-'

'There's something else you should know.' Stanwell cut across him sharply but calmly. The tone of his voice had changed. 'Laura is there.'

Rowe heard it as he was moving the phone away from his ear to end the call. He didn't say anything as he brought it back but knew Stanwell would be sure of his attention. When he did speak, he found his own tone had changed and almost certainly betrayed his thoughts.

'Great. She can handle it then.'

'You misunderstand me, Mike. She was at Fenwood last night as a visiting officer. She is technically a witness.'

The bird, as Rowe had become sure it was, had begun chattering to its friends in the still-dark morning. The idea of further sleep had quickly become absurd.

'You should've told me that first' he said.

It was Stanwell's turn to be silent.

7

'Who's at the scene?' Rowe surprised himself with the question.

'DC Meredith is doing the preliminaries and awaiting the arrival of the senior officer.'

'I'll be there.'

ROWE TOSSED THE PHONE back into the passenger seat and turned on the car's interior light. He gave his unshaven visage a brief once-over in the mirror. Lately he'd been sleeping in the car more nights than not, finding it preferable to sleeping in a flat that hadn't felt like home for some time. It was impossible to deny that his face was showing it.

The car itself was a black 1986 Rover Vitesse. It had a comfortable, unmistakably old school interior with plush seats and the kind of walnut embellishments that had fallen out of favour around the time the world wide web was invented, or possibly earlier. Rowe had picked it up at a bargain price a few years before, shocked by how low its mileage still was and the generally favourable condition the car was apparently still in. It was only later that he was alerted to the fact that these models had been used by the British police in the 80s and early 90s. That information came mostly from people who believed his purchase to be a display of either nostalgia or irony.

Rowe's only addition to the vehicle up to that point had been a CD player, into which he mostly inserted albums by obscure songwriters who were either from Texas or sounded like they should be. Otherwise, the car was virtually in its original state, which meant it could be viewed as either impressively retro or embarrassingly outdated depending on the onlooker's perspective. Rowe had been known to talk up the

Vitesse's longevity when in sympathetic company, but the fact was its undercarriage was in the process of rusting irretrievably and its past two – or possibly three, when he thought about it – MOT certificates had been granted via a no-questions-asked connection with a friend's regular mechanic.

In the preceding few weeks, Rowe had made a habit of parking the Vitesse up on quiet back roads within walking distance of a different rural pub each night. He'd walk to the pub, take a seat in the corner of the bar where possible and stay there amid the warm, dimly lit bustle until closing. He never drank a huge amount – at thirty-seven he probably drank less than half the amount he had a decade earlier. He hadn't been what he would call an alcoholic, but he often thought of a quote he'd once read in an interview with an ageing rocker who certainly had been: something about it taking the guy ten years and about £50,000 to realise it was the pub he liked and not the drink. Rowe liked the quote, but he also knew the drink wasn't totally redundant to him. He wasn't ready to do without it entirely.

Rowe certainly liked the pubs though. He liked their British tradition as community living rooms and the generally convivial, neutral environment they provided. The slow demise of the old school boozer versus the rise of the gastropub was sad in its own way, he thought, but he found it also had the effect of creating a smaller, quasi-exclusive club of drinkers – particularly in country pubs. Sometimes he found that aspect of his country's culture was misunderstood, whereas in Ireland – the country of his parents – it was celebrated. He thought it suited him in any case.

Rowe got out of the car and stretched as the darkness was beginning to retreat. Often, he slept with the driver's seat reclined but the previous night simply folding his arms and closing his eyes had been enough. He'd grown used to the cold and had learned to sleep in all sorts of places and positions over the years, but that didn't stop his body seizing up. Maybe he should keep a blanket in the Vitesse. A well-built six foot tall but certainly not a giant by modern standards, his body nonetheless always craved freedom after a night in the car.

Rowe wearily tousled his hair. He would ordinarily head home for a shower and breakfast, but on that morning he would take advantage of the fact that people mostly expected dark, wavy, Irish hair to be haphazardly presented. The one thing he would need though was coffee, and soon.

He stretched a final time and got back in, starting the old Vitesse's engine.

Two months earlier, Detective Inspector Mike Rowe began a period of paid leave from Oxford police – leave tagged with the prefixes 'gardening' or 'compassionate' depending on who you spoke to.

Prior to that leave, Rowe had been working on the alleged suicide of a fellow officer, PC Hannah Crockett – a case that was intended to represent his last activity as a member of the police service. His appetite for the work had long since disappeared if it had ever really existed at all.

Rowe's father, Brian, had carved a sterling career in the service. A combination of what Rowe supposed was restlessness, a lack of other options, pride and a culmination of the eternal father-son struggle had led him to attempt to follow the same path. As the years had passed though, he could honestly say he had never really enjoyed a second of it. He had hoped his experience would improve as he progressed through the ranks and assumed more responsibility – and thus, more autonomy – but if anything, he had gradually concluded that the opposite was the case.

It may have been that integrity was a more prevalent characteristic during his father's time in the service, but it was not something Rowe had encountered very often himself in the police. In fact, those of robotic mind and lacking in conscience within the ranks seemed to him to increase in number by the day. Even the 'good' ones who had joined the service for the 'right' reasons appeared to him to be guilty of a lack of self-awareness at best.

Naturally, these views and Rowe's occasional expressions of them, privately or publicly, did not sit well with either his peers or superiors. Detective Chief Superintendent Judith Carne in particular was keen to expedite Rowe's resignation, which he had submitted just prior to Hannah Crockett's death and after a lengthy self-exploration. Brian Rowe's name still being sacrosanct within the walls of the Oxford Police building, Carne was keen for the resignation of a legend's son to be as seamless as possible and had assigned Crockett's apparently straightforward suicide to him in what she evidently considered to be a show of magnanimity.

The case, though, was not straightforward. At least not to Rowe. Although all the physical and circumstantial evidence was consistent with the 24-year-old PC having hanged herself in the living room of her Fenwood flat, Rowe was more interested in the fact that Crockett had twice attempted to call Detective Chief Inspector Neil Vickers somewhere around her estimated time of death.

Vickers was someone Rowe had never liked and actively avoided interacting with, a task made more difficult by the fact that the DCI was essentially his boss and acted as a kind of assistant-cum-lapdog to Carne. As part of his investigation, Rowe had requested phone records for both Crockett and Vickers as well as a formal interview with Vickers, who could not provide proof of his whereabouts on the night of the death. Carne had denied these requests outright and swiftly assigned the case elsewhere so that it could be formally closed as a suicide, which chimed with the coroner's report.

Rowe's response to Carne had been bitter and angry, bordering on explosive. But before further action or recriminations were possible, another incident occurred which resulted in Rowe's paid leave and, ultimately, changed the complexion of his future.

AT THE TIME OF the investigation into Hannah Crockett's suicide, Rowe had been in a relationship with a colleague, Detective Sergeant Laura Cross, for almost two years. To his mind, meeting Laura on the job had been the only bright spot of an otherwise deeply disenchanting period of his life.

They had worked together a lot at first and even partnered in CID for a while, but as their relationship endured, they agreed, and endeavoured to work together less. The desire not to risk burning out what had grown between them was just another motivation for Rowe to leave his place of work.

As negative as he was towards his occupational surroundings generally, Rowe considered the part of his life that Laura inhabited to be the most intensely positive thing he'd ever known. The sheer weight of that positivity contrasted sharply with a road travelled that had otherwise been littered with disappointment and obstruction. The power of it scarcely seemed real at times, something which, if he were being truthful, frightened him.

Laura Cross was tall, striking and of a tough but reserved nature. She was five years younger than Rowe and, like him, had grown up in the Fenwood area, herself the daughter of a policeman. Her hair was a thick, dark mane, and her eyes gave away very little to those not accustomed to reading them. Rowe knew she didn't exactly share his distaste for the job, but she had tried to understand it and had chosen not to stand in the way of his desire to leave. In many ways they were each other's counterpart – dark, resolute, introverted and, at times, deceptively insecure. A lot of unspoken understanding could pass between them, but equally, both had built walls the other was unable to scale.

On the morning after his as-yet-unresolved altercation with Carne over the Crockett case, Rowe was woken in his studio flat by a call from Neil Vickers who was calling on behalf of the DCS. He informed Rowe that, in the early hours of the morning, Laura had been the victim of an assault and attempted kidnap outside her home. She had not been able to identify the masked assailant responsible and anything that might be used to trace the attacker's vehicle had apparently been strategically disguised. There was no apparent motive. Apart from a few bruises Laura was mostly physically unharmed afterwards, which Rowe was relieved to find when he had been to see her later that morning. However, the incident had a psychological effect on her that troubled Rowe. And the fact she had not called him after it happened was equally concerning to him.

Carne had taken the opportunity to place both Laura Cross and Rowe on compassionate leave (although some debated how 'compassionate' Rowe's was). Elsewhere, the Hannah Crockett case was quietly closed as a suicide, a footnote Rowe was no longer as concerned about as he previously might have been.

Over the next two months, Laura had returned to work relatively quickly but gradually reduced her contact with Rowe. She no longer visited his flat, which was the main reason he was spending less time there than ever. She had told him she needed time and space to deal with her thoughts after the incident. At first Rowe attempted to maintain daily contact with her to convey his love and support, but it soon became clear to him, perhaps only intuitively, that it was not what Laura wanted. Eventually he started limiting his check-ins to the occasional text message, deciding that giving her space was the best course of action. Increasingly these went unanswered.

Rowe didn't think at first that he and Laura were drifting apart. Instead, he wanted to believe that the ramifications from Laura's attack were entirely the reason for the shifting sands. He increasingly sensed a distancing as time went by though, and just two weeks earlier had been told by one of his few remaining friends in the service that Laura had been seen with someone else. Before hearing that news, Rowe had arrived at Laura's flat a couple of times in the hope of reopening communication but had found her to be out when he wouldn't usually expect her to be.

Rowe hadn't seen or been in contact with Laura for several weeks and the news from his friend had pushed him back into his shell, he knew. The apparent unravelling of the most positive thing in his life had contributed to the deterioration of his mental state and left him leaning on a crutch that manifested itself as the nightly lone pub treks. He felt isolated and empty most of the time – which was no surprise, as all he was doing was hiding.

As he eased the Vitesse off the muddy verge it had been resting on, Rowe had the idea that Carne must be aware of his mental state to some degree. She was certainly aware of his desire simply to be granted his resignation as he had confirmed it by letter a few weeks earlier, receiving no response. It begged the question of why she was so intent on assigning him to 'one last case' again, considering how the previous one had gone even before the attack on Laura had happened. It didn't make sense to him, and he suspected Carne would at the very least have contingencies in place to ensure he didn't take the new case in a direction that she would find disagreeable.

In his present frame of mind, Rowe had no interest in the case or any other. If it weren't for Laura being involved, he wouldn't be going anywhere near it, and he knew it. As he headed east towards Fenwood, bleary-eyed on the silent back roads, he thought of all the things he wanted to say to her and whether he could really say any of them. Perhaps things would become clearer in his mind when he saw her.

Perhaps just seeing her would be enough.

4

HE EMERGED FROM THE single tracks and back roads, almost creeping up on the town from its northwest edge and skirting one of the newer housing estates that had been tacked on in the name of progress at some point in the last twenty years. Rowe preferred the back roads and villages to the suburbs and the town, despite living his entire life in Fenwood. The space helped him to think.

A Terry Allen CD, *Lubbock On Everything*, played on the car stereo at what Rowe deemed a reasonable volume for the hour. Despite his distaste for the associations made with country music – which he professed not to like – Rowe had a long-held fascination with Texas and the dustier corners of North America in general. The songwriters from those places spoke to him most, as did the authors of western fiction, of which he hankered to be one.

One of the prime underlying reasons for his resigning from the police was that he wanted the time to complete his first novel. Or start it, to be more precise, as he had never completed a first chapter he was remotely satisfied with. That was something Rowe blamed on the time constraints and stresses of his job, regardless of the fact his writing efforts had been in similar stasis since his late teens.

Rowe's fixation on the American west had been a source of mirth among some of his colleagues, as had his inability to progress with his writing. He had still never actually crossed the Atlantic or seen any of the places he was attempting to write about. That was a fact that nagged at him to a point, but he didn't see it as being as vital to what he wanted to achieve as others seemed to. Still, most saw his writing ambitions as a waste of time – a pipe dream.

He was dressed today as he normally was – a light brown durable workers' jacket with fleece lining, dark and hard-wearing jeans and working boots. He found these things comfortable and useful, but some saw them as further evidence of his attempting to Americanise himself. Rowe had never cared what others thought.

After stopping to buy a self-service coffee at the first petrol station he found that was open, Rowe rolled the Vitesse through the industrial end of Fenwood at almost 5:30am. Grounds Way had been built wide to accommodate lorries turning in and out of the labyrinthian avenues situated at regular intervals on either side of it, but at that time of the morning traffic of any type was virtually non-existent.

The right turn into the unnamed cul-de-sac that held Fenwood police station was fairly deep into the industrial zone, but not as closely connected to the town centre as one might expect an important public amenity to be. Filling much of the side of the road opposite the turning were empty commercial units that it had once been planned would create a separate shopping area and thus spread people and traffic further out from the claustrophobic town centre. A not unusual story of an English market town trying to find a solution to a new volume of inhabitants and new modes of transport it was never built for.

Rowe slowed and made the turning into the cul-de-sac. The rectangular station building sat on the left corner of that road and Grounds Way, with the front entrance to the public reception desk on one of the short ends of the oblong in the cul-de-sac, making it not immediately obvious what the building was if you were driving past and didn't already know. Rowe knew the building well from the outside, and the inside up to a point, although he had never worked within it on any consistent basis and hadn't set foot in the place at all for several years.

An austere, three-storey, beige brick structure from the mid-1980s, the station was built to replace its original, charmingly inadequate forerunner in the centre of town which in more recent times served as the private office of an accountancy firm. The newer and much larger edition was seen as a progressive move for the town combined with the new retail units, which it was hoped at the time would eventually serve to expand the centre of Fenwood. Sadly, both latterly represented a dismally failed strategy and, with all the shop units closed, the station was one of the increasing number nationally that were being phased out.

The station was at that point open only three days a week – Monday, Tuesday and Wednesday – and operated only on the ground floor. The upper two that had previously served chiefly as office space had long since been given over to storage of either surplus or obsolete equipment from other stations and departments in the county. These items had probably been deemed entirely useless for some time but would likely only be removed when the building was demolished in the next few years, which it inevitably would be. Rowe contemplated that on his arrival, along with the idea that the station could be deemed unlucky to have a cell death on its record, considering the lack of activity the place saw at that stage of its existence.

Whilst it was no surprise that town in general was quiet at that hour, Rowe was somewhat confused by the absence of any obvious police presence outside the building as he came to a stop near the front entrance. An unmarked car was parked on the road in front of the main door, straddling the double yellow lines on the road but with no one inside it. A light was on immediately beyond the glass doors of the station but nothing and no one was visible inside. There were no officers guarding the door and nothing to suggest anything of interest had happened in the building recently. The station was not due to be open on that day – Thursday – and Rowe could maybe understand not wanting to draw attention to the place, but he had been led to believe it was the scene of a death, nonetheless. He thought the building should have been essentially locked down and cordoned off, possibly even the entire street seeing as it was a dead end in which no other businesses operated. As the streets got busier, it was vital things were handled correctly. He wondered whether those inside the station were waiting for him as the officer in charge to make a call on it, and why common sense so often seemed an alien concept these days.

Rowe also wondered who the unmarked car belonged to. It was a dark-coloured police issue Audi A6, certainly at the more sought-after end of the unmarked range. Not the sort of vehicle that would be entrusted to the lower ranks or possibly anyone that Rowe would usually consort with at all. Detective Constable Joanne Meredith was apparently inside – according to what Stanwell had said – but Rowe did not think it was likely she had arrived in one of these. Not at all in fact. He mused that it could possibly belong to the coroner before deciding that was unlikely too. Rowe realised that his speculation only served to underline how little he actually knew about the scene he had arrived at.

He moved further on down the road, beyond the Audi and parked on double yellows himself. Ultimately, he wasn't interested in whose car was whose and whether anyone had bothered securing the scene. On the journey over, Rowe had decided he wasn't going to get involved in the cell death after all. His sole priority was seeing Laura and talking to her. He had no interest in dancing to Carne's tune – she would get fed up and accept his resignation sooner or later. It didn't matter.

He got out of the car and looked up at the building. Something told him that going into the place when he was trying to leave what it represented behind was a bad idea. But the fact Laura was in there gave him no choice. And he was used to living with bad ideas.

5

IN PARKING WHERE HE had, the Vitesse was positioned on the other side of the open gate to the station's car park. Walking through the car park, Rowe saw two patrol cars and a riot van lined up in designated bays with a couple of private cars on the opposite side of the rectangular area, which could hold maybe nine vehicles at a stretch. He presumed one of the private cars belonged to Meredith. Laura's blue Volkswagen Golf, which he knew she still drove, wasn't visible anywhere.

In between the two patrol cars was a gap filled by both a set of external fire escape stairs that served the higher floors as well as providing access to the roof and by a staff access door that stood slightly ajar. Rowe knew the door led to the heart of the ground floor including the interview rooms and custody suite. It was no surprise to him that it, too, was unguarded.

Reaching the open door, he nudged it further open and stepped in. He was in a corridor with another door at its far end which required a key card to access – or usually would if it hadn't also been standing ajar. There were key card doors on each side of the corridor that opened into other rooms, but these doors were both shut. The corridor was representative of much of the rest of the building with its tired grey decor and uninviting smell. A mood of grim resignation somehow hung in the air, like an employee who hadn't had a pay rise in a decade and was being rewarded with redundancy. It was chilly, and Rowe didn't believe that was simply because the door had been left open. The station felt like an abandoned building, which by his reckoning was essentially what it was at that point.

He walked ahead to the second open door and, nearing it, heard voices coming from the direction of the custody suite, which he knew to be beyond the door and to the right. Stepping through and turning right, Rowe saw the distinctive figure of Joanne Meredith standing at the doorway of the suite. She was talking to someone inside who was hidden from Rowe's view. Meredith seemed to clock his approach out of the corner of her eye and turned to face him, looking very slightly flustered, Rowe thought.

'Joanne.'

Rowe used her first name, fearing ranks or surnames might imply that he was interested in being involved in the case, which he wasn't. Meredith was a young DC in her twenties who was of the geekier and more modern stripe of officer, extremely earnest about doing as instructed and conscientious about procedure. Her hair was naturally a dark red and she was short and wide at the hip with robust-looking arms that filled her suit jacket. Rowe thought she was the kind of person that made Body Mass Index calculations redundant as she was exactly the size and weight she was meant to be. Evidently, that hadn't stopped some unkind mockery from her colleagues, which possibly fed into the permanently stern look on her face and the hair she tied back so severely in an apparent effort to be taken seriously.

'Detective Inspector. Glad you could make it.' The comment came out straight, but Rowe detected muted sarcasm and found it didn't bother him.

'Looks like either I've missed the party, or it hasn't got going yet,' he said. 'Where's Laura Cross?'

Meredith eyed him for a split second through her clear-rimmed glasses before answering, as if he were jumping ahead.

'DS Cross was in a meeting room and I'm not aware of her having left.'

Rowe briefly juggled the possible inferences and implications of her wording. Meredith continued before he could respond.

'I haven't spoken to her, but I have taken preliminary statements from others present at the time of the incident. Have you been given the details? If not, I should probably fill you in before you speak to anyone.'

These last few words were delivered with an extra importance, which Rowe took as an attempt at a warning. What of, he had no idea. He felt inclined to go around opening doors until he found Laura. But something about Meredith's curious manner, the lack of basic procedure, the unusual car outside and the as-yet-undisclosed activity in the custody suite held him back. He decided it might be worth at least finding out what was going on.

'Okay,' he said.

'Well,' Meredith flipped the pages of a notepad that had appeared in her hand. 'The deceased is a male, 31 years old, identified by his driving licence as James Michael Burnell of an address in Somerset. He was brought in at around 1am after reports of drunken disorder in the centre of town. According to the officers who brought him in, he was unable to communicate coherently so was placed in a custody cell with the intention of release when he'd sobered up. The custody sergeant checked on his condition every fifteen minutes until 2:30am when he appeared unresponsive. An ambulance was called but he was pronounced dead at around 3:00am. There is no official word yet, but the death appears to be from natural causes.'

'This happened three hours ago? When did you get here?'

'Uh, around 3:30am, guv.'

She dropped her gaze as she said it. Rowe hadn't been contacted until an hour later, which he presumed meant much debate and political wrangling had occurred in the interim. He knew that would've been out of Meredith's hands, but it remained an awkward fact, nonetheless. It also raised some other questions.

'Stanwell said something about the coroner. Is the body still here after all this time?'

'Yes. I believe there was an, uh, issue with the coroner's availability. And they would have needed you to be here before they took the body in any case, guv.'

Rowe ignored the undisguised barb.

'What was Laura doing here?'

'A far as I have been able to ascertain, DS Cross was visiting with another officer to discuss a case.'

'Who else was here? It must have been quiet at that time.'

Meredith checked her notepad and Rowe got the feeling it was to buy time.

'The custody sergeant, obviously. The two officers who brought Burnell in. Plus one other.'

'Steve Symonds?'

Rowe asked it quickly enough that Meredith couldn't hide her surprise.

'Uh…yes, DS Symonds was the other officer present, guv.'

At that moment, the person Meredith had been talking to when Rowe arrived peered around the doorway at them. It struck Rowe that Meredith was effectively blocking his access to the custody suite, and the face that regarded him from it extended no more of an invitation. It belonged to an apparently very tall and slender black man with a shaved head, who might have been in his mid-fifties, wearing a tailored black suit and a humourless expression. Rowe felt there was an unsettling air about the man which went beyond his intimidatory size and the glare of superiority.

'Detective Inspector Rowe,' Meredith said to fill the silence, 'this is Commander Grantley. He leads a Scotland Yard task force that have the deceased's name flagged as part of another investigation.'

Yard. That one word explained almost everything in Rowe's mind. The cloak and dagger lack of procedure, the car, the in-house politicking that delayed things…and his being used as a puppet to sign off on whatever convoluted situation lay within the custody suite, no doubt. In his head he kicked himself for not realising sooner.

Rowe stepped to his left in order to see around Meredith and past Grantley into the custody suite. The wiry Commander was blocking much of the view, but Rowe could still see two minions behind him, both as apparently joyless as their boss. They stared at Rowe but didn't acknowledge him. The demeanour of the trio gave the distinct impression that they were tolerating Rowe's presence out of professional courtesy, but the courtesy was finite.

Rowe thought his instincts had been correct: going there had been a bad idea. He had voluntarily walked into a scene which was not, and was never likely to be, under his control and he would be forced to deal with the consequences of that. But as much as Rowe wanted to wash his hands of it, he had to admit his curiosity was piqued.

Flagged as part of another investigation. While such an occurrence wasn't totally unheard of, it would normally be something followed up in the days after an incident – and then probably over the phone or by e-mail. Burnell wasn't going anywhere. Yet a car had been dispatched from the Yard in the small hours of the morning and was on scene well before Rowe had arrived. Possibly before he'd even been contacted.

'The deceased is in cell number two.'

Grantley broadcast this information in a booming yet somehow hollow voice to no one in particular. Rowe placed the accent as South London but with an attempt to hide its origins. He found many senior officers spoke that way.

Rowe took the invitation to enter the custody suite, thinking it might be the only way he would ever know exactly what Carne had tried to drop him into there. He walked past Grantley and turned left in front of the two minions, who were arranged in front of the custody desk. The three cells were on the other side of a small gap, with two directly in front and one opposite and to the right. The door of the cell diagonally opposite him was open, propped back against the cell wall with a weight to prevent it closing.

He stood in the doorway and surveyed the space. The cell was a square about eight feet by eight feet, with a bench, topped by a thin rubber mattress, against the far wall. A toilet unit stood exposed next to it, with a basin built into the opposite wall, to the right of the door. At the top of the back wall a small, barred window let in a token amount of the early signs of daylight.

Rowe didn't step inside, although it was clear that others had done so from the multiple footprints visible on the otherwise bare, off-white floor that chimed with the grey-blue walls. Meredith had said the ambulance crew had been there. The dead man lay on the mattress on the bench. He was on his side, facing the wall and wrapped tightly in a much-washed orange blanket that Rowe presumed had been on the mattress.

Sticking out from the blanket at one end were black trainers and at the other end was sandy blonde hair of medium length. Burnell appeared to be of approximately average height or below, as far as could be told from his position.

'Can I go in?'

Rowe asked the question without looking round.

'Yes, but don't touch anything.'

Grantley had silently approached, and Rowe could feel him hovering behind like a disapproving butler. He took one step inside and a glance around was enough to tell him there was nothing else in the cell. The toilet and basin were empty, and the walls and floor showed no obvious marks besides the footprints on the latter. He felt Grantley's eyes watching his every move and was then aware of the presence of the two minions at the door also. One was basically a smaller, younger version of Grantley, possibly someone who aspired to be like him. The other was far more brutish, with a wide, bulky frame – not all of it muscle – and close-cropped hair. Rowe thought the second man resembled a rugby player he'd seen on TV once, possibly French. He also thought the man looked like it had taken intensive training simply to stop him chewing on the furniture, let alone join a specialist team in the Met.

All three men were wearing guns under their jackets. Rowe had seen it when he first walked past them into the suite. There were certain specialist teams from Scotland Yard who were licenced to carry firearms, but they were few and far between. He felt it was yet another very odd and disquieting detail to add to the morning's events.

Rowe stepped across to the body and leaned over it. Burnell's face was young-looking. His mouth was open. If he had drooled on the mattress it had dried. The man could still have been asleep if it wasn't for the unmistakeable mask of death he wore. Rowe had seen enough.

'The coroner will be here for the body shortly,' Grantley announced from the doorway.

'Has the scene been fully cleared?' Rowe asked.

Grantley glowered but before he could respond, Meredith piped up from where she had joined the throng.

'There was full CCTV coverage, guv. Everything is recorded.'

'That's not what I asked.' Rowe paused and looked back at Grantley. 'What room is Laura Cross in?'

'She has been allowed to leave.'

'Why?'

Rowe glanced at Meredith who looked away and shifted uncomfortably.

'DS Cross had no pertinent information. Most of those present have now given statements and been excused.'

Grantley's expression and body language suggested the conversation and Rowe's tour of the scene were finished. Rowe had almost decided he was probably okay with that considering the way things were going, but Grantley's final sentence gave rise to another thought.

'Is Steve Symonds still here?'

6

ROWE DIDN'T BOTHER TO knock as he entered the interview room, which was in a block of four positioned on the other side of the station closer to the front entrance. It was a square, deliberately basic room with a table and two chairs huddled against the left wall. Detective Sergeant Steve Symonds, in uniform, sat on the far side of the table, facing the door.

Symonds was around thirty years old, taller than Rowe, with blonde hair and athletically built. He had only been in the job for a few years, but Rowe was aware that he had risen quickly in terms of assuming responsibility, ensuring he became part of the in-crowd where and when required. Symonds had worked almost exclusively out of Fenwood until the reduction in its operating hours, whereafter he'd been shifted around local stations depending on requirements, but he remained one of the few officers with a regular attachment to Fenwood. Rowe did not have any specific history with the younger man, other than knowing that Symonds was the type of officer he'd usually prefer to be a million miles from if he had a choice.

But at that moment there might have been something more specific: Steve Symonds was the man Laura had been seen with two weeks earlier, and the previous night the two of them had been present in the same, sparsely populated station in the middle of the night where someone had died. Rowe didn't like any single part of that equation.

As Rowe stepped in, Symonds had his arms folded and looked tense. For the briefest of moments Rowe thought he saw fear in the eyes of the DS, but it was hard to tell. The expression changed from surprise to something approaching contempt just as quickly. It occurred to Rowe that Symonds must have been in the room for some time. He shut the door behind him.

'Why did Laura Cross come here last night?'

'Why do you think?' Symonds retorted. A dark but apparently tired smirk appeared on his face.

Before the smirk had faded, Rowe took two fast steps, reached down and grabbed Symonds by the collar with his left hand. That kept his right free which he used to punch the man hard in the left side of his face. Symonds reeled in his chair and struggled to push Rowe off him as his face turned red from the blow.

'You fucking idiot!" Symonds hissed. "There's a camera in here!"

By then, Rowe had a two-handed grip on him then and Symonds was offering resistance, if not as much as Rowe might have anticipated.

'What happened here last night, Steve? This scene is a fuck up. And I'm guessing by the fact you're the only one still here that you're part of that fuck up."

Symonds didn't respond. He looked like he was trying to regain his composure. Rowe moved closer to the man's face.

'Start talking or the next one won't be a friendly love tap.'

Symonds eventually spoke in a low voice, which was remarkably controlled for someone who had just been punched in the face.

'Fuck off, Rowe. You're a miserable pisshead who's scared of the job. Laura's finally got you sussed. That's why you don't know where she is – why you never know.'

As Symonds spoke the last two words, there was a knock on the interview room door. It took a moment or two for Rowe to register the two things separately and, just as he did, the door opened. Assistant Chief Constable Nicholas Stanwell took a step into the room.

Stanwell surveyed the tableau before him and frowned with the avuncular style that accompanied most things he did. His silver hair, distinguished features and old-school upright posture were all part of the humble gravitas he generally radiated.

'Ah, Mike. Glad I found you.' Stanwell said it with his standard diplomacy, politely choosing not to acknowledge the grip the two men at the table still had on each other. 'Perhaps we should have a chat in private?'

Rowe paused momentarily before letting go of Symonds. He straightened himself up, turned his back on his simmering opponent and walked out of the room. He heard Stanwell shut the door and follow him.

They walked out of the staff access door which Rowe had first entered through and turned left. At the end of the car park was a gate through to a compact courtyard which housed a rusting bike shed but was mostly used by any smokers that worked in the building. There was a bucket on the ground that was peppered with ancient cigarette butts. As they came through the gate, Rowe turned and looked at Stanwell, whose face still showed the trace of a frown.

'Look Nick, I don't know what's going on here,' Rowe said. 'Laura's gone. No real procedure has been followed and this team from the Yard are clearly in charge. I'm not having any part of it.'

'I'm sorry, Mike,' Stanwell sighed. 'It seems things are different from the brief I was given. Commander Grantley's Special Deployment Unit are taking the lead on this one. They apparently released DS Cross because she was not an eyewitness and therefore had no useful information. And they have decided to keep personnel and regular procedure to a minimum while they continue with their associated enquiries.'

Stanwell cleared his throat as a form of punctuation.

'The good news is there is virtually nothing that you need to do on this one bar signing it over to Commander Grantley's team from a local perspective. DC Meredith has all the information we require at this point – it is unambiguous stuff. There will be a routine coroner's inquest of course, but essentially Scotland Yard can take it from here.'

Rowe stared at him.

'I'm not signing anything over. This isn't my case.'

Stanwell glanced back over his shoulder at the sound of a shoe scuffing on tarmac and seemed to acknowledge someone on the other side of the gate. Rowe adjusted his view and saw the spidery figure of Detective Chief Inspector Neil Vickers looking back at him. Vickers was hovering as if he were trying to find the way into the building, even though it was evident he was eavesdropping on their conversation. He nodded in a greeting which Rowe ignored.

'DCI Vickers advised me of the change in circumstances a short while ago, hence my making the trip down here to let you know' said Stanwell as he turned back to Rowe. 'After our phone conversation this morning I spoke to Chief Superintendent Carne and had you confirmed as the local lead for this matter. I regret that things aren't quite as we had originally thought, Mike. But in the long run this makes our lives easier I think.'

Rowe didn't say anything at first. He looked over at Vickers, who was still hanging around by the gate, then back at Stanwell.

'How does everyone know this thing is so straightforward?' he asked.

Vickers took a step forward impatiently, as if ready to provide a patronising answer, but was then joined on his side of the gate by Meredith, who looked mildly exasperated.

'As I said, guv, the whole thing is on CCTV. Start to finish.'

7

THEY SAT IN A SMALL back office situated directly behind the reception area and the public-facing front desk. There were two monitors on a desk plus a laptop, which Meredith was sitting in front of, while Rowe perched to her left on a threadbare swivel chair. Stanwell and Vickers were not with them – Rowe presumed they were standing awkwardly with Grantley and his bag men somewhere, awaiting the arrival of the coroner.

It hadn't been made clear why Vickers had turned up, but Rowe was working on the assumption that it was a double whammy of keeping an eye on him while sucking up to officers from the Yard. The DCI hadn't looked impressed at Rowe's request to see the CCTV footage, but as the coroner was yet to arrive Stanwell had suggested it was a good use of his time.

Rowe was in no doubt that both Vickers and Carne had known the Special Deployment Unit (and he wondered what the hell that even meant) would be in charge of the cell death, and that was why they had been so keen for him to be the 'local lead' on it. In his bosses' eyes, it would limit his opportunity to embarrass them. He had some sympathy for Stanwell, however, who had clearly seen the case as an amicable resolution to Rowe's feud with Carne, or as close as they were likely to get. The old man had a propensity to be too nice in these situations and had possibly been downright naïve in thinking anything would be allowed to happen on

Rowe's terms. Nonetheless, Rowe had known Stanwell for a very long time and admired the integrity he had shown in arriving at the scene to act as a mediator at least.

The way in which Grantley and his team had assumed control of the entire case still irked Rowe. Officers with potentially key information had already left the building and it was clear Meredith had only been allowed to cover the extreme basics before Rowe arrived. And when he had, he'd been treated like a competition winner whose prize was a day out to visit a dead body. On the topic of the body, for reasons yet to be satisfactorily explained, it had by that point been in the cell for almost four hours. Rowe reflected that the frustration from all these things was part of the reason he had gone after Symonds the way he had. Or perhaps it was just that he just didn't like Symonds.

It was approaching 6:30am as Meredith brought up the CCTV feed from the early morning hours on the laptop. In contrast to most of the other contents of the building, the equipment they were using seemed very new, practically state of the art in fact. Rowe knew virtually nothing about that type of thing and was grateful that Meredith seemed at home with it.

'Ok, this is the custody suite main camera at 12:38am, when Burnell was first brought into the station,' Meredith said as she clicked the mouse a few times and images appeared on both monitors. One monitor showed the various cameras available in grid form, and the other was a full screen view of the custody desk in colour.

Burnell was seen from the back, flanked by two uniform officers – a man and a woman – seemingly keeping him upright. The camera perspective was from above the door to the custody suite and showed a frontal view of the custody sergeant, a woman who looked to be in her forties with bleach-blonde hair that was tied back. Meredith clicked the mouse again and a second angle appeared, one from the wall adjacent to the door, showing a side view of the protagonists and the mini gangway through to the cells beyond them.

At Rowe's request, Meredith scanned through Burnell being processed. As Burnell was apparently unable to communicate sufficiently, they saw a high-speed version of one of the officers fishing the driving licence from his wallet and the custody sergeant filling out paperwork. Rowe noticed that along with the usual pocket items and belt, Burnell's coat was confiscated, which was irregular. People in holding cells were normally allowed to keep coats and jackets, especially at colder times of year. The coat was a black padded affair with distinctive green and red diamonds on the back, which reminded Rowe of the kind of thing he and his friends wore as kids in the 80s and early 90s.

Rowe didn't ask Meredith for any names of those on the screens, he simply watched the monitors wordlessly. Meredith set the footage to normal playing speed again as Burnell was led to his cell. As she did so, she deftly toggled between the second camera angle they had seen and two new ones.

The first of these two cameras was positioned at the left end of the row of cells and showed the doors to all three with Burnell's cell – cell 2 – being the furthest away on the left of the shot. At the far end, directly facing that camera, was another door which clearly did not belong to a cell. Rowe knew from his previous involvement with Fenwood that the door led to a cupboard containing cleaning products and other assorted practical items intended for keeping the cells at an acceptable level of cleanliness. He presumed it still did.

The second of the new angles was from a camera located directly above the door of cell 3. That camera was focused down on the door of cell 2 opposite. It seemed all the cells had an individual camera focused on their respective doors, although not all were live in that instance.

From these two new perspectives they saw Burnell helped to the door – which the custody sergeant unlocked – then helped inside. From the door camera they saw him being rested on the bench-cum-bed and the orange blanket wrapped around him by the custody sergeant. It seemed an unusual level of care and another small detail that Rowe found slightly odd. The officers then withdrew, and the door was closed and locked.

Without prompting, Meredith then fast forwarded through the next ninety minutes or so, which meant they could still see the custody sergeant performing her checks through the hatch on the cell door every fifteen minutes, albeit in fast motion. Meredith let the footage play again at around the 2:30am mark, when it was obvious the custody sergeant had gone back to the cell twice in quick succession.

'The custody sergeant – Sergeant Rachel Worth – said that Burnell's breathing had been heavy up to this point, like he was in a deep sleep,' Meredith said as she toggled between the camera angles again. 'Then it seemed to stop, and she became concerned.'

Rowe didn't respond.

They watched as the two other officers reappeared and Worth unlocked the cell door. Worth seemed to check Burnell's pulse and then, after a brief exchange with the officers, started using her radio, presumably to call an ambulance. A minute or so later, Steve Symonds appeared looking slightly anxious and a bit red in the face. He seemed to have a lengthy conversation with Worth. Meredith scanned through again until around twenty minutes later when a two-person ambulance crew appeared on all four camera angles in turn as they moved through to the cell. The two officers and Symonds were still present. Laura Cross was nowhere to be seen. Worth seemed to take the lead in explaining the situation to the crew who then performed, what looked to be, superficial checks on Burnell.

Rowe had wondered why the body was still in a sleeping position when he saw it, but, watching the footage, he decided it wasn't all that surprising. Burnell was clearly dead, and as everyone was still following procedure at that point, Rowe could understand them not doing anything which could contaminate or erase useful evidence of the cause of death at the inevitable inquest.

More standing around and discussions continued on the monitor, with various members of the assembled coming and going at different points, until Meredith paused it.

'Seen enough, guv?' she asked.

Rowe breathed in deeply and sat quiet for a second with his arms folded.

'What makes this CCTV so special?' he said at last.

Meredith stared at the screen and wrinkled her nose but didn't reply. Rowe tried again.

'What I mean is, why is this enough for us and for Grantley's team on its own? CCTV isn't deemed 100% reliable as evidence, and this doesn't show us anything that happened before Burnell entered the building. It's incomplete at best.'

'Well, guv. We are hopeful of retrieving the town council's CCTV footage of Burnell being picked up in town once they are in the office later this morning. There will be body cam footage from the two officers too, and we also have their statements. As for the reliability of the footage we have here, it's a Lockscreen system.'

Rowe rubbed his eyes and realised he was on the verge of desperation for more coffee.

'And for those of us who speak English…'

'Lockscreen, guv. It's a CCTV system that's being trialled at a number of stations around the country, and Fenwood is one of them. I'd have thought you might have heard about it. It was in the Oxford newsletter.'

'Must have missed that issue.'

He thought Meredith looked disappointed in him.

'Well. Lockscreen is a government-sponsored secure program that cannot be altered or modified either in real time or later. Camera footage is fed back into a central hub which is not controlled or accessible by any individual station or building that uses the system. All the users can do is allocate which cameras they wish to feed into it, usually every 12 hours. It is possible for stations to do this more often, but it's not straightforward, and most stick with the same cameras pretty much constantly anyway.'

Meredith continued:

'The feeds are stored in the central hub, as they happen, on a constantly rolling basis. They can be viewed from the Lockscreen app – as we've just been doing – but cannot be edited in any way. The footage is literally locked in. The purpose of it is to ultimately ensure that CCTV within police stations and other public buildings is beyond reproach and as reliable as it possibly could be.'

'Right,' said Rowe. 'But you said this is a trial. Why would it be considered reliable if it's not even been fully tested yet?'

'Lockscreen feeds were accepted as evidence by a judge earlier this year in an assault on an officer case. The trials have been going on for some time. Early versions of it are already fully implemented in some government buildings, we're now just waiting for it to be written into law that all police stations should adopt it.'

'So... does this thing only operate inside the building?'

'At Fenwood, yes guv.'

'Why?'

Meredith shrugged. 'I suppose they are just trialling the internal aspect of it here.'

'Okay,' Rowe sighed. He wasn't sure he understood much of what he'd just heard. He went back to the case in hand.

'Where was Burnell picked up?'

'The market square I believe, guv.'

'How was he transported back here, by car?'

'Yes, guv.'

Rowe gazed at the paused image on the screen, which included the figure of Steve Symonds in its cast.

'Why is Symonds still here but no one else?'

'Not sure, guv. I think he was helping the SDU – the Special Deployment Unit – with something.'

For the life of him, Rowe couldn't imagine what that something would be.

'Okay, one last question. Why was Fenwood chosen to trial this Lockscreen thing? It's open less than half the week and has the staffing levels of a corner shop.'

Meredith shrugged. 'I suppose they're trialling it at stations of varying sizes, guv.'

Rowe nodded. Fair enough, he thought. No one could ever be expected to know how or why decisions like that were made at the higher levels of police and government.

'Well, time to go and see our fearless leaders' he said, making to get up and then stopping. 'Although, there's one more thing I'll need first…'

Rowe found Stanwell, Vickers and the SDU members in the custody suite, standing silently at the door of cell 2 as the recently arrived coroner and his assistant loaded Burnell's body into a black bag within. The coroner was an expressionless man of about forty while his assistant was younger, also male, but with no more evident charisma. Stanwell saw Rowe coming and intercepted him before he reached the group.

'So, Mike, are we all sorted now?' The joviality in the Assistant Chief Constable's voice was somewhat out of place in their surroundings. 'I think Commander Grantley and his team are keen to get going now the coroner has arrived.'

Stanwell gave a small nod in the direction of the three Met officers, who were stone-faced and pretending not to be listening in.

'If you're satisfied, we can get this all signed over.'

The thin figure of Neil Vickers appeared at Stanwell's shoulder. He had naturally olive skin and thick, jet-black hair which had caused Rowe to wonder more than once about his lineage. The DCI was holding some paperwork and glaring at Rowe.

'This needs to be wrapped up now, DI Rowe.' Vickers said it in a low voice. 'Otherwise, you will be hindering the work of the Special Deployment Unit and Scotland Yard.'

Rowe beamed at him.

'Well Neil, with that in mind you'll be pleased to know that I've decided to take the case.'

Stanwell's frown returned while Vickers' glare became fused with incomprehension.

'I'll need to speak to the officers who brought Burnell in, plus the custody sergeant,' Rowe continued. 'Also, DS Symonds and DS Cross. And I'll need to see the results of the coroner's inquest, when they become available.'

The young assistant who was setting up a gurney to transport Burnell's newly bagged-up body on looked sharply through the doorway at Rowe as he said it.

'Last but not least,' he continued, 'I'll need a forensic review of all the CCTV footage, including body cams and the council recordings once they've been handed over.'

Vickers had become irate.

'Ludicrous,' he spat. 'You're not in charge here, Rowe. The SDU are and all the essential details from a local standpoint have already been completed by DC Meredith. You will sign this over now and allow Commander Grantley's team to conduct their important work.'

Rowe stared back at him silently. Attempting to diffuse things, Stanwell raised a patient finger to Vickers and gently guided Rowe out of the custody suite, then far enough into the corridor that they were no longer in earshot.

Stanwell spoke softly.

'Mike, I'm glad you're on board now but we really don't have much of a say in all this. It's a great shame but it seems the real investigation is a much wider picture than we had imagined and something that only the SDU are privy to. Hence the irregular protocol.'

'Irregular protocol!' Rowe shook his head. 'Nick, you know I'm not exactly a stickler for the rules, but this lot are taking the piss.'

'I'm sure they have their reasons, as odd as it might appear to us. They answer to a higher power, as it were. And if we're talking protocol, Mike, I'm really not sure what others might make of your encounter with DS Symonds earlier.'

Rowe eyed the older man but didn't respond.

'That's not any sort of a threat, Mike. I'm just saying that the scene is what it is, and, in the circumstances, it is better off in the Yard's hands than in ours. I hope you know me well enough by now that I wouldn't be saying this if it wasn't best for us all.'

Rowe rocked back on his heels and stared at the ceiling.

'Yeah. But I don't like this. The fact no one who saw Burnell alive is still here bugs me. And I still don't know why Laura came here last night. Vickers and Carne seem very eager to push this thing away and they want me to steer the cart. You said yourself that I don't have a choice. Considering everything that happened with the Hannah Crockett case, it feels wrong. Like I'm being set up.'

'I'm certain that's not what's happening.' Stanwell said. He then visibly softened, sighed and it was his turn to look up at the bowing ceiling tiles. 'Listen. Let me see if I can buy you, say, 48 hours extra just to satisfy your curiosity. The Yard might not go for it, but I don't mind asking just to remind them we exist.'

Stanwell smiled tiredly as Rowe thought about the offer.

'Alright,' Rowe said eventually.

The Assistant Chief Constable nodded, turned and walked back into the custody suite. Again, Rowe felt a small pang of gratitude that he had the old man in his corner. He guessed that the situation would probably have been heading south even faster without him there.

Rowe walked out of the station via the staff door, through the car park and onto the street. He walked up level with the station's front entrance and looked around. It was a chilly November morning, getting on for seven thirty with people and vehicles starting to appear on the road and pavements, on the way to places of work and other routine destinations.

Diagonally opposite the corner on which Fenwood police station stood was a public car park, which was beginning to fill up. Officers working out of Fenwood had used it in the past when the station was busier. A thought briefly crossed Rowe's mind that Laura's car may have been there when he arrived, which was why he didn't see it, and she had then avoided seeing him as she left. He dismissed it as overtly paranoid.

Even so, he was tired of wondering. He took out his phone and sent a message to the woman he hoped was still his significant other. He thought she might be sleeping at that time but had to trust she would see it when she woke up.

> Hey. Been given this cell death thing.
> Be good to talk later. Trees at 8pm maybe?

The 'Trees' was short for the Three Trees Hotel on the bypass to the east of Fenwood. It wasn't far from town but virtually no locals ever went there as it was difficult to reach by foot and its bar had all the atmosphere of a doctor's waiting room. It was strictly for business types passing through and perhaps the odd local firm's Christmas party. That made it ideal for a quiet drink if you didn't want to run into too many people you knew. It also wasn't anywhere most people would choose for a date, so meeting there didn't necessarily imply romanticism. Rowe hoped it was a neutral suggestion.

'Ah, Mike. Good news.'

It was Stanwell, emerging from the station car park. Rowe put the phone back in his pocket, the message having been sent, and walked back to meet him by the gate.

'Commander Grantley's team have no problem with a two-day extension for you to dot the I's and cross the T's' Stanwell said. 'DCI Vickers had a somewhat different perspective but ultimately the SDU don't see what harm it will do, and they of course welcome a thorough approach. So, shall we give it until close of play tomorrow? You'll still have the assistance of DC Meredith obviously.'

Behind them, the coroner and his assistant were preparing to leave, the body having been loaded into their dark-coloured vehicle. Rowe wondered how often the coroner himself personally collected bodies. At the same time, Grantley and his minions emerged from the staff door and moved towards the gate. They paid Rowe and Stanwell no attention as they passed.

'I'll see what I can do with the time,' Rowe said. 'Thanks, Nick.'

'Not at all. You were right that we should do this properly. Do what you need to, and we can put this all to bed.'

Stanwell winked and patted Rowe's shoulder. Rowe nodded slightly and Stanwell walked off in the direction of the big public cark park. He acknowledged the SDU team as they sat in the Audi, which in daylight was revealed to be a colour known as Typhoon Grey. Rowe watched him go and then noticed the large minion who reminded him of a rugby player staring at him from the

Audi's drivers' seat in a manner that couldn't be described as cheerful.

Rowe knew the SDU trio had no interest in his investigation – such as it was – and that they had only agreed to the 48-hour extension purely *because* they couldn't have cared less about it. He also knew Vickers wouldn't have made a scene about Rowe's involvement in front of them because he desperately wanted to impress the London superstars. It could be deemed a hollow victory, Rowe thought, but Stanwell had scored it, nonetheless.

The Audi performed a three-point turn, drove to the end of the road and turned left towards the bypass. Heading back to London. As it disappeared, Meredith walked out from the car park.

'So, guv, what's the next move?'

It was a safe and practised question. Rowe doubted whether her heart was in it.

'I want you to set up separate interviews with the two officers that brought Burnell in. This afternoon at Oxford if possible.'

'Ok.' She jotted something down in her notebook. 'Anything else?'

'Yes. Get a copy of that Lockscreen CCTV for the last 24 hours – or access to the original, whatever. Nail down the bodycam footage if you can and get the request into the council for their street CCTV. Tell them it's urgent.'

'No problem, guv.'

'I'll meet you at Oxford around midday. In the meantime, I'll go and see our other friend.'

Rowe took a piece of paper out of his pocket and held it up. It had an address on it that Meredith had given him after they viewed the CCTV. She nodded in understanding.

'I'll go and see about the Lockscreen access,' Meredith said. 'Catch you in a bit, guv.'

She disappeared back into the station in a business-like fashion, her short and broad legs eating up the tarmac. Rowe mused that in the circumstances it might be useful having a DC who was thorough.

He took out his phone again. He wasn't expecting Laura to have replied yet but found himself to be nervous about the possibility all the same. To his surprise, a message was waiting.

Ok. I'll see you there.

It occurred to Rowe that it was the first message he'd received from her in weeks. It was a start, he supposed. He walked back down to the Vitesse, stopping as he reached the drivers' door and looking back at the simultaneously remarkable and unremarkable edifice of Fenwood police station again. It was a strange building, and he had the feeling that strange things had happened inside it. And maybe still were happening – other than Meredith, only Vickers and Symonds remained within its' walls at that moment.

That fact wasn't lost on him.

8

THE HOUSE HE WAS looking for was on the end of a row – the left-hand end if looking from the street – of six relatively new houses. All the houses closely resembled the others on the development in which they resided. It was one of the sprawling and winding newer estates built on the edges of small towns all around the country in recent years, which tended to have the population of a village in their own right. Rowe reflected that these estates were the kind of place homebuyers were increasingly forced into, like middle-class shanty towns where everything looked the same, while anything remotely unique or characterful elsewhere became progressively unaffordable.

He was depressed by these surroundings but had spent a lot of time in very similar locations thanks to the nature of his work and, it couldn't be denied, his age. Most of his childhood friends lived in these types of pop-up neighbourhoods for the various reasons of raising families on a budget, trying to qualify for school catchment areas and to simply get a foot on the property ladder. He knew that in a way he was fortunate not to have needed to juggle such things in his life so far, but the lack of soul in these places ate at him even so. He felt it acutely. Rowe guessed there remained a slim possibility that such areas would one day radiate nostalgia like the hill from the old Hovis advert, or even war-era terraced streets, but he had his doubts.

He had parked further up the road and out of sight of the house so that his approach to the front door wouldn't be observed. There was no gate but small, wire metal fences surrounded postage-stamp patches of grass on either side of the short path. Rowe stepped up to the door and knocked. While it was not aggressively early, he guessed that the owner of the house would be asleep. Sure enough, it took three attempts at knocking and several minutes for the door to be answered.

A woman opened it a few inches and peered out. She had bleach-blonde, wavy hair that fell over her shoulders and wore stylishly framed glasses.

'Yes?'

She looked both tired from sleep and suspicious of the caller.

'Sergeant Worth? DI Rowe from Oxford. I'm completing the enquiries related to the cell death at Fenwood. I understand you were the custody sergeant on duty.'

Rowe raised the ID badge that was around his neck. He had found it under a seat in the Vitesse earlier after a long search. Rachel Worth glanced at it then shook her head blearily. She didn't open the door any further.

'I spoke to the DC at the station,' she said. 'It's all on CCTV. Sad thing for a young guy but I suppose he had a heart issue or something.'

'Gotta love CCTV.'

Worth looked confused and impatient.

'Mind if I come in?'

Sighing, Worth opened the door wider and stepped back. She was barefoot, wearing black leggings and a baggy white t-shirt. Rowe shut the door as she stood in front of him with her arms folded.

'Why was the custody suite open on a Wednesday night at Fenwood?' Rowe asked.

Worth initially looked taken aback by the question, then answered as if dealing with a slow-witted child.

'Because we're on a rota with the other county stations.'

'Right. But Fenwood's only open three days a week. I guess the other stations take a big share of the rota.'

'It's not up to me,' she shrugged. 'Will this take long? I haven't had much sleep and I thought this had already been covered.'

'Not long. Shall we sit down?'

Worth didn't reply but led him into the living room which was through a door next to where they stood. Rowe could sense her annoyance with him, along with the fact that she was not overly impressed with his appearance, unshaven in yesterday's clothes as he still was. There was no offer of tea or coffee as they sat down. Rowe sat forward on the sofa just inside the door while Worth perched on an armchair in front of the living room window, looking like a bird that could take flight without warning. The front room was tidy and modern-looking; Rowe thought it probably looked identical to several million others in the country.

'What time were you allowed to leave the station today?' he asked.

'About five or five thirty, I think. Why?'

'Just getting things clear in my head. Did you speak to the Special Deployment Unit at all?'

Worth paused before answering.

'You mean the team from the Yard? No. Not that I remember.'

Rowe wasn't taking notes. Just watching the woman's reactions.

'What time did they arrive at the station?'

'I'm not sure. Can't have been long before I left. I really didn't have much to do with them – they liaised with DC Meredith.'

She folded her hands together on her knees as if to stop them from doing anything unsanctioned.

'What made you think there was something wrong with James Burnell when you checked on him at 2:30am?'

'He didn't respond to my attempts to call his name, and he didn't seem to be breathing.'

'What was DS Cross doing at Fenwood last night?'

'I don't know who that is. An officer came in to talk to DS Symonds, was that her?'

'I didn't say it was a "her" but yes, it may have been. Did that strike you as strange?'

'No, not really. Two officers on a late shift talking about a case I suppose.'

'You didn't speak to DS Cross then?'

'No. Why would I? I mean, she wasn't there to see me.'

'Did you see her leave the station?'

'I was a bit busy with a dead man in a cell to keep an eye on her.' Rowe could detect the sarcasm in Worth's response. Her voice had risen, and she seemed suddenly aware of it.

'What was DS Symonds doing there?'

Worth made a face as if it were an odd question. Rowe's expression had not changed.

'He's been working out of Fenwood quite often recently. You'd have to ask him what exactly he was working on.'

'Do you know Steve Symonds well?'

'I know him from the station but that's about it. Why does this matter anyway? A man died in the cell. It's tragic but none of us could have expected it. Steve wasn't even there.'

The last sentence hung in the air. Rowe decided not to acknowledge it but left a gap that Worth couldn't have failed to notice.

'Just a couple more questions, Sergeant Worth,' he said eventually. 'What do you know about the Lockscreen system?'

Worth shook her head with exasperation.

'Nothing. Other than that stuff in the newsletter.'

'Has anyone informed James Burnell's family?'

Worth cocked her head to one side.

'I would've thought that was a job for whoever is investigating. Possibly you.'

Rowe smiled and made to get up.

'Ok. Thanks, Sergeant. I'll be in touch if there's anything else.'

Worth strode into the hall to show him to the door. He said 'goodbye' but got no response. He thought her hands looked unsteady as she opened the door to let him out.

9

AFTER THE VISIT WITH Rachel Worth, Rowe stopped at his flat near the centre of Fenwood for a shower and to fuel himself before he headed to the Oxford station. Something had told him it was important to see Worth as early as possible, as if things might hinge on it somehow. He wasn't sure why.

His flat was more of a studio apartment – a converted office at the back of an old glove factory at the bottom of a hill. The factory had been totally converted into flats that were designated as 'luxury' and were all significantly larger than Rowe's, which bore all the hallmarks of an afterthought that had possibly been intended for a janitor or similar custodian. Although the flat suffered from several issues, its size did at least have the benefit of bringing it into a somewhat affordable rent bracket. Generally, the cost of renting in Fenwood was prohibitive, particularly to lone renters. Rowe may not have spent many nights there in recent weeks or months, but the practicality of the flat's location – a short walk and even shorter drive from the centre of town – could not be denied.

It was roughly a thirty-minute drive into Oxford, which gave Rowe time to think about the cell death. One thing he decided was that he would need help if he was going to use the time he'd been given as productively as possible. He parked in an available space at the rear of the building, which was old and grandiose by the standards of police stations. A four-floor Headington stone structure that fitted well amongst the traditional student digs and heritage buildings on the edge of the city, Rowe had always presumed that it had been owned by the University at some point up to and possibly including the present day. Most things of any value in Oxford tended to be, either directly or indirectly.

The station was a bustling place in the daytime, something which Rowe attributed to it being the only station in at least the county, if not further, where any significant police work happened on a regular basis. And, he supposed, even that was up for debate. The interior was far more modern in appearance than the exterior, with glass doors and walls complementing contemporary furnishing. Its décor had enjoyed far more attention in recent years than that of the Fenwood station, that much was certain.

He used his badge as a key card to open the staff access door at the rear, which opened at the foot of some stairs that he then climbed to the second floor. When he got there, he swiped again to access a glass door, which opened into a wide, open-plan office. He threaded through the sea of desks and the hubbub of conversations and ringing phones, deflecting any sharp glances at the interloper, and made for the far corner of the office near the front of the building.

'Right, that's it. I'm finding that swindling watch salesman in Benidorm and getting my money back.'

Jim Ferry sat at his desk, looking to Rowe's eyes like a cross between a Weeble toy and Penfold from the Danger Mouse cartoon, holding his watch to his ear and shaking the wrist it adorned.

'Hmmm,' Ferry muttered. 'Seems to be ticking. Which means it actually is before noon and you're in the office. But then…yes, I suppose pissing the bed must be especially awkward when you sleep in your car.'

'Hello, Jim,' Rowe said, stopping in front of the cluttered desk. 'No accidents in the car yet, believe it or not. How's tricks?'

'Give it time. Everything here is just rosy, thanks. The firm thwack of objectives being achieved resonates through the corridors.'

'I'd expect nothing less.'

'So, what's the emergency behind this super-human achievement? You being here I mean, not controlling your bladder.'

Ferry was a rotund, greying teddy bear type in his late fifties. He was on the cusp of retirement and, Rowe suspected, keen to be noticed as little as possible as the long-awaited day of his 'freedom' approached.

Ferry had completed his training and early days of service with the Metropolitan Police but had taken a posting at a small-town station in the Cotswolds as soon as possible. Rowe's educated guess was that it had been the kind of place where Ferry and a handful of others like him settled neighbourly disputes and returned lost wallets, and the only strict targets revolved around the upkeep of the coffee machine and adherence to the sandwich rota. The station had closed some years ago – along with many like it – and Ferry was given the choice of returning to the beat in Oxford or taking a desk job in order to see out his remaining years in the job. He had elected to become a civilian Crime Analyst. He remained in reserve as an officer for emergencies, but otherwise it was clear to Rowe that a spot in the corner and a well-beaten path to the kitchen had long since overcome any urge Ferry may have once had to hit the streets.

Rowe liked Ferry a lot. To Rowe's mind, the veteran was nothing like the newer breed of apparently brainless automatons who seemed to arrive in the job on an endless conveyer belt, nor the self-righteous narcissists and unscrupulous vultures who populated the middle and senior ranks. In some ways, Ferry was the classic old-school beat bobby, although possibly with more interest in building relations with publicans than with the community. Behind the wisecracks and sardonic exterior though, Rowe knew Ferry was very bright and often sought his perspective on cases. Ferry was one of the only colleagues Rowe had been in contact with during his leave period and would likely be in the same category once Rowe's resignation was granted.

'I've got the cell death at Fenwood from this morning,' Rowe said. 'Don't know if you heard about that. Carne gave it to me to make herself look magnanimous and me look respectable.'

'Well, she's on a hiding to nothing there then.' Ferry was leaning back in his chair with his hands behind his head. 'I did hear the basics of it. Thought you were done mate, what made you take it on?'

'Laura was apparently there. I really went to see her. But she'd already gone when I arrived and before I knew it Vickers appeared, and I was told it was signed and sealed. The scene was screwed and some team from the Yard had taken over before I even got there.'

'The Yard?' Ferry's eyes widened. 'Why are those clowns involved?'

'No idea. The dead man, Burnell, was apparently part of another investigation. I've been told nothing. But Stanwell at least eked out an extra 48 hours from them so I can make sure I'm not getting shafted.'

'Good old Stanwell. In the wrong job that bloke. You said Vickers graced you with his presence so I'm guessing he poked his nose in?'

'Yup. He was running around after the Yard crew mostly. I thought he might spontaneously combust when I refused to sign it over.'

Ferry chuckled as he sat forward again and rested his hands either side of a battered keyboard.

'You spoken to Laura about it?'

'Not yet. Trying to get a picture in my head first. Speaking of which, I might need to use your research skills.'

'Uh oh. Mate, I'm hoping to get out of here alive in a few months. Don't drag me into your sordid world of degradation and infamy.'

'Relax. It would just be a few facts and figures from the databases. Nothing extra-curricular.'

'Oh yeah…'

Rowe smiled. 'I'll be in touch.'

'Oh, I know you will, you owe me at least three pints.'

Ferry winked at him, and Rowe waved as he started back across the room to the door.

'Best get those car seats shampooed,' Ferry called after him, loudly enough to illicit confused glances from the room.

Rowe came back down the stairs and turned into the office where most of CID worked, which was on the first floor. It was a smaller room than the one Ferry inhabited, with four sets of four desks that faced each other equally spaced out, plus a glass-walled office on the far side of the room opposite the door.

Meredith sat at one of the desks in the middle of the room, upright, on the edge of her seat, and staring at her computer monitor. Rowe thought it gave her the air of a high-marks student eager to impress a teacher, only at that moment no one else was in the vicinity. As a rule, Rowe wasn't generally a fan of working with others, especially officers like Meredith whom he perceived as being over-keen. But the circumstances were irregular, and with that in mind, he wanted to strike a balance between utilising her enthusiasm to his advantage and keepings things light to avoid putting pressure on her – especially as it was not yet midday, which had been their agreed meeting time.

'Hi, Joanne,' he said as he walked over from the doorway. 'How's it going? We set for this afternoon?'

Rowe slumped into the chair next to hers and she started slightly.

'Hello, guv. Yes, all good. PC McMurray is coming in this afternoon and PC Shehzad is already here. Oh, and I got a copy of the Lockscreen CCTV as you asked. Still waiting on a response from the council. The bodycam stuff should be available soon too.'

'Ok, thanks. Tell the council we need that footage ASAP, they're obstructing an important investigation…that kind of jazz. Same with whoever has the bodycam feed. We don't have long.'

'Yes, guv. How did it go with Sergeant Worth?'

'It went. Might mean more when I hear what the others have to say. What room is Shehzad in?'

PC Sarfraz Shehzad was in a cramped office adjacent to the main division room. Meredith had taken the view that an interview room wasn't required as it was not a formal meeting. Rowe hadn't cared either way.

Shehzad was a young constable who hadn't been in the job very long, and as a result he sat up attentively when Rowe and Meredith walked in. He was shorter than Rowe with big, round eyes and cultivated facial hair.

'PC Shehzad.' Rowe nodded in greeting as he sat down on the other side of the room's bare desk.

'Sir,' Shehzad replied briskly.

'What time did the Special Deployment Unit arrive at Fenwood this morning?'

Shehzad was visibly surprised, either by the question or the lack of preamble or both. Rowe had his arms folded and was leaning back in his chair, while Meredith appeared to be taking copious notes in the seat next to him. The PC answered after a few seconds.

'Uh...I'm not sure exactly, sir. PC McMurray and I were given permission to leave not long after they arrived, so maybe around 5am.'

'Who gave you permission?'

'Sergeant Worth, sir. The custody sergeant.'

'Where did the initial call regarding James Burnell come from?'

'I believe it was a local business owner – Palace Kebabs – concerned for his welfare, sir. PC McMurray and I didn't have any contact with that person though, we were just dispatched to the location. We found Mr. Burnell in the town square and, on assessing his condition, escorted him back to the station for his own safety.'

'You didn't call an ambulance?'

'No, sir. We felt it was clear he was intoxicated. We assessed his condition again with the custody sergeant back at the station also.'

'I see. Why were you and PC McMurray on patrol out of Fenwood on a Wednesday night?'

'Sir?'

'Rather than Oxford. Or Banbury. Or anywhere that isn't borderline derelict and on the verge of closure?'

'I don't know, sir. The rota comes from our commanding officer.'

Rowe asked a few more questions with regards to timings and the discovery that Burnell was no longer breathing, but Shehzad's answers didn't provide anything that hadn't already been evident on the CCTV. He was thanked for his time and allowed to leave.

While they had been talking to Shehzad, PC Estelle McMurray had arrived, and Meredith showed her into the room. She was another younger officer and was tall and thin with very dark hair tied back conservatively. McMurray was similarly eager to be helpful in the way that her patrol partner had been and gave almost identical answers to the same questions. Their story was very simple, and they seemed surprised that they were being asked about it again after Meredith had spoken to them earlier. They were of the view – as apparently most people were, Rowe ascertained – that it had all been documented on the CCTV. Rowe might have been beginning to share that view if it weren't for a few small factors – not least the SDU and their still-opaque yet supposedly vital "wider" investigation.

He and Meredith reconvened at her desk once McMurray had left. Rowe suspected that the Detective Constable was increasingly viewing these further enquiries as a dead end and probably a complete waste of time. That was as good as confirmed a moment later when she checked through her e-mails.

'Still no reply from the council, guv. I chased them up after you said to earlier. I don't think they see it as a priority sadly. I'll keep trying.'

Rowe thought she may as well have added "but I don't see the point".

'Make sure they don't fob you off, Joanne,' he said. 'These people are jobsworths. I'm sure they won't want to be seen as wasting police time in a major operation.'

Meredith made a face.

'It's not really "major" though is it, guv? I mean, Burnell was clearly intoxicated and more than likely had a pre-existing condition. Everything is on CCTV, and we've already seen there's nothing untoward there. At the very worst, if there were negligence or foul play of any kind involved then the SDU will find it as part of their investigation. I hate to say it guv, but I think we're just shuffling paper for the sake of it now.'

Rowe nodded while staring at his hands, then looked up and drew his swivel chair closer to hers.

'That's the point though,' he said. 'The SDU aren't investigating. We – mostly you – have done all the interviews that are going to be done. We watched the CCTV, they didn't. They had one interest and that was shutting this down and getting Burnell's body out of there. Ask yourself why that would be.'

She gazed at the ceiling for a second as if she were doing as he suggested, then looked back at him.

'Guv, why did you ask PC Shehzad and PC McMurray what time the SDU turned up? You could've just asked me, I was there.'

'Same reason you should always ask a question. To see what answer you get.'

Meredith made another face.

'Well, it was 5am anyway, guv. Pretty much on the dot.'

'That's basically what Rachel Worth said. Although you'd think a specialist team from the Yard showing up was akin to the bin men coming round for all the attention she paid them. You know, Fenwood might be a reasonably big building, but it's been a tiny police station for a while now. These days it's open almost exclusively for lost dogs and parking disputes – and only three days a week at that. Pretty soon it'll close completely. How often do you think it's necessary for the custody suite to be open on a Wednesday night at a place like that?'

Meredith shrugged.

'Hardly ever would be my guess,' Rowe continued. 'Anyone heading for a cell at that time would either be brought here or to Banbury. There's a reason the suite at Fenwood was open last night but I'm damned if I can see it.'

Rowe exhaled. Meredith didn't offer anything in response to his ruminations.

'How much did Grantley ask you when he got there?' Rowe asked after a pause.

'Not a lot to be honest, guv. I gave them a brief rundown, but they were mostly interested in the body. I guess Commander Grantley must have got the details from whoever he spoke to here.'

'But he let certain people leave without informing you?'

She looked momentarily sheepish at the question.

'Apparently yes, guv. He did ask me where you were a couple of times though.'

'Nice of him to think of me. Did he ask any actual policeman questions? Like what was a bloke from Somerset doing smashed off his head on a random Wednesday night in Fenwood? Or whether anyone had bothered to call forensics?'

'No, guv.' Impatience was creeping back into her voice. 'It wasn't a crime scene though. If it were, questions like that might have been more relevant.'

'Did Grantley tell you what their investigation was about?'

'No, guv. Like I said –'

'Because,' Rowe cut in, 'for all we currently know, Burnell could have been the Pablo Escobar of Somerset who someone had a hit out on. Or a Russian spy. Or maybe he was just someone Grantley didn't like very much. Point being, we know precisely jack shit about the guy. Yet I was expected to sign this over with no questions asked…nothing to see here.'

Rowe used his fingers to put the last few words in quotation marks.

'Well...I hate to say it,' Meredith ventured, 'but that kind of brings us back to the CCTV, guv. The SDU may well have something bigger to look at with Burnell, but even so, what happened at Fenwood is quite clear cut. It's not for us to worry about.'

'Ah yes. The bulletproof CCTV which is being trialled at a lemonade-stand station like Fenwood for no apparent reason. Where would we be without it?'

Meredith didn't answer. She seemed weary of the conversation.

'Ok, here's the plan...' Rowe went on. 'First, see what you can dig up on Burnell. Bio, criminal record, recent occupation etcetera. It'd be nice to have some idea of why he was in town. Second, maybe ask around about how often custody suites have been open at smaller stations in the county in the last year, if you can. And lastly, find out how many cell deaths there have been in the UK in the last two years – custody suites only. Then...I promise you can get back to solving crimes.'

Rowe smiled wryly, remembering he really needed Meredith's assistance at that moment. Meredith dutifully took note of all he'd asked for in her book. He knew she wasn't really on board with the case, but he hoped he could keep her attention until the end of the following day.

'Ok, guv. What will you be doing?' Meredith asked.

It was a fair question, although the tone could have seemed mildly insubordinate had Rowe cared enough to interpret it in that way.

'I'm gonna see if I can get someone to open Fenwood back up for me. Seems like a good time to get to know the place better.'

He smiled again and winked, then stood up and headed for the stairs, the back door, and the Oxford station car park.

10

ROWE EASED THE VITESSE into a space towards the rear of the public car park that sat diagonally opposite Fenwood police station. The time was approaching twenty minutes past two in the afternoon. Using a phone number he had found in the internal police directory he still had access to, Rowe had arranged to meet one of the reserve, public-facing desk supervisors at the building in order to gain access to the place and had arrived early.

Whilst he was aware that Meredith viewed their investigation as somewhere between highly frivolous and an attempt by Rowe to be as disruptive as possible on his way out of the job, he was determined to use the slim time extension they'd been given to ensure he wasn't being stitched up in any way.

The car park was mostly full of cars belonging to those who worked locally, and possibly a few shoppers willing to make the five-minute walk into town. It was a free car park – a perk which Rowe suspected was unlikely to last, particularly as there had been an increase in people simply dumping and abandoning vehicles in it over time. As if to underline the point, he spotted a decaying caravan crumbling in the back corner, not far from where he had parked.

Rowe walked out from the car park, crossed the road and headed into the side road towards the station. It didn't appear that anyone had arrived to meet him yet, so he went and stood in the station's car park at the side of the building.

The two patrol cars were still in place but otherwise there were no signs of life. The staff access door was firmly shut. He looked up at the outside of the structure. On the first and second floors, boxes and discarded equipment were visible in pretty much every window, evidently piled high. The occasional lighting fixture was visible but little else. How long the building would be allowed to exist solely as a glorified dumping ground was anyone's guess, but Rowe knew that the topic would already have been discussed by the Thames Valley Police hierarchy, along with local councils and community groups ad nauseum. The station had essentially become a redundant eyesore, mostly offering equally redundant services to the public. It had long outlived its usefulness. It was that image that Rowe was struggling to reconcile against the drama that had recently occurred in its custody suite.

He wandered back around to the station's entrance and found a short, round woman standing near the front entrance doors and gazing around testily. She was not in uniform and looked to be approaching middle age.

'DI Rowe?' She made the enquiry whilst studying his general appearance with some hesitation, her eyes coming to rest on the badge around his neck.

'Yes, that's me.'

'I think I'm to open up for you.' She looked closer at the badge. 'I'm Mary Drinkwater, I help with the front desk here.

'Hello Mary, call me Mike. Thanks for coming down.'

They shook hands briefly while Rowe concluded that using civilians to man the desk at a police station was a sure-fire indication that no one cared about the station in question.

'Wait here.'

Mary disappeared round to the car park – and the staff access door, Rowe presumed – then a minute later reappeared inside the front doors. She unlocked them and Rowe stepped in to join her. She stood awkwardly there in the reception area, clearly awaiting some more detail from him as to the purpose of his visit.

'Are you looking for something specific, DI Rowe?'

'I'm investigating the cell death here this morning. Thought it would be helpful to take in the atmosphere.'

'I thought that was all done now.' Mary looked both blank and mildly agitated. 'I was told everything had been cleared?'

'I'm afraid not. Do you have keys to everything in here?'

'No, just the staff door, and the front door. I have a key card for the internal doors down here but that's all. Where do you need to go?'

'Can I borrow your key card?'

'Well…I suppose so.'

She retrieved it from her pocket and handed it to him. Her expression as she did so conveyed her wariness of the situation.

'Right,' she said. 'I'll wait here for you then, shall I? Just let me know when you're finished.'

The implication in her voice was that the clock was already ticking.

The front desk was on the left of the reception area and Mary unlocked a staff door next to it and walked through to the back office where Rowe had viewed the CCTV footage with Meredith earlier, as if to busy herself. Rowe used the key card to access the door which led to the main body of the ground floor that held interview rooms and the custody suite.

He set off down the central corridor, passing the four interview rooms on his left, and eventually coming to the custody suite further down on the right. The door was predictably locked and could not be accessed by key card alone, and the suite appeared empty through the door's narrow glass pane. The floor looked like it had been freshly mopped – Rowe had an image of Vickers enlisting the help of Symonds to tidy the place up once everyone had left that morning.

It was what Rowe had expected to see, and he hadn't made the trip simply to look over the scene again anyway. After all, there hadn't been much to see when the body was in situ. He moved on past the suite, almost to the end of the corridor where he arrived at the door to the back stairway. Surprisingly, he found it was unlocked and didn't require key card access. As he pushed the door open, cold and stale air hit him from the space that extended up to the top floor. He thought it was a reliable indicator that no one used that part of the building with any regularity at all.

Rowe ascended the stairs to the first floor and was met by an identical door to the one he had come through at the bottom, only the one in front of him was locked. There was no key card access facility – clearly the building had installed that after these floors were put out of use – therefore it had simply been locked by a key which was in the possession of an unknown person.

Thinking that Mary had most likely fired up the Lockscreen system in order to track his movements, Rowe had a quick look at his surroundings and saw no cameras in the stairway. Even so, he guessed she was probably wondering what he was doing on the stairs and thought there was a strong possibility she could appear at any moment.

He reached into his jacket pocket and pulled out a half-size chisel that he had brought with him from the car. In the past he had employed it for jemmying locks and windows of varying sizes when, in his view, circumstances on the job had deemed it necessary. He used it to force the wooden door as quickly as he could. Any damage it caused or mess it made didn't concern him. He believed it was clear that nothing of any real value was stored on the floor and most things there were probably broken anyway, so a broken lock would be unlikely to raise a significant number of eyebrows.

The lock eventually gave after a few attempts and the plastic handle, which had been rendered useless, hung loose. Rowe put the chisel back in his pocket, glancing back down the stairs to ensure Mary hadn't appeared, then went through the door.

The air was cold and stale, having apparently not been heated or ventilated in an eternity. And, as he had expected, the space was a mess. It had previously been an open-plan office but had now been stacked high with boxes, broken office furniture, outdated and possibly obsolete computer equipment and various other useless workplace paraphernalia. Whilst it was a certainty that anything of any use or value would long ago have been pilfered by those who worked on the ground floor, the sheer amount of detritus that confronted him suggested equally that that floor, and the one above it, had become a dumping ground for other stations as well as the one he stood in. He moved steadily among the items and cast quick glances over most of them, seeing nothing of any great interest anywhere.

The large space was one of two open-plan areas that were separated by a central bank which contained two glass-walled offices and a photocopier room, which also provided access between the two main working areas. There was also a break room, a storage cupboard, and staff toilets, all of which occupied the same quarter of the floor as the back stairwell. Rowe quickly checked all these rooms along with the two offices and didn't find anything unexpected. The offices were cold, silent and lifeless, housing bare desks and shelves that contained dog-eared textbooks or homeless chair casters. Rowe moved through the copy room into the other open-plan space, which was smaller than the first, and found another jungle of boxes and junk. The stale smell prevailed, and the cold air had begun to hassle him.

He hustled quickly back across the cluttered floor to the stairway and cautiously looked out for signs of Mary approaching. There were none, but he didn't want to push his luck. He closed the door behind him, the plastic handle hanging impotently, and took the stairs quickly up to the second floor. As he reached the door, he could see through the glass panel that it was a similar story to that which he had just encountered below. A sea of dumped, tired furniture and items that had not been particularly impressive when they were new, let alone at that point in their existence. Still, he wanted to clear the floor as he was there. The chisel came out again and he got to work.

As he wedged the tool into the door jamb, an urgent sound broke the cold hush. Startled for a second, he was relieved to find it wasn't an alarm going off or a sudden intrusion by Mary Drinkwater, it was his phone ringing in his pocket, its volume accentuated in the silence. Rowe took out the phone and looked at the number. It was from Oxford station, and he hoped it was Meredith with an update. He answered.

'Rowe.' He said it quickly and quietly.

'DI Rowe, this is DCI Vickers. I've just been informed that you are back at Fenwood station for some unknown purpose. As far as I'm concerned this was not cleared with me or the SDU from Scotland Yard and –'

Rowe ended the call and turned his phone off. He had no interest in anything Neil Vickers had to say on any subject and did not have the time to chat in any case. He returned his attentions to the lock but was nonetheless intrigued that Judith Carne's loyal assistant had discovered his whereabouts so quickly. It was possible Mary had called around asking about him, but Rowe thought it was unlikely she would cast a net that would reach Vickers so quickly.

Which left Meredith as the only probable source.

He decided to continue the mental debate later. The door eventually gave, and he stepped into the room. The layout of the second floor was identical to the first and Rowe took a similar route as he explored it. He walked through the larger space, checking the break room, storage cupboard and toilets on his way. He checked the glass-walled offices and the copy room, all of which could have been the exact ones he had just seen below. Aware of the need to hurry, he almost wasn't going to bother venturing into the second open-plan space as he could see perfectly well that it was full of yet more boxes and surplus equipment.

However, as he contemplated leaving, Rowe realised something looked odd. He stepped into the space, examining the right-hand far corner of the room from where he was standing. It was overloaded with boxes which were piled noticeably higher than they were elsewhere across the two floors, and it made the room appear an unusual shape. Like it was foreshortened somehow – at least, more so than its counterpart on the first floor. Rowe was considering that it was simply an illusion created by the way in which the myriad boxes had been stacked in that particular place when a voice came from behind him. It sounded harsh in the dead quiet.

'Hello? DI Rowe?'

He turned to see Mary Drinkwater standing in the doorway of the copy room with the building keys in her hand. She gazed around the room beyond him and jingled the keys.

'I need to get going now…if you've seen enough.'

Her unspoken implication was that he'd seen more than enough. Rowe briefly wondered whether Vickers had phoned the station or if Mary had just got fed up with waiting.

'Right,' Rowe said. 'Yes, I think so.'

'I can see why no one comes up here anymore,' Mary continued as if he hadn't spoken, still looking around the room. 'Makes one wonder how the door locks could ever have got broken.'

Rowe simply raised his eyebrows in response, then walked out past Mary. He didn't see any benefit in further discussion but felt her eyes burning into him as they walked back to the stairs. She overtook him as they reached the door and made an exaggerated point of moving the deceased door handle up and down as she opened it. They made their way back down to the reception area and Rowe returned her key card and thanked her for her help again.

'Probably not worth getting those locks fixed now' he said with a smile as he opened the front door. 'Not sure this place has much longer left.'

Mary's eyes were cast down in a clear indication that his departure was overdue.

Rowe walked back in the direction of the public car park. As he went, he pulled out his phone and turned it back on. Not surprisingly there were two missed calls from Vickers on it. He ignored them and called Meredith's mobile number instead, the young DC answering after three rings.

'Hey, Joanne,' he said, as airily as he reasonably could. 'Any joy with the CCTV and the other stuff yet?'

Meredith seemed to hesitate before responding.

'Not yet, guv. But I should have something ready first thing tomorrow.'

'Ok, no worries.'

Rowe had hoped to be able to study either the council's CCTV and bodycams or the lists he had requested and follow up on them where necessary, both later that day and the following morning. But he also knew pushing Meredith at that point probably wouldn't help. And, in the event she didn't come up with anything, Jim Ferry remained his back-up plan. He changed the subject.

'Has Vickers talked to you today?'

Meredith hesitated again.

'Yes, guv. He wanted to know where you were. I said I didn't know.'

'Thanks, Joanne. Don't get yourself in the bad books on my account though. See what you can get hold of, and we'll talk first thing tomorrow.'

They said their goodbyes and hung up. Rowe paused as he reached the Vitesse and rested a hand on its roof. He didn't know how Vickers had learned of his whereabouts and he found it troubling. There was no way he was heading back to Oxford just to be harassed by the man anyway. Time was getting away but, realistically, there wasn't much more to be done until Meredith came up with at least part of his wish list. So, the other option was home.

He needed space to think about Vickers and the cell death, of course. But there was something more important he needed to think about as well.

11

AT 8PM SHARP, LAURA Cross was sitting in a stiff-looking white chair in the corner of the Three Trees Hotel bar. The bar was essentially merged with the hotel's lobby and reception area, which meant it was easy for Rowe to spot her when he walked through the revolving door at the main entrance. It was a serviceable if not spectacular room, reflective of the hotel itself. All in cream with minimalist décor, the space was certainly big enough to accommodate a large number of guests, but he felt it equally gave off a vibe akin to a sterile holding area for people undergoing clinical testing.

Rowe had seen many hotels become like that in recent years. Places that were of a perfectly reasonable standard to continue to attract patrons but that had been marred by repeated attempts at rejuvenation and modernisation which ultimately stripped them of any character or warmth. He felt it was a particular shame that the Trees had succumbed to the atmosphere-free trend as its bar had once been a lively open secret among locals who occasionally grew bored of the drinking holes in town. In that particular moment though, its bland mediocrity suited his needs.

The table Laura was sitting at was one he would have chosen himself had he arrived first. It was against the wall and not far from the left-hand end of the long bar which extended across much of the back wall. The table was also slightly at an angle so that it wasn't directly overlooked by anyone else seated in the bar. A few other tables were occupied but it was generally a quiet night in the Trees bar, which Rowe estimated would be par for the course in its newer incarnation.

Laura – sitting with her back to the bar to give her a view of the room, he guessed – looked up at him when he was a few feet away and smiled opaquely. At least, he couldn't read it. Rowe hadn't seen her in weeks – had barely seen her meaningfully since she was attacked outside her home – but it felt like he was meeting her for the first time all over again. She was dressed casually, with her hair falling over her shoulders like a painting of a rough sea. To his eyes, she looked incredible. He had never been able to think clearly when it came to Laura, and things on that score had not changed. But for a few seconds his mind settled itself into an approximation of calm. For the first time in a long time.

She stood up as he got to the table and gave Rowe a quick hug around the neck before he could think about how to start off. She sat back down, and, after a brief and awkward exchange in which he acknowledged her full glass of wine, Rowe headed to the bar to get himself an ale. While he stood there, he decided the quick hug was probably more positive than negative, and the fact she was drinking also definitely leaned towards the former. He returned to the table with his drink and sat down in the opposite chair.

'So, how are you?' he asked.

The words felt banal and hollow in his mouth, but he didn't know what else to say.

'I'm doing okay, thank you.'

She sounded sincere to him.

'I managed to get some sleep earlier,' she continued. 'How are you?'

Laura pushed her dark hair back from her face and took a sip of her wine. Rowe was finding it hard to think again.

'Oh, you know.' He smiled, compounding the vacuousness of the response. 'Had a busy day myself. That's why I wanted us to meet up. Trying to get my head around the cell death.'

He realised he couldn't have cared less about the cell death at that moment. It seemed like a distant memory.

'Yeah. That's odd that they gave it to you, what with everything that went on with the Hannah Crockett case.'

Her eyes met his and moved away again.

'That's what I thought too. I wasn't gonna get involved but it doesn't look like I have a choice. They wanted me to sign it over to a team from the Yard, but I squeezed another couple of days out of it. Or rather, Stanwell did. If my name has to be on it, I at least want to know what happened.'

He took a sip of his beer to try and cease his babbling.

'Makes sense to me. Not sure how much help I can be though.'

It was a difficult moment. They had slipped straight into work talk because it was easier than anything else – and it was the pretext on which the meeting was happening – but there was an elephant in the room that had to be acknowledged. The only question was which route Rowe would take to get there. One thing he knew for sure was that he would have to be quick; everything always showed on his face before long.

'Do you mind if I ask a couple of things?' he began after a pause. 'I've spoken to the officers that were there and I think I know less now than when I started.'

'Yes, sure.'

She took another sip.

'Ok. How come you were at Fenwood last night?'

There was no non-accusatory way to phrase the question that Rowe could think of.

'I went to see Steve Symonds' Laura said without hesitation. She didn't seem defensive. Her eyes, which had been fixed on her glass, came up and met his. 'I was coming off a late shift and he wanted to consult with me on a case.'

An expression that he guessed was both stony and sad flashed across Rowe's face and he knew she had seen it. She always did. Everything showed on his face. As if in response to the expression, she leant forward slightly and spoke more quietly.

'It wasn't anything like that, Mike. Steve has been contacting me a lot and we did meet up once, as friends. That was all. One of the reasons I went to Fenwood was to tell him there couldn't be anything else to it.'

'You had to go there to tell him that?'

Rowe instantly regretted the question.

'Maybe not. But I wanted to make it clear.'

He was silent for a second.

'And what did he say?'

'Nothing – we didn't get that far. I got there sometime between quarter past and half past two and we went into a meeting room. I was later than I said I'd be, and he seemed a bit put out. Steve started talking about the case but there wasn't much to it. I was surprised at that because I'd also had a message from the top floor saying it was important for us to liaise on it.'

'The top floor?'

'Yeah, Oxford. No name but it was from the senior management office.'

'Right.' Rowe made a mental note of the detail.

'So anyway, we can't have been in there more than a few minutes when the general alarm went off. He told me to stay put and I did. He came back about twenty minutes later and told me what had happened. I offered to leave but he told me I should wait for DC Meredith, who was on her way at that point.'

Laura's explanation told Rowe where Symonds had been before he appeared on the Lockscreen footage when Burnell's death was discovered. But he wondered why the man had been red-faced on the CCTV – almost embarrassed. Suddenly the case was intriguing him again.

'What case was Symonds working on?'

'Some burglary in Fenwood. Seemed straightforward to me. I don't know why I was needed.'

'Why didn't Meredith speak to you?'

'Steve basically blocked her off from coming into the room. He told her I hadn't seen anything and knew nothing about Burnell being brought in. Which was true, but I could have told her that.'

'So, what time did they let you leave?'

Laura drank some more wine.

'Straight away, pretty much. Once Meredith had gone elsewhere Steve said I should go. He seemed quite flustered, so I didn't ask any questions, I just went.'

'Did you talk to the team from the Yard before you left?'

'No. I went straight out of the fire exit that opens onto Grounds Way. You know, on the opposite side of the building from the station car park. To be honest I couldn't be bothered to get involved with any of it.'

Rowe nodded thoughtfully.

'Have you heard from Steve Symonds today?'

Laura shook her head.

'No. Did you talk to him?'

'Briefly.'

Rowe drank more of his beer and didn't expand further. He was grateful Laura didn't press him either, and she changed the subject instead.

'So, do you think there's more to the cell death then?'

'I'm not sure yet. The scene was a joke. The Yard team wanted it kept quiet and Vickers is trying to shut me down. No surprise there. I don't like it anyway. And as much as I can't wait to get out, I'm not signing it over just because Vickers says so.'

They fell quiet for a while and sipped on their drinks.

Rowe bought them another round and, in taking the drinks back to the table, checked the room for prying eyes and eavesdroppers. He couldn't see any obvious signs and wasn't sure if he expected to. It was a private rendezvous between two people who had been – and he hoped still were – very close. No one else mattered.

He settled back at the table with the drinks. They had slipped into the shop talk easily enough at the outset, but he wasn't sure what to say next.

'Mike...'

Laura's voice jolted him out of his inner dialogue.

'I want to say I'm sorry. The last two months have been very hard, but I never should have shut you out. After the attack…I didn't know what was happening to me. I thought I could tough it out but, actually, I was terrified, and I had no idea how to cope with it.'

She averted her eyes from him as they became damp, and he felt his own do the same.

'I went back to work to distract me, but it didn't help.' She gulped from her glass. 'I've felt like I was drowning ever since it happened. Probably should have talked to a counsellor or something.'

'Jesus…I'm sorry. Why didn't you talk to me?'

His voice was gentle, but he could feel a note of desperation in his throat. Guilt mixed with something like grief.

'I don't know.' A tear fell. 'I didn't know whether I wanted to be around anyone or not. Or whether they'd want me to be. Stupid, I suppose.'

Rowe reached across and took her hand firmly.

'I'll always be here to listen.'

'I know…I know. I still need time with this, Mike, but I want to start rebuilding things. I've missed you. I'm sorry.'

She wiped her eyes and straightened up in her chair.

'You don't need to say sorry,' Rowe said. 'I've missed you too, but we're here now. Let's keep talking from now on, OK? If you're ready to.'

Laura agreed that they should. They talked some more about her problems and decided to keep in touch over the next few days, especially if she was feeling particularly down. Rowe wanted just to hold on to her for as long as possible, and even though it was hard for him to fully understand what she was experiencing he could see she still needed time. He wouldn't rush things, as hard as that might be.

They finished their drinks, and it seemed the right time to leave if they were to be taking things step by step. They stood and hugged again. That one was longer and felt more like old times to Rowe. He kissed her on the cheek. Her hair smelt just as it always had.

When they parted ways, Rowe felt he had a lot to think about. It seemed like a new path had emerged that hadn't been there before, one which they both had to navigate without a map. It was somewhere to start at least, but whatever it was he wouldn't let it go. He'd had a long time to think about all of it recently and knew that how he felt about Laura had never been in doubt. He didn't think that real love ever was.

There was one other person still occupying his mind at that moment – albeit a far smaller part of it – and that was Steve Symonds. Even if Rowe's immediate instinct was never to think about the man again, the fact was that he needed to know a lot more about him. He believed Laura when she said there was nothing between them, but Symonds' role at Fenwood the previous night was troubling to Rowe. He was determined to figure out exactly why.

Mike Rowe walked out of the Trees bar with some bounce in his step and a smile pulling at the edges of his mouth.

12

THE CLOUDED, COLOURLESS LIGHT breaking through the gap in the curtains gradually woke him, and Rowe stirred. It took him a few seconds to realise he was in his own bed. For the first time in several weeks, he had gone home to his flat and slept there rather than in his car on some quiet back road. He hadn't felt the need to be elsewhere and, as he swung his feet to the floor, had no doubt that it was a direct result of the emotional and restorative meeting with Laura the previous night. Things weren't back to normal by a long shot, but he thought maybe they had a chance of getting somewhere close.

He looked at the clock on the bedside table. It was 7am – his body clock had clearly anticipated the imminent alarm. Rowe knew there was a lot he needed to do today if he was going to get even half the answers about the cell death that he wanted. He felt energised. He reached for his phone, which had been charging next to the clock, and typed a message to Meredith.

    Hey Joanne. You able to talk this morning?

He thought perhaps it was too early to be bugging her, but time was tight, and the message was at least light in tone. He got up and went straight into the shower. When he came out his phone was flashing to indicate he had a message. He picked it up, hoping it was a swift response from Meredith, and even allowing

88

something in the back of his mind to speculate that it was Laura continuing their reconnection from the night before.

When he opened the home screen though, it turned out not be a message but an e-mail to his personal account.

Detective Inspector Michael Rowe

This e-mail is notification that the Fenwood cell death investigation has now been closed by Oxford Police and passed to the Special Deployment Unit at Scotland Yard.

Your resignation from the Service has now been approved and confirmed. You are to report to Detective Chief Superintendent Carne's office at 0830 on Friday 12th November for processing of documentation and return of personal identification.

Detective Chief Inspector Neil Vickers

Office of Detective Chief Superintendent Judith Carne

Rowe stood still as he read through the message a few times. As it had come from Vickers, his first instinct was to ignore the missive and call Meredith to try and get a bead on things. But he quickly realised there would be no point. Meredith had probably been slow in gathering the information he requested because Vickers had told her to be. Most likely the pressure from Vickers started when the DCI and Meredith had been two of the last three people left in the Fenwood building the previous morning. Rowe thought that would certainly explain Meredith's obvious reluctance to continue with the investigation.

Rowe got dressed and went into the kitchen. He made some instant coffee and ate toast while he considered the situation. He decided there was one option worth trying.

Taking out his phone again, he searched for the number he wanted and called it. An unfamiliar female voice answered.

'Hello, this is Assistant Chief Constable Stanwell's line.'

'Hi, this is DI Rowe from Oxford CID. Is Nick available?'

'No, I'm afraid not, DI Rowe. The Assistant Chief Constable began a period of annual leave today.'

Rowe was in equal part surprised and not surprised to hear it. On the one hand, Stanwell hadn't given any indication of an imminent absence the day before. On the other, most people in senior roles in the public sector seemed to Rowe to be almost constantly on some sort of leave. And he could hardly complain, having just been on an ill-defined, impromptu sabbatical himself after all.

'Ok, no problem. Thanks anyway.'

He hung up. Stanwell was not contactable. Rowe knew the man had no mobile phone barring his obligatory service-issued one which would be turned off while he was on leave. It struck Rowe that it was typical of Vickers to pull something of that nature when Rowe's only senior ally was not around, and he cursed himself for not being prepared for the eventuality.

The coffee was starting to have some effect. The e-mail had been a blow, but he still felt the get-up-and-go in his legs that had been there on waking.

He downed a second cup before he left the flat.

13

HE TOOK THE STAIRS at Oxford station two at a time on his way to the top floor. When he got there, Rowe used his badge to swipe his way into the almost deathly quiet open-plan area. It was the same size as the two floors below only far more sparsely populated and mostly devoid of the activity generally associated with people and offices. The desks that were out in the open were manned by a smattering of senior-ranked officers who stared studiously at their computer monitors as if the very fabric of society depended on it. Rowe had no doubt that some of them thought that was indeed the case. It was just before 8:30am.

He walked across the office, past a couple of glass-walled rooms which contained more deathly-earnest members of the senior ranks. He ignored the sour glances cast by some of the assembled - he guessed he probably had even less respect for them than they did for him. Ahead of him, Neil Vickers emerged from a corner office adjacent to Judith Carne's and started in Rowe's direction with purpose. The door to Carne's office was closed and the venetian blinds shut.

'DI Rowe, Chief Superintendent Carne is currently in another meeting – '

Vickers stopped talking as Rowe brushed past his shoulder. It wasn't hard enough to start a physical confrontation, but it was enough to piss him off, which had been Rowe's intention. In one movement he opened the office door and stepped inside. Detective Chief

Superintendent Judith Carne was sitting behind her desk with her hands clasped on top of it. In the chair opposite Carne, with his back to Rowe, was another of the indistinguishable senior ranks, who turned his head in a disgusted manner at Rowe's sudden invasion. Their body language suggested it had been a relatively casual meeting, although Rowe wouldn't often have associated the word with Carne.

The Chief Superintendent was a slim and tall woman in her early fifties with grey hair that had once been blonde. Her face was expressionless – the only way Rowe had ever seen it – and gave away nothing of her inward emotions. Carne gave off an almost cliched air of intimidatory dominance, which, whether it was deliberate or not, was something else Rowe had little time for.

'Well, I'm here,' he said.

The seated senior officer turned back to Carne who was regarding Rowe silently.

'We'll continue this later,' she announced finally, not taking her eyes from Rowe. After a moment, the senior officer seemed to twig the statement was directed at him. He dutifully stood, moved impatiently past Rowe and out of the room, shutting the door behind him.

'Please sit down, DI Rowe.'

Carne had the practised, business-like delivery of a career police officer. It reminded Rowe of Grantley's speaking voice in that it lacked the distinction that she probably hoped it possessed.

'No thanks.'

Vickers thundered into the room at that moment, clearly taking the senior officer's exit as an excuse to insert himself into proceedings. He hurried across to the far end of Carne's desk, his long and thin legs making it a short journey, and turned to face Rowe, making a triangle of the three of them. Rowe thought he looked mildly distressed that he hadn't been expressly invited to join in.

'Why has the Burnell case been passed to the Yard already?' Rowe asked Carne, ignoring Vickers. 'They granted us two extra days and DC Meredith and I were in the middle of them.'

'Firstly Rowe, it's not a case.' Vickers hissed the words out. 'It was a preliminary enquiry into an unfortunate cell death, clearly from natural causes. You were generously granted an extended period by Commander Grantley's team in which to conduct this enquiry, but it has now been decided that that extension is unnecessary.'

'Oh, you performed Burnell's autopsy yourself did you, Vickers?' Rowe enquired. The DCI's olive complexion started to turn red as Rowe continued. 'Why was the extension deemed unnecessary? Meredith requested further information yesterday, some of which was based on the follow-up interviews we did. I'm not willing to sign this case over until I see that information.'

'DC Meredith did nothing of the sort, Rowe. I spoke to her and as far as she's concerned your enquiries were a waste of time. In any case, none of the information you asked her to procure would have been received within the given timeframe. Meredith has now been assigned to more pressing tasks.'

Vickers gave a glimmer of a smile in an obvious attempt to regain his composure. Rowe considered his suspicions that Meredith had been being pressured from the start to be confirmed. Their part of the supposed investigation never stood a chance. But he wasn't letting it go that easily.

'At the very least,' he said to Carne, 'we need to see the CCTV footage from the street before this is handed over. At this moment, we have no context at all for Burnell's death.'

No one responded. Carne seemed to be letting things play out.

'What you're doing is reckless at best,' Rowe went on. 'In a way I hope you're just passing the buck to the Yard to cover your arse. Otherwise, this is even more fucked up than I thought.'

Carne stared at him, her eyes inscrutable and narrow. It was Vickers that spoke next, his voice surprisingly steadier than it had been.

'Yesterday, DI Rowe, you conducted several either informal or unsanctioned interviews with officers who were present at Fenwood at the time of the cell death.' He took out a notebook and read from it. 'One of these interviews involved an intrusive visit to the home of a custody sergeant...'

Vickers looked up at Rowe as if to underline the seriousness of the accusation, before continuing.

'...one involved an unprovoked and violent attack on a fellow officer...'

Rowe's jaw tightened. He wasn't remotely surprised that Symonds had gone crying to Vickers and didn't care, but he could see where Vickers' melodrama was heading.

'...and one took place amid the consumption of alcohol by both parties. If indeed this were a 'case' as you seem so keen to characterise it, DI Rowe, that would be considered fraternising with a witness.'

Rowe said nothing. Carne filled the silence, as if collaborating on a rehearsed piece with Vickers.

'Mr Rowe,' she said, making a point of dropping his rank, 'please hand your identification materials and service mobile phone in now. The Fenwood matter is now with Scotland Yard and your contribution is at an end. DS Symonds will not be pressing charges with regards to the assault. My suggestion is that you stay away from police buildings and former colleagues for the next few weeks. Your presence while the SDU are completing their work could be deemed a distraction and any indication that you have interfered in any aspect of their work will be met with police action. In that event, you will of course be treated as a private citizen although your past indiscretions within the service will be taken into account.

'There was a time when you served this constabulary with an unconventional yet admirable effectiveness, Mr Rowe. But your time with the service is now complete and you are kindly asked to leave the premises immediately.'

A trace of a smile appeared on Vickers' face again and he took a step forward. Rowe turned, opened the door and walked out of the room.

'Your badge and phone, Rowe,' Vickers' called as he marched after him.

Rowe crossed the open-plan space and went out through the door. He took the stairs quickly all the way down to the back exit, aware that Vickers was behind him but probably not wanting to chase him in a way that might cause a scene.

As he pushed out through the back door, Rowe took the badge from his neck and tossed it, together with his phone, into the row of short hedges that stretched across the rear wall of the building.

Vickers must have seen the act through the glass and came scurrying out as Rowe neared his car. On reaching the Vitesse, Rowe called back to him:

'Fetch.'

After fishing the items out of the hedge and glaring bitterly at the Vitesse for a few moments, Vickers had finally gone back inside the building. Rowe sat in the car and considered things for a while.

While it wasn't a shock to him that Vickers had undermined the investigation, it hadn't occurred to Rowe that the man had been following him as well. That was the only real way, he decided, that the DCI could have known about his second trip to Fenwood station and the meeting with Laura. Rowe considered calling her to tell her what had happened but thought better of it. He would drop her a line later and only tell her if she asked about his day. Baby steps, for the time being.

As he thought about it, his personal phone that was on the passenger seat bleeped to indicate a new message. He picked it up and saw it was from Jim Ferry.

> No running in the building, young un

Ferry had obviously seen or been told about the commotion as Rowe had been pursued down the stairs past his floor. Rowe chuckled dryly at the message and replied.

```
            Working the big cases I see.
      Won't be able to solve them for you now.
                Pint later TJ?
```

TJ Hooker was one of the TV policemen Rowe liked to compare Ferry too, having heard of his exploits as a younger officer. Ferry replied within seconds.

```
            Great minds think alike.
                Vernon at 6?
          Have info that may interest
```

Rowe responded again, agreeing to the meeting place and time. At the very least, he thought, he and Ferry could celebrate his last day over a drink, but his friend's mention of potentially useful information intrigued him too. Ferry had suddenly become the only ally Rowe had in the service that he could readily talk to.

He knew it would make perfect sense at that point to forget the cell death and focus on fixing his relationship with Laura. But he also didn't like what he'd just learned in Carne's office. If Ferry had something, he needed to know what it was.

14

THE ADMIRAL VERNON WAS one of the few pubs left in Fenwood that could be considered traditional in any true sense of the word, and as a result was largely patronised by the more traditional-minded drinkers in the locale. It was slightly detached from the centre of town which Rowe found generally made it a solid combination of busy but not overrun. It was a late 18th century building in a string of other similar structures with a small front door, low ceiling and durable, lived-in oak furnishings. It was one of the places where Rowe and Ferry had met often.

Rowe thought the place fitted Ferry's character perfectly. The clientele tended to be stubborn, sardonic, and ruthless; anyone attempting to engage in conversation with the regulars needed to ensure they were adequately equipped to do so. Ferry thrived in such an environment, as Rowe had witnessed many times, and he enjoyed it even if he wasn't quite the practitioner that Ferry was. What he really loved was the concept of the communal living room in which people could escape their actual living rooms. Places like The Vernon were dying out, he was aware, but their appeal remained undimmed in his mind.

He stooped through the entrance just before 6pm and scanned the room for Ferry. Not seeing him, Rowe ordered a pint of Timothy Taylor Landlord and stayed put at the bar. He had spent most of the day catching up on chores at his flat for the first time in a while, which he had found oddly therapeutic. He had also exchanged brief messages with Laura; she had got word of his meeting at Oxford that morning and had asked if he was okay. He had briefly run through events, and they agreed to discuss it when they next met. Rowe found it was an easy exchange but also a warm reminder to him of what it was like to have Laura there to talk to.

After leaving Oxford and before going home, he had headed directly to the local council offices in Fenwood to enquire about the missing CCTV footage. His lack of identification had been a hindrance and he never made it past the reception desk. Rowe wasn't even sure why he'd gone there but mostly attributed it to simply wanting to shake things up after having learned of Vickers' skulduggery. Afterwards, he realised it was a fool's errand; today should have been the first day of the rest of his life, yet he was still allowing something to block his road.

Ferry breezed in as Rowe took the second gulp of his pint. He arrived alongside Rowe at the bar, carrying a brown A4-sized envelope with documents of some sort protruding from it and started earnestly examining the ale pumps.

'Seen better cask ale in a mosque.' Ferry deadpanned in the direction of the barman, a wide man in his fifties who feigned exasperation at the quip.

'Another Landlord, landlord.' Ferry winked at the man who gave a grim smile as he started pouring.

'Careful with that joke, TJ, it's an antique.' Rowe sighed. He paid for Ferry's beer, knowing that was what was expected, and they moved to a table near one of the wooden frame windows at the front of the pub.

'So that's you done then mate?' Ferry asked as they settled onto creaking chairs.

'Yup. Sorry I didn't bring any leaving cakes in.'

'Oh, it was noted.'

Ferry raised his glass.

'I don't mind saying you're a one-off, Rower. You'll be missed.'

'Cheers, Jim.' Rowe smiled and raised his own pint in acknowledgement.

'Hope you had a nice chat with the top brass before you left,' Ferry said after taking a sip. 'She's very fond of you.'

'Wouldn't call it a chat exactly. Think I made the mistake of trying to do actual police work again.'

'I thought you didn't like police work? Or police for that matter.'

Rowe sat back, still holding his pint while Ferry warmed to the topic.

'The thing about you, Rower, is you're so desperate to be a maverick cop that you think anyone who isn't is the enemy. I mean, we both know the job has its fair share of arseholes but we're not all like that. Some of us actually got into this lark to serve the public and, on occasion, actually do that very thing.'

'Jim, you got into it when helping little old ladies across the road and teaching school kids the phonetic alphabet still counted as police work. Even you have to admit that both the job spec and the preferred candidates have changed since then.'

'Maybe.' Ferry shrugged with faux haughtiness and reached for his beer.

'Somewhere along the line the modus operandi changed,' Rowe continued. 'The job stopped being about service and became more about control. The image of the honest beat bobby died when the corner shop stations like the one you and your compadres ran were shut down. Most of the types who join up now have axes to grind…prejudices. And the rest just want the power it grants them.'

'I'm sure you're right, Mr. Peace, Love and Understanding. But what about Laura? Does she count among this new breed of thugs and psychopaths?'

'Nah. She went into the family business because she knew she'd be good at it. I guess she and you are part of the third group – people in the job for the "right" reasons,' Rowe made quote marks in the air with his fingers, 'and who don't like to think about how messed up their colleagues really are.'

Ferry smiled and then took a drink so as to create a pause.

'You talked to her yet?'

'Yeah. Last night. She's doing okay. The attack thing hit her hard but she's tough.'

Ferry nodded and winked earnestly. He had known Laura Cross for longer than Rowe and had always looked out for her. Rowe knew the older man had been worried about her in recent times.

'So,' Rowe said more brightly, 'what's in the envelope? One of those giant leaving cards signed by the whole top floor?'

'Nope, just boring cop stuff I'm afraid.'

Ferry slid the envelope across the table, so it was lying between them.

'Well, this is basically useless to you now mate, but I took the liberty of doing some digging after our chat yesterday. Once you said Vickers was snooping around, I knew nothing much would be allowed to happen in his orbit. So, I dug up what I could on Burnell and did some research on cell deaths at small stations around the country. It struck me that that kind of thing is quite rare. Stop me if you've covered this stuff already.'

'Not at all. In fact, I asked Meredith for almost the same thing before Vickers put the kybosh on it.'

Rowe knew Ferry generally couldn't resist reading up on his cases but was still pleasantly surprised at the effort that had been made.

'This isn't going to come back on you, is it?' Rowe asked. 'I know you've got one eye on the gold watch.'

'Doubtful. I spend my days rummaging around databases for no reason. Can't see why anyone would suddenly take an interest in what I do at this late stage in the game.'

'True.' Rowe nodded at the envelope. 'Anything interesting come up?'

Ferry winced slightly. 'Nothing earth-shattering. Burnell had no immediate family as his parents are both dead and there are no siblings. He had employment of a sort – working for a website that transcribes meeting notes etc. for businesses. Not regular work and I'm guessing money was an issue. No criminal record and no other pertinent info to be found.'

'You get an address?'

'It's in there.'

'Thanks. Anything on the cell deaths?'

'Hard to say without looking into each one in depth, but in sheer numbers they've averaged around two or three per year in the UK in the last five years. More than I expected. Mostly natural causes, a couple were drug related. Nothing too lively.'

Rowe mulled it over.

'What about prior to the last five years?'

'More like one or two a year. Not significantly different.'

'But different.'

Ferry nodded, acknowledging the point. They went quiet for a few moments as Rowe considered the new information. He spoke eventually.

'Thanks for doing this, Jim.'

'No worries. Not sure what use it is though, you being a free spirit now and all.'

'Well, I started off curious about this thing...now I'm just pissed off. Vickers had been following me. Or having me followed, at least.'

'What?' Ferry looked up mid-gulp. 'Why's he doing that?'

'To make sure I don't cause a stink after the Hannah Crockett thing, I guess. Guess I must have been getting dangerously close to the truth on that.'

'Are you sure you're being followed?'

'He somehow knew I met Laura last night and that I paid another visit to Fenwood in the afternoon. He's shadowed my every move since yesterday morning. I don't think Carne knows about it – even she wouldn't agree to something like that. I think it's his deranged paranoia at work.'

'So, what are you gonna do?'

'Find a quiet spot to do some reading. And keep my eyes open.'

Rowe downed the last of his beer and grabbed the envelope as he stood up.

'You leaving already amigo? It's my round.'

'You can get them next time,' Rowe said, seeing Ferry's statement for the bogus play that it inevitably was. 'And anyway, you've already reached your usual limit.'

Ferry chuckled and saluted Rowe as he left.

15

THE VITESSE WAS PARKED one street over from The Admiral Vernon, among a throng of limestone houses. Night had fallen, with the streetlights shining on the pavement. Rowe scanned his surroundings as he walked to the car but couldn't see any signs of Vickers or anyone else watching him. He thought that Vickers may have lost interest due to Rowe's credentials being removed but felt it also didn't hurt to put it to the test.

He reached the Vitesse and got in, constantly observing his immediate surroundings. He started the engine and moved off, winding through the streets until reaching a road that led out of Fenwood to the northwest. Then he travelled fifteen miles or so, traversing back roads and single-track lanes in a direction he hadn't driven for years. Despite that fact, he felt strangely attuned to the large expanses of quiet that he passed through. He continued into that territory, negotiating increasingly remote and expensive villages and hamlets where streetlights were practically unheard of.

Eventually, Rowe slowed and turned right off a quiet road onto an even quieter and narrower one with only fields on either side. It was not sign-posted. The road was long and straight until it curved to the right after 300 yards or so. Reaching the curve, Rowe slowed and performed a turn in the road until he was facing back the way he had come. Then he accelerated forwards as fast as he was able back to the junction and stopped. No other vehicles or signs of life were visible. He waited. After a minute or so he turned the car again and headed back up to the curve. He kept going for another 300 yards, then stopped again. Then repeated the same trick; turning, driving as fast as possible back to the junction, waiting, turning again, then heading back the way he had come.

Further down the road than before, Rowe pulled over into a passing place and stopped. He turned the lights off, killed the engine and waited again. Nothing stirred around him from the road or from the open fields that were exposed, in part, by moonlight which was unimpeded by any overhanging trees. After a few minutes he restarted the engine but didn't turn on the headlights, and moved off, using the moon's light to make very slow progress and ensuring he didn't miscalculate the road ahead. After a couple of minutes, a dull glow came into view in the distance. As the artificial light nullified the effect of the moon's illumination, Rowe turned his lights back on and sped up until the source of the new glow came into view.

It was an old, compact, two-storey building, and the light was emanating from within it. A simple, sparsely lit sign hung from a pole out the front which read 'The Bear and Rifle' at its top and 'Free House' at its bottom. Rowe kept driving past the pub. Another 200 yards ahead he slowed and turned left onto a farm track that curved back, parallel with the road and which was shielded from it by a high hedgerow. There was enough room at the side of the farm track for the Vitesse to edge in without blocking access for another vehicle, although Rowe was hopeful that that scenario wouldn't arise, as the barns visible at the end of the track appeared to be derelict.

He killed the lights and the engine again, then sat still for a while and listened. On the roads leading out there the traffic had become naturally quieter, but one car had stayed with him. It had been a fair way behind, but its headlights could be seen in the dark. To test whether it was a follower or not, Rowe had taken a series of random, nonsensical turns that he knew would still lead him roughly in the right direction. The car had disappeared shortly after. Nonetheless, he had performed the checks he could be doubly sure that no one was still lurking at a distance.

Rowe had not seen the car for at least fifteen minutes, and after a while sitting silently on the farm track, he was satisfied it was not close by. While the thought could have been deemed paranoid, it was still possible that the car had been following him but had backed off for some reason. Still, he couldn't wait forever. He got out of the car and walked back to the pub.

No vehicles passed him on the road as he arrived at The Bear and Rifle, although a good number were parked on the gravel stretch at the front of the pub. A middle-aged couple emerged from the front door as he approached and paid him no attention as they drifted to their car.

Rowe thought he had only been to the pub once before, possibly as long as ten years earlier, but he couldn't be sure. It fitted the stereotype of the country gastropub that maintained a smaller yet healthy core of drinking clientele so as to retain its status as a pub, rather than a restaurant. It was one of those affluent hostelries in the sticks that Rowe viewed as being one wealthy regular's raised eyebrow away from becoming exclusively focused on dining. Despite that, upon entering Rowe found he still liked the pub and was reassured by the mini club of drinkers that occupied its bar area.

He caught the eye of the young girl behind the bar and asked for a pint of Old Hooky. When it appeared he paid for it and headed for a small table and short stool the other side of the large open fireplace which was lit and giving off a welcoming warmth. It was an old school, casual area in stark contrast to the clearly renovated dining portion of the pub, which he could see was doing a decent trade at that time.

Rowe took the envelope that he had brought with him from under his arm, removed the printed documents held within it and spread them on the table. The first pages showed the personal details of James Burnell, including his home address, typed into a summary - by Jim Ferry, Rowe presumed. He scanned the opening lines:

```
James Andrew Burnell.
Born 12th September 1990 to Derek and Susan
Burnell in Taunton Hospital, Somerset.
Employed by RiteUp.com online transcription
service since 2016.
Burnell inherited family home in Somerset on death
of both parents in a road accident 03.06.15.
No obvious links to Fenwood.
```

Rowe stared at the page for a long time, re-reading it to ensure he was seeing it correctly. He sat back and gazed blankly at the room around him as he thought. A moment later he was brought out of his semi-trance by a face at the bar. It was that of a young man that he had seen before, but he couldn't think where. Rowe was good at remembering faces but not always good with context. Maybe he'd seen him in another pub somewhere. Either way, he didn't especially like the coincidence at a moment when he believed he was being followed.

He didn't stare at the man. Simply went back to reading through the documents. The other pages were all listings with brief details of each cell death at smaller stations over the past few years. Rowe scanned through them, making a mental note of the occasional interesting detail but nothing jumped out at him in the way that the first page had. He stole the occasional glance at the bar but had not seen the young face turn his way yet. The man appeared to be on his own.

Rowe went back to the papers. Just as he was deciding there was no further information of interest in them, his eyes shot back to a single word in one of the cell death summaries.

Coroner.

Without moving his head upward, Rowe looked back at the young man at the bar and caught him averting his gaze. Then the face came back to him: it belonged to the coroner's assistant from the previous morning who had helped take Burnell's body away. They had briefly locked eyes when Rowe had announced he would want to see their final report.

It came to Rowe that it was the same man who had been in the car following him earlier and who had then backed off for some reason. He surmised that the man had probably been checking all the pubs in the area and finally stumbled on the right one. Why it was that particular man that was following him, Rowe didn't know.

He waited until the face wasn't looking in his direction. Then he subtly collected the documents back into the envelope, sipped the last of his pint and was gone.

The pub had two rear exits for customers – one which led from the dining room to the smoking area and one which opened from the bar area onto a patio with outdoor seating and a garden beyond. The patio was lit from ground level despite not being in use at that moment, but the garden behind it was in darkness. Rowe was in the garden, standing behind one of the tall hedges that divided the grassed area about halfway down. From his vantage point, he could see both rear exits of the pub.

It took less than two minutes for the man to emerge, cautiously, from the same door that Rowe had. He seemed to scan the area, and, for a moment, Rowe thought the man wasn't going to investigate the whole garden. But then the supposed assistant to the coroner stepped down from the patio and began to edge around the perimeter of the lawn, eyes moving constantly. Rowe had settled into a crouch behind the hedge and could see the man was roughly his own height but wirier in build. As the man drew closer, Rowe shrunk further back behind the hedge and remained motionless. Instead of turning into the gap between the tall hedges though, the man continued past, at which point Rowe took the opportunity to move out from his hiding place.

Rowe darted out behind his follower and stabbed the sole of his right boot into the back of the man's knee. The leg that received the blow gave way and Rowe used his forward momentum to grasp his opponent round the neck from behind. But despite his disadvantageous position and the swiftness of the attack, the man reacted unfathomably quickly. He seized the arm that was across his throat and spun around, rising up as he did so. Rowe tried to react by grabbing the man's neck again with his free right hand but found himself in an identical hold immediately. They each tried to block the other's left arm until both were gripping that of the other. They stood rigid like that for a few seconds, staring.

'Why are you following me?'

Rowe rasped the question as best he could, but the man's hand on his throat was solid. There was no response.

'Who are you?' Rowe croaked with some effort.

The man didn't speak. Rowe was unnerved by his calmness. He could feel from their physical proximity that his opponent probably had the edge over him; he sensed a level of training beyond police self-defence or the very basic karate that Rowe himself had learned as a teenager. It was palpable. He didn't understand why the man hadn't yet made a move to gain the upper hand.

'Tell Vickers I'm coming for him.'

Rowe forced out the words as a final push to incite a reaction from his silent adversary. However, all that came across the young man's face was a look that resembled confusion before it dissipated into a kind of black amusement.

Loud voices sprang forth from the smoking area at that moment. An inebriated couple had appeared and were lighting cigarettes. Rowe and the man maintained their respective grips on each other, standing unseen in the dark as they were, but the interruption had taken some of the intensity out of the stand-off. In an instant, the man removed his hand and evaded Rowe's grasp, spiriting away past him in the darkness.

Rowe stood in the same spot, confused and rubbing his throat. He looked around him and saw nothing and no one in the garden. Then he heard the sound of a car starting followed by hurried tyres on gravel.

Slowly, after a minute or so, he retrieved the envelope from behind the hedge where he had left it and ventured back towards the pub. No one seemed remotely interested in him as he re-entered the bar, suggesting the confrontation in the garden had gone completely unnoticed. An older couple were sitting at the table he had previously occupied, so he walked over and took a seat among the drinkers at the bar. He saw no sense in retreating to his car at that point.

Once again, he had some thinking to do.

16

THE NEXT MORNING AT 7am, Rowe was in the Vitesse on another long and quiet stretch of country backroad. He was parked in one of the makeshift laybys that those types of single-track lanes have – a generally rutted and uneven surface which could be tricky to negotiate in very wet weather, especially when potholes weren't readily visible. That morning was only damp however, and he had found a flattish stretch on which to stop.

Fifty yards ahead on the same side of the road was a house out on its own. Rowe presumed its address was technically attached to one of the neighbouring villages, even though it wasn't physically situated in any of them. He wasn't sure though as he hadn't needed to search anywhere for the specific address of the house. It was a place he'd known for a long time.

The home belonged to Assistant Chief Constable Nicholas Stanwell. It was a picturesque, early twentieth century affair which comprised three wide floors, the highest of which had been converted from attic space. Impressive by most standards except perhaps those of other country manors in the area. It was set back from the road with a generously proportioned driveway that stretched the full width of the house, while at the rear a large conservatory had been added at some point which looked out on the broad back garden. Beyond that, the house was surrounded only by fields owned by a farmer who was Stanwell's closest neighbour and who resided roughly a hundred yards further down the road. There were no significant structures in the visible vicinity that didn't belong either to Stanwell or the farm.

Stanwell – who was four years past the traditional police retirement age of sixty – had been a close confidant and friend of Rowe's father, Brian. Stanwell's own father had been a prominent lawyer and politician in the area, and the house had been passed down from him. Rowe remembered coming to the place countless times when he was growing up. Stanwell had been someone who encouraged Rowe to join the police at a time when Rowe was doubtful about it and his innate rebelliousness was taking over. The older man had always been an empathetic ear, and his gentle approach had been instrumental in Rowe's decision to follow in his father's footsteps.

The house held other memories for Rowe: abundant food, revelatory (to him) music from Stanwell's deep and varied vinyl collection, a general warmth that he had always felt within the place. The matriarch Gloria – Stanwell's wife, who had died two years earlier – had cultivated most of it. Their daughter Sarah had felt like a sister to both Rowe and his brother Devon.

As he looked at the house, Rowe felt like all of that was a very long time ago.

Rowe watched and waited. He had slept in the car in its spot near The Bear and Rifle the previous night and hadn't been home. As a result, he was stiff and tired. He had taken an educated guess that Stanwell would be at home on a Saturday morning and that he, despite being on leave, hadn't gone away anywhere. Sure enough, lights came on upstairs around 7:30am and, as it got closer to eight, he saw the front door open and someone who resembled Stanwell step out to retrieve milk bottles from the step.

Rowe started the car. The light was creeping on and although the road had been deserted since he arrived and he was fairly sure no one had seen him there, it was time to get out of sight. He turned the wheel fully to the right and edged out of the layby, stopped, reversed back, then headed back down the lane away from the house. After a short distance he turned right up an unmarked mud and gravel track that lay between two hedgerows and was barely wide enough for the tractors and other farm vehicles it was intended for.

He followed the track along the length of the field to its right until the guiding hedge eventually curved a sharp right along the back edge of the field. Halfway along that stretch, the track became wider and the hedgerows taller. An ancient, moss-greened shed which Rowe had always known to be there stood next to the hedge. He guessed it belonged to the farmer and that whatever it held couldn't be worth a great deal judging by the state of repair it was in. There was a rough, well-worn rectangle right in front of the shed where Rowe parked the Vitesse. He knew parking there was a calculated risk – he was relying on the fact that Stanwell was still friendly with the farmer if any questions did happen to be asked. Rowe just hoped they were asked before the car was shunted or dragged unceremoniously back to the road.

He got out and looked around. There were no human beings in sight and no vehicles could be heard from the road. A horse neighed from the direction of the farm. He locked the car and walked around to the other end of the shed where there was a purposely made gap leading into the field behind Stanwell's house. The field was ploughed so Rowe made his way round its left edge where some grass still existed, trying to avoid the heaviest mud where possible. Rowe knew there were ways a person can walk without attracting attention but being on open ground in a muddy field certainly made that more difficult. He quickened his pace as best he could.

Coming round to the side where the house was, Rowe walked briskly alongside the tall wooden-slat fence that spanned the back of Stanwell's property and looked for a particular spot. He found what he was looking for almost straight away: there was a gate built into the fence which he was glad to see had not been overgrown and was even more glad that its bolt was not padlocked when he tried it. Cautiously, he pushed his way through into some foliage which soon gave way to the lawn beyond. He examined the back of the house before stepping out into the open. There seemed to be movement in the kitchen, on the left side of the house as he looked at it.

Rowe quickly stepped out and across the lawn diagonally, past the conservatory and directly towards the kitchen door that opened onto a small back patio. As he drew closer, he saw that Stanwell was indeed in the kitchen, busying himself at the sink with his back to the door. He was wearing a chequered shirt tucked into expensive-looking jeans, which by Rowe's estimate was as casual as the man's attire ever got.

The kitchen was a large, rustic affair with an aga oven and sturdy wooden finishes. Rowe tapped on the door's glass window. Stanwell was ten feet or so away, but he stopped what he was doing abruptly and half-turned towards the door in surprise. He smiled upon realising who it was that had knocked but Rowe thought there was hesitance in it, perhaps understandably. Hs father's friend dried his hands with a tea towel before striding over and opening the door.

'Mike! To what do I owe this pleasure at such an hour on a Saturday?'

Rowe thought Stanwell looked genuinely pleased to see him.

'Hello, Nick. Sorry to turn up like this. Can I come in?'

'Of course.' Stanwell moved back, allowing Rowe to step inside. 'Dare I ask what necessitates the cloak and dagger arrival? Haven't seen you at this door since you used to play out the back with Devon and Sarah.'

Stanwell was still smiling but something in his face suggested that he had realised the memory might not be one Rowe welcomed. Rowe's older brother Devon had disappeared ten years earlier while posted in Afghanistan with the British Army. He had been close to an explosive device that detonated but his body was never found. He was presumed dead. Stanwell's daughter Sarah, meanwhile, was alive, married and living in London – Rowe thought she was working in the legal profession somewhere, but he had lost track of the details over the years.

Before Rowe could respond to his first question, Stanwell asked if he wanted coffee.

'Yes please. Just black. I came to the back door as a precaution…it's a long story.'

'Coming up. Go and have a seat in the conservatory and you can fill me in when it's brewed.'

Stanwell winked and Rowe did as he was told. He walked out of the kitchen, through the large, high-ceilinged living room and into the almost equally generous and airy conservatory that connected to it. The conservatory held a couple of relaxed, white-cushioned chairs and a bamboo two-seater affair and offered a panoramic view of the garden. Rowe stared out at it for a few seconds before sitting down in one of the cushioned chairs. Stanwell appeared after a short while and deposited two coffee mugs on a low table in the middle of the sunroom before settling into the chair opposite Rowe's.

'What's up then, Mike? I heard about what happened yesterday morning, naturally. I'm sorry I wasn't around but I'm not sure I'd have been much use anyway. For what it's worth, I'm sorry to see you go.'

Rowe held up a hand.

'Thanks, but we all knew the day was coming. I was the one who wanted to leave after all. As for the cell death thing, I know you did what you could.'

Stanwell smiled and they sipped their coffee in polite silence until Rowe got to the rub of his visit.

'I guess what I'm here about is somewhat related,' he said. 'At the little meeting yesterday morning I found out that Neil Vickers had been following me. I wasn't totally surprised as I know he was paranoid about my involvement anyway, especially after I linked him to

Hannah Crockett's death. But it seemed a bit extreme even by his standards.'

Stanwell said nothing but made it clear he was listening.

'That was one thing,' Rowe went on. 'What was odd is I was followed again last night. And not by Vickers, or even Steve Symonds who seems to be weirdly in his pocket somehow, but someone else. And he seemed like he was trained.'

'Trained?'

Stanwell raised a bushy eyebrow.

'Yeah. I don't know in what exactly, but he wasn't job, and it was more than just basic stuff from the training centres. I think he could've put me down quite easily but for some reason he chose not to.'

'How odd.' Stanwell's eyebrow remained raised. 'I presume you made some, uh, polite enquiries and that's how you discovered he was a bit handy? How did you pick him out in the first place?'

'Something like that. Picking him was easy – it was the same guy who was assisting the coroner at Fenwood the other morning.'

'Really? Are you sure he was following you? Seems very odd if so.'

'He followed me to a pub in the middle of nowhere – I saw him hanging back. I'm sure it was him, coincidences like that just don't happen. But the fact he was the coroner's assistant could make a kind of sense. It's possible that Vickers – or Carne, more likely – either want or have control over Burnell's autopsy and they don't want other eyes on it. This guy, whoever he is, is working for them and they're trying to warn me off. Or maybe it's Grantley pulling the strings. Either way, it raises a lot of other questions. And you can see why I'd want to keep a low profile today.'

Stanwell sat back. He puffed his cheeks out and ran a hand through his hair.

'Well. I'll admit it's all very, very strange and irregular, Mike. Bizarre in fact. But I'm not sure there's much to be done short of reporting this fellow to the police – which I'll presume isn't currently an option. Do you have anything else to link this to DCI Vickers? Or anyone else?

'Not yet. Although I intend to keep digging.'

Stanwell frowned. 'I'm not sure that's a statement for my ears.'

'There's something else too,' Rowe said, continuing as if Stanwell hadn't spoken. 'I went back to Fenwood on Thursday afternoon to take a look around the higher floors.'

'What made you do that? As far as I know it's just a junk pile up there these days.'

'Curiosity I suppose. And yes, it is mostly a junk pile. But something on the top floor looked out of place. Couldn't put my finger on it but it was like the dimensions of the room were wrong. And I didn't have time to check it out.'

'Right...and how does this connect to the other matter?'

'Vickers somehow knew I was there even though no one had told him. I'm pretty sure it was him that had my visit curtailed.'

They continued to talk, and Stanwell fetched more coffee. The older man sat attentively while Rowe offered additional background, including the suspicions he held regarding Steve Symonds and the motives of the Scotland Yard team. Sensing he may simply be being humoured at that point, Rowe wound up his summary to allow Stanwell to consider the situation and respond, which eventually he did.

'Well, I can see the predicament and I empathise with your curiosity completely, Mike.' Stanwell had sat forward, hands clasped between his knees. 'It's a confusing one. You wouldn't have been such a good DI if you weren't intrigued by it. Sadly though, I think this is going to be one of those events you simply have to file away as someone else's problem and have done with it. As you know, I had hoped the cell death would all be very straightforward but that ended when the SDU got involved. I can only apologise for dragging you into it like I did. As things stand, however, the case is now outside of all our respective remits and, unless you are willing to make an official report over being followed, there is no realistic action you can take except the obvious.'

'Which is?'

'Do as Chief Superintendent Carne suggested and take some time away. Forget all this noise. As much as it pains me to see you resign from the service I would much rather you were happy. You have your entire life ahead of you now. This current issue is only delaying you from living it.'

Stanwell smiled a sympathetic smile. Rowe was sitting back in his seat, aware that his body language told that he knew a valid and sensible point was being made. Possibly sensing the same, Stanwell continued.

'I've never told you this, Mike, but there were a couple of times in the early days when your dad and I considered quitting altogether. Some blustery old goat – not unlike I am now – would shut down a case we were on or reassign it elsewhere. We both still had that fiery will that so many start out with, so we talked about getting out and working in private security or opening a pub together or something. Never quite had the gumption to do it, I suppose. After a while we learned to pick our battles. It's very political in the police, Mike, as you know, but that doesn't mean you have to be a politician to survive it. It's more about rolling with the punches…and letting someone else carry the load every now and then.'

Rowe didn't have any response at that moment, and Stanwell was warming to his nostalgic bent.

'You're very similar to Brian, Mike. I know I've said that before. You're more, er, single-minded than him, but the resemblance is still strong. He was basically fearless and had a very strong sense of justice. He certainly didn't agree with a lot of what we had to do as police, although I will grant you that things are worse now than they were then. It's not the same service I joined, although some would argue it still serves the same purpose. I think your dad had fallen out of love with it a bit…by the end. Perhaps he was starting to share some of your misgivings.'

Rowe looked back at Stanwell steadily.

'I don't think so,' he said. 'My Dad wouldn't hear a word against the police. In hindsight, I think he just found it hurtful that his son didn't fully respect his profession. Maybe he thought that meant I didn't fully respect him as a person, which couldn't have been further from the truth.'

Stanwell looked at the floor and nodded.

'I must admit, I struggled with some of your characterisations of the service at times.'

Rowe smiled slightly. 'I'm sure. All I really wanted was for anyone in positions like that – police yes, but others too – to think a bit more. Why am I doing this? Who am I here to help? What gives me the right? That last one was the kicker. Being in a position of power gives you permission to do certain things, but having the right is different. Like this cell death problem – what gives Vickers, Carne, Grantley or whoever the right to just push it away or gloss over it? Where's the thought for James Burnell's family? Does anyone care?'

Stanwell tilted his head but didn't speak. They fell silent as both neared the end of their refilled coffee mugs. A small number of birds chattered in the leafless trees outside on what was still a grey morning.

'Crikey,' Stanwell said out of the quiet. 'Must be almost fifteen years since we lost Brian and Aoife. Seems like only last week we were all guffawing together in here.'

Rowe looked up from his mug.

'I found out Burnell's parents also died in a car crash, in 2015,' he said, electing not to mention the specific date.

'Did they?' Stanwell met Rowe's eyes in surprise at the detail. 'There are some incredibly tragic things that befall us in this world – some more so than others.'

Stanwell sat back again in thought.

'I know it's been a dreadfully long time, Mike,' he said, 'but have there been any more developments concerning Devon?'

Rowe finished the last of his coffee, then shook his head.

'None.'

There had been a handful of unverified sightings of Devon Rowe shortly after his disappearance, but none of them were ultimately deemed credible and there had been no more since. The trail, if one ever existed, was cold.

'Please let me know if you ever do hear any more. He was a very good lad.'

Rowe nodded. He then stood up from his deep chair.

'Thanks for the coffee, Nick. And thanks for listening. Apologies again for barging in so early.'

'Think nothing of it.' Stanwell stood up himself and shoved his hands in his pockets. 'It's nice to have the company – drop by any time. Do think about what I said though, old chap. Nothing good can come from stirring things up anymore. Time to start again.'

Stanwell gave one of his trademark winks. Rowe saw a trace of sadness in the eyes of his father's old friend. It occurred to him that maybe he hadn't given enough thought to how difficult things had been for the man, existing alone in a big house as loved ones and friends slowly disappeared from his life.

'I will.' Rowe smiled back and made his way out towards the back door again. As he opened it, Stanwell took its weight.

'Give Laura my best, will you?' he asked. 'She's one to keep hold of.'

'Absolutely. And yes, she is.'

Rowe said goodbye and went back the way he had come – across the garden, through the gate in the fence and around the edge of the ploughed field. He emerged through the gap in the hedge, walked around the shed and was glad to see the Vitesse was apparently untouched.

He got into the car and spent a while thinking back on the conversation he had just had. Stanwell was a confidant and Rowe knew deep down his advice to leave things be was sound. But there were things about the exchange that niggled at him – he just couldn't put his finger on exactly what they were. He guessed he would work it out, given time.

Rowe's phone bleeped in the silence of the resting farmland. A new message. Rowe took the phone out, hoping it was Laura but half-expecting it to be Vickers or someone else he would rather ignore.

It turned out to be from Jim Ferry, and it contained three words:

```
Symonds is dead
```

17

JIM FERRY'S HOUSE WAS in the Dunfield Circle area of Fenwood. Rowe parked three streets away from it, shortly after 10am. He got out of the car and, as he did, momentarily noticed a black car moving into a space behind him at the far end of the street. He pretended that he hadn't.

The street was part of a sprawling section of wartime and post-war housing on the edge of town, most of which was quiet and largely inhabited by older people and those soon to qualify as such. A lot of the houses were bungalows or close-quartered terraces with waist-height walls bordering compact front lawns. It struck Rowe that the economy of space wasn't far removed from the modern housing he saw on estates like the one that Rachel Worth lived on.

There had been a light rain, and the pavement was damp. Rowe walked up the street, away from the Vitesse and the black car he had seen. At the end was a T-junction where he decided to bear right, continuing in that direction whilst periodically checking to see if the black car or its occupant were anywhere in sight. Confident that neither were, he crossed the road and jogged a few yards to a path that ran between the end of one row of houses and the corner of another street. On the path he settled back into a fast walk, which he thought was less conspicuous than a jog. If whoever was in the black car was in fact following him, Rowe accepted there was a good chance they already knew where he was headed. However, his rationale was that it didn't hurt to be cautious.

Doubling back along the path behind the houses he had just passed, he weaved his way through, staying alert and moving quickly, until he turned onto the street where Ferry lived.

Rowe had responded to Ferry's message first to check he was at home and second to say he would be there directly. He had also a sent a message to Laura, simply to make contact again – and because the news of Steve Symonds' death had concerned him. He hadn't mentioned it in the message because he wanted more information first, which was why he was on the route he was.

Reaching Jim Ferry's house, he headed down the short path that led to the front door, then side-stepped to the wooden gate that accessed the passage at the side of the property and led to its rear. He pushed through the garden gate and saw Ferry waving at him through the dusty window of a shed at the far end of the lawn, which was where he had said he would be waiting. Rowe walked over to the shed and entered through the door at its right-hand end.

'Ah, the prodigal son returns,' said Ferry with false surprise.

Ferry was sitting on a rickety-looking wooden chair at a small-scale white patio table and holding a mug of unspecified liquid to his lips. There was a similar chair next to where Rowe stood, and on the table sat a Thermos, a hip flask and a second mug.

Rowe looked briefly around the shed and saw tools and various garden items that were covered in cobwebs and dust that had long settled and that were haphazardly shoved towards the back of the structure. Underneath the window was an old, similarly unemployed workbench, beneath which a prehistoric lawnmower lay dormant. It was apparent that Ferry had at some point cleared space for the table at which he was sitting, at the expense of the items the cramped shed was intended for. Rowe noted that a cheap digital radio sat on the workbench while empty real ale selection boxes cluttered the floor and a dog-eared Playboy calendar from 2012 hung on a nail next to the window.

'Welcome to the man cave, muchacho. Snifter?'

Ferry raised the hip flask from the table and waggled it.

'Thanks. You didn't have to tidy up on my account.'

Ferry poured coffee into Rowe's mug and topped up his own, then did the same for each with whatever the hip flask contained. As he did so, Rowe glanced through the glass and saw Ferry's wife Angela looking back at them from the kitchen window.

Ferry had suggested they meet in the shed for reasons of privacy, but Rowe knew their presence would not have been welcomed in the house in any case. Angela Ferry viewed Rowe as a bad influence on her husband, whom she in turn viewed as a kind of pitiable jester, in her more charitable moments. Rowe's invitations to their home were few and far between. He imagined that Angela hadn't set foot in the shed for decades, if ever, and had probably actively lobbied for its demise.

'So, what's the word on Symonds?' Rowe asked as he carefully settled on the moribund chair.

'Strange one.' Ferry leant forward and spoke in a hushed tone that surprised Rowe in its seriousness. 'He was found this morning in his car at the bottom of a steep hill near the quarry out by Billingmoore. Apparently looks like he veered off the road and flew down through the trees there. Hit a fair few of them on the way down too. The car was a mess and so was he. No other vehicles involved, so they say.'

'When did this happen?'

'Hard to be certain yet as there were no witnesses, and no reports came in. But they're thinking it could have been as far back as Thursday night.'

'Thursday? How come no one saw the car earlier?'

'Seems it was out of sight from the road. A dog walker spotted it from a field on the other side in the early hours. Symonds wasn't due on shift yesterday and he lived alone, so no one knew he was gone.'

Rowe looked out of the window blankly.

'I know that stretch of road,' he said. 'Someone would have to be going at a hell of a lick there to veer off, clatter though the trees and hit the bottom.'

'Maybe he was drunk, these things do happen.'

'Symonds didn't drink. He was one of those fitness freak types. But drunk or sober, I'm telling you; it'd be near impossible to have an accident like you've described on that road.'

'Brakes failed?'

'Possible. Let me know if you hear anymore after it's been checked out. But if you ask me the timing is very convenient.'

Ferry looked at him.

'Not very convenient for Symonds I'd say. Are you saying this might be linked to the Burnell thing? Bit of a leap and, I'd guess, impossible to prove.'

'I don't think it's a leap. Symonds was the only one they kept back after everyone else had gone on Thursday morning. Laura said he seemed flustered when the thing happened. And now he's dead, quite possibly within 24 hours of Burnell.'

Ferry didn't respond but stared at his mug thoughtfully.

'Well, it's something to consider, mate,' he said. 'Not sure what you or I can do about it though. If there's been foul play, I'd imagine the investigation will turn something up.'

'Like my investigations into Crockett and Burnell's deaths did you mean?'

Ferry frowned. Rowe leant forward and spoke more quietly.

'I was followed here today, Jim. And I also had a tangle with a guy last night who followed me to the middle of nowhere. Someone's trying to get to me, even now when I'm not a copper anymore.' Rowe sipped from his mug, wincing slightly at the strength of its secret ingredient. 'I went and saw Stanwell this morning – he agrees with Carne that I should make myself scarce for a while. I was close to agreeing with him before I got your message.'

'Followed here? My address isn't a state secret, sadly. But that does sound dodgy I grant you. Who was the guy last night?'

'I don't know, but if I had to guess I'd say he was a stooge roped in by Vickers. Seemed like he was just there to try and intimidate.'

'Jeez. Never a dull moment with you is there. So, what now?'

'Think it's high time I paid someone a visit.' Rowe stood up and drained more contents from his mug. 'Thanks for the coffee, TJ. I'll be in touch.'

'Anytime, Rower. The man cave never closes.'

Leaving Ferry's house the same way he came in, Rowe checked the road before venturing out into full view. He didn't see any people or vehicles that looked out of place but went back to his car by the same route he had taken earlier anyway. There was no black car at the end of the street when he reached the Vitesse. Even so, Rowe was sure it would be somewhere close by.

He had decided that it didn't matter in any case. As far as Rowe was concerned, being followed to the next place he was headed wouldn't be an issue.

18

THE VITESSE CAME TO a stop around fifty yards from the entrance to the Oxford police station car park. It was midday on a Saturday and parking was at a premium in town, but the largely residential street that the rear of the station backed onto still offered a handful of spaces between the driveways of its houses.

In his wing mirror, Rowe saw a black car – a Mercedes – glide past the end of the street. He was confident it was the same one he had seen near Ferry's house in Fenwood as he had observed it trailing behind him at a distance on his journey to Oxford. He hoped it would reappear again shortly.

Neil Vickers' car – also a Mercedes, but a silver convertible – was in the station car park as Rowe had expected. Rowe thought the car suited the man; someone who put image above all else in his quest for power and success. In Rowe's eyes, Vickers was a bullshit merchant of the highest order; someone who would arrive early in the office and leave late purely for the sake of appearances. As laughably transparent as such tactics seemed to Rowe, he also knew they had probably contributed to Vickers' rise in the ranks and the fact the DCI had come to be the trusted sidekick of Chief Superintendent Judith Carne. The predictability of the DCI's sucking up meant he was very likely to be in the office on a Saturday, which was Rowe's purpose for coming.

Rowe waited. He calculated that whoever was in the black car would have had time to notify Vickers of his presence. Ultimately, Vickers would have no choice but to confront him, blowing the cover of whichever goon was behind the wheel of the black Mercedes as he did so. The waiting continued for longer than Rowe liked though, and after a while he had to admit that if Vickers was aware of his presence, he was either showing restraint or avoiding him.

As he waited, Rowe's phone vibrated in his pocket, and he took it out to find a response from Laura to his earlier message. She suggested they talk on the phone later that day. That was fine by him. Just as he turned his thoughts back to the situation at hand and a potential alternative strategy, he saw Vickers emerge from the back door of the station. It had just gone 12:30, which Rowe presumed meant that a half day of doing nothing constructive was apparently enough for his former boss on a Saturday.

Vickers appeared relaxed and seemed to have the air of a man without a care in the world - possibly of someone finally free of a burden, Rowe speculated. Vickers didn't glance in Rowe's direction or even seem to consider he might be being watched. He wasn't in an obvious rush either. If he was bluffing, Rowe had to admit it was a surprisingly good act.

The DCI got into his Mercedes, started it up and proceeded to the exit of the car park. He turned right up the one-way street, away from where Rowe was parked and towards town. Rowe started the Vitesse and moved out swiftly to follow the car closely. He wanted Vickers to see him. The Vitesse edged up tight behind the

Mercedes as it headed for the junction at the end of the street. Rowe flashed his headlights. He saw Vickers give an irritated glance in the rear-view mirror, which quickly turned to surprise and then anger when he saw who was doing the flashing.

Rowe put his indicator on and pointed to the right-hand side of the road, which had a single yellow line and was unoccupied for thirty yards or so. Grudgingly, Vickers slowed and pulled over, right side wheels up on the curb so traffic could pass, and Rowe slotted in behind him in the same way.

Their drivers' doors opened at the same time, and Rowe got out just as Vickers was marching towards him.

'What is this?' Vickers demanded. 'I hoped you would have got the message by now, Rowe.'

'Hello, Neil. Not nice being followed, is it? Time you gave me some answers.'

'I don't know what you're talking about, but this is harassment, Rowe. Expect a visit from uniform.'

A cyclist rolled past and gave them both a quizzical look. Rowe stared back at the man until he'd gone, then grabbed Vickers' arm and shoved him towards an alleyway they were standing a few feet from. The alley was split into foot and cycle paths and enclosed on either side by high Cotswold stone walls. No one else was nearby.

'Enough bullshit, Vickers,' said Rowe, getting close to the man's face. 'You've been having me followed since at least Thursday. I want to know why, and I also want to know what the fuck this Burnell case is really about.'

Vickers was up against the wall on the footpath side of the alleyway, with Rowe's right hand pressing hard on his chest. He had a slight height advantage, but Rowe thought Vickers would be reticent about a physical altercation, in case it later came back on him unfavourably.

'Now this is assault,' Vickers replied bitterly. 'You're a bigger moron than I thought, Rowe. You're imagining things. Burnell was – '

Vickers let out a sharp, wheezing grunt as Rowe punched him squarely in the gut. He bent over, coughed and held his stomach as he gradually got his breath back.

'How's that for assault, Neil?' Rowe said. 'Thing is, I know Burnell's death was crooked and it's only a matter of time until I figure out why. And I've got a feeling that Steve Symonds' death was linked to it. Oh, and obviously I know you've been trying to undermine me ever since I found out you were connected to Hannah Crockett's death.'

Vickers' eyes blazed at the last statement, but he didn't respond between wheezes. Rowe took it as a tell.

'One thing I want to know,' Rowe continued, 'is why you're still following me now, after I've left the job? You can't tell me Carne authorised that.'

Vickers' face was red with anger and humiliation, but Rowe saw confusion in it at that moment too. The DCI nursed his stomach, gathering himself while he looked at the floor, and spoke barely audibly.

'OK...look. I had a tracker put on your car after I heard you were assigned to the cell death. One of those cheap GPS ones off the internet. I then had it removed while you were in the meeting with DCS Carne and I yesterday.'

Rowe thought back. His car had been left unattended on the side road outside Fenwood police station for some time, and then later in the Oxford station car park. A tracker could have been planted at either of those times, and then possibly removed in the Oxford car park when he returned the following morning. He guessed it didn't matter exactly when the tasks had been carried out and by whom, but he felt stupid for not considering the tracker as a possibility before. He realised Vickers was still talking.

'It wasn't an official move...frankly, I didn't trust you after the Hannah Crockett case and I had to ensure you weren't going to embarrass us. Which of course you attempted to. DCS Carne didn't know about it, but I believe she would have understood my reasoning.'

'That's nice, Neil. But you might want to try again. I'm still being followed by at least one clown pretending to be an assistant to the coroner. Tell me what that's about and what Grantley's team are actually doing.'

'I don't know what the fuck you're talking about.' Vickers spat the words and the venom of his delivery caught Rowe off guard. 'You tried to ruin my career over Hannah's suicide so I kept an eye on you while I reasonably could. Justifiably, I think. Now you're just an idiotic loose cannon who looks even more pathetic without a police badge. Trust me when I say I couldn't care less about what you do as a civilian; it was one of the new PCs that saw you and Cross at the Trees that night in case you were wondering. I was never privy to the SDU investigation because it's confidential...all I know is if you fuck with them, Rowe, you'll be sorry. And as for Symonds, if you're so sure there was foul play involved then I can think of someone with a good motive...someone who assaulted and threatened him on the same day, perhaps.'

A crooked smile appeared on Vickers' face, appearing as if he sensed he had the upper hand and was warming to it.

'As you were advised yesterday, Rowe, now would be a good time to make yourself scarce. From what I hear, you're even less popular around here than you were before, if that's possible.'

Rowe said nothing but had moved back slightly. Vickers straightened his clothes and pushed Rowe's resting hand away. As the DCI made a move back toward his car, he looked back at Rowe once more.

'If you touch me again, the tough guy act won't seem quite so entertaining. It's time you fucked off.'

Vickers adjusted the knot of his tie in what Rowe presumed was an attempt to re-establish his poise, then strode back to the Mercedes.

Rowe watched him get in, rev the engine, and drive off. He was more confused than he had been before he came.

Rowe did a brief sweep of both the outside and inside of the Vitesse just to be sure there was no longer a tracker attached. There wasn't and he didn't really expect there to be. He sat in the drivers' seat and took out his phone, calling Jim Ferry. The veteran answered swiftly.

'I know my dulcet tones are irresistible,' Ferry said, 'but it is the weekend, mate.'

'Jim, sorry to bug you again.'

'Let me guess, another favour? How'd it go with your friend?'

'You guessed right. And I'm not sure how it went. He fessed up to tracking me between Thursday and Friday morning but denies all knowledge of anything after that. He also claims he doesn't know what the Yard team are doing on Burnell. So, if it's possible, I need you to try and find out.'

'Right. And how are you proposing I do that?'

'Maybe use your access…your contacts. Call in a favour or two. I wouldn't ask if I didn't think it was important.'

'Can't you just go up the Yard and knock on the door? Might be quicker.'

'I'll owe you big time, Jim.'

Ferry scoffed theatrically. 'Oh, won't you just. This is my retirement on the chopping block here – possibly more if Angela gets wind of it.' He exhaled audibly. 'Alright. Let me have a poke around and see if any of the geriatric fish in my pond are still biting. I'll try and drop by the office this afternoon.'

'Thanks Jim. It's appreciated.'

They said their goodbyes and hung up. Rowe did feel he was pushing it with Ferry, but also that he didn't have much of a choice all things considered.

He thought back on his encounter with Vickers. It seemed odd that the DCI would admit putting a tracker on his car – a risky move for someone so obsessed with his own image and progression through the ranks – if it wasn't true. He could simply have denied the whole thing, as Rowe had expected him to. On top of that, a GPS tracker was quite different to following someone in person. The 'coroner's assistant' and whoever was in the black Mercedes clearly had a far bolder approach. They weren't just monitoring his movements, they were making themselves known, if not outright attempting to intimidate their target. It was a completely different mindset to that which Vickers had admitted to.

Rowe thought that if Vickers was telling the truth about the tracker, it was possible – even likely – that he was also being truthful about everything else. His reaction to Rowe's allusion to Crockett – and the fact he had referred to her as Hannah – suggested his connection to her was more personal than anything else. Vickers had also seemed confused by, and dismissive of, the idea that he would know anything about the SDU's investigation. And it didn't seem to have occurred to him that Steve Symonds' death might not have been an accident.

Whether his initial assessment of Vickers' responses was correct or not, Rowe decided that there was little mileage in pressing the DCI further at that point. He knew his only option was to focus on the reasons for Burnell's death.

The fact that Rowe no longer had a badge was an obvious problem, and consequently Jim Ferry's help would be essential. But there was still one avenue he felt he could explore on his own.

19

THE PALE SUN STRUGGLED to free itself from behind a wall of mid-afternoon cloud as Rowe stood outside a relatively new house on the edge of six other similar ones. The left-hand end as you looked at it from the road.

As he moved down the short front path, he caught sight of Rachel Worth sitting on the same sofa that he had sat on two days earlier. She was wearing what looked like a white dressing gown and was holding tissues in the palms of her hands, on which her forehead was resting. He knocked on the door and waited. After a minute or so it was opened a few inches and Worth peered through the gap.

'You shouldn't be here.'

Worth rasped the words in a hoarse stage whisper. Rowe thought she looked much more tired than the last time he had been at the house. Her hair was a mess, and her eyes were red-ringed and bloodshot, like she had been crying for a very long time.

'Guess you heard the news about Steve Symonds,' he said flatly.

Worth looked wounded, and when she replied it was in a faltering tone.

'I have nothing to say to you, Rowe. You're not job anymore. Like I said, you shouldn't be here. In fact, you should go as far away from here as fucking possible.'

The words could have been construed as threatening, but Rowe realised that even though Worth was clearly grief-stricken, she was also terrified.

'I need to know what happened at Fenwood,' Rowe said. 'Someone's been following me. You and Symonds were the only two regularly rostered officers there that night. Tell me what Burnell's death was about.'

Worth's demeanour suddenly became even more distraught.

'You're being followed?' she asked, incredulous.

'Yeah. I don't know who by.'

'And you came here?! Get the fuck away from me Rowe, and don't ever come back.'

She slammed the door, punctuating her sentence. Rowe stood there for a few seconds then walked back down the path, scanning the area as he did. He had been careful on the journey over but couldn't be sure if he had totally given his follower the slip.

It had been a risk, he knew, but the visit had at least confirmed his suspicions that Worth and Symonds had been close. On his first visit she had become prickly at his questions about Symonds and pretended she didn't know who Laura Cross was. On the second she was clearly devastated over the younger man's untimely death - and she was scared of something. Rowe didn't think it was a stretch to conclude that she saw herself as a potential target for whoever had killed Symonds. And he thought she might well be right.

Back in the Vitesse, which was parked at what Rowe deemed to be a safe enough distance from Worth's house, Rowe took out his phone and opened the police

141

directory he still had saved into it. He scrolled down to the number he wanted, then dialled. The professional voice that answered had a quality about it that was very slightly sweet, which he noticed for the first time.

'DC Meredith.'

'Joanne, it's Mike Rowe.'

There was silence from Meredith's end.

'I'm guessing you've caught up on everything by now,' he said. 'The case is gone, I'm gone, that's that. Problem is, I'm being followed, and I think it's connected to the cell death. I'm asking a lot here, but, if you still have it, it would really help me to see the CCTV footage again.'

Rowe knew the footage was police property and may even have been officially held by the SDU at that point, but he also knew Meredith had originally downloaded it from the Lockscreen database at Fenwood onto a memory stick, which he hoped she still had. After a long pause, she spoke.

'I can't help you, Rowe.'

'I've already seen the footage, Joanne. I just need to see it one more time. It could be crucial.'

'Please don't call this number again.'

The line went dead.

20

TAKING A CIRCUITOUS ROUTE in the vague direction of town, Rowe kept an eye on his mirrors. He didn't spot anything obviously suspicious all the way back to his flat, which either meant the follower's tactics had changed or that they were leaving him be for some reason. He presumed they must know where he lived anyway, but he also accepted that he couldn't be certain of much at all at that point.

He parked in the narrow, designated space outside his front door which was barely big enough to accommodate the Vitesse's long front end, got out and let himself in. There were items of post on the mat that amounted to a couple of bills and several advertising circulars. He gathered them and threw them onto the table a few feet in front of the door that he used for eating, writing, reading and just about everything else. To his left was the basic kitchenette area that looked out on where his car was parked and a door that led to the bedroom and bathroom. To his right was a living area that comprised an old leather sofa, a low lounge chair, a cluttered coffee table, a TV stand with a modest widescreen set on it and two sets of over-flowing bookshelves against the front and side walls – one laden with books and the other CDs.

The books were mostly his favoured western fiction – Cormac McCarthy, Larry McMurtry and Zane Grey interspersed with more modern titles like Tony Hillerman detective novels and non-fiction books about

Native Americans and the Old West. The CDs were mostly Texas songwriters like Terry Allen, Guy Clark and Robert Earl Keen along with others in a similar vein, interspersed with rock and metal albums from the 80s and 90s. Rowe was heartened by the fact that Laura had tolerated most of his music and even liked some of it.

He was fond of informing anyone who saw the contents of these shelves that their western theme was not related to country music or its culture, although the Hank Williams boxset he owned was hard to miss.

Being at the flat and looking at these things tended to remind him of his own, thus far failed writing exploits, which he guessed may have been another reason he didn't come home as often these days.

He sat down at the table, took out his phone and called Laura Cross's number. She answered after a couple of rings.

'Hi Mike.'

'Hey. You at home?'

'Yeah, I am. How are you?'

'Doing OK. Just figuring things out. And you?'

'Same. Thanks for ringing.'

The awkward exchange was followed by an awkward pause before Rowe spoke next.

'You heard about Steve Symonds?'

'Yes, I did. It's unbelievable. Just a horrible thing to happen.'

'Mmm.'

'What's that noise for?'

'I'm not sure it was an accident.'

'What do you mean? Look, I know you didn't like Steve, but-'

'I think it's linked to the cell death. I've just been to see Rachel Worth again – she was in bits. And scared too.'

'Scared of what?'

'Don't know yet. I've been trying to find out. But it's tough with a lot of avenues being closed to me now.'

'Well…I mean, these things happen. It could just be a terrible accident. You might be reading too much into it.'

'Did you know Worth and Symonds were a thing?'

'I'd guessed. She wasn't very friendly with me.'

Rowe was quiet.

'I think you should be careful,' he said after a while. 'Something is wrong here.'

'Careful of who? I've been through a lot, Mike. I'm pretty good at keeping my guard up these days.'

'OK, I know. I'm sorry.' And he was. 'You wanna meet up again and talk? Maybe tomorrow night?'

'Yeah, sure. I'd like that.'

'Fine. I'll be in touch tomorrow and we'll figure it out.'

'OK.'

'Take care. I love you.'

'I love you too.'

They said goodbye and disconnected. Despite their minor disagreement on the cause of Symonds' fate, Rowe saw the exchange as another gentle step forward for them. Meeting up again would be valuable. He knew he needed to understand more about what she had been through, and he found himself looking forward to trying.

Whatever else was happening in Rowe's life, he felt that things were slowly regenerating between he and

Laura. He thought that was something important for him to hold on to at that moment.

While he waited to hear any news from Jim Ferry, Rowe spent the rest of the afternoon into the evening trying to distract himself. He read some more of a book about the American frontier that he had been slow to get through. He even opened his last attempt at the first chapter of his own book and read through it again, making note of a few ideas for the progression of the story. It wasn't much, but by his recent standards he thought his efforts represented a high level of constructive productivity, all things considered.

Eventually though, his mind turned back to the day's events. He couldn't ignore them, even if his hopes of learning more ultimately depended on Ferry's enquiries being successful. He considered his options while he showered and made himself a microwave dinner, finally deciding on a course of action while he ate.

Rowe went into the bedroom and changed into a dark blue tracksuit he hadn't worn in years, along with black trainers and a charcoal beanie hat. It was dark outside as it was approaching 9pm, and it wasn't as if he was known for dressing in bright colours, but he thought it best to wear something no one would readily associate with him under normal circumstances. Or that would be easily identifiable on camera.

He came back out into the main flat and locked the front door. Then he withdrew back through the bedroom and into the bathroom. It was a claustrophobic space with just a shower cubicle, toilet and sink. Rowe unlocked the window above the toilet cistern and pulled it open, then stood on the toilet and climbed out into the alley at the back of his flat. The alley had once been a service access point for the old glove factory but latterly housed storage sheds for the occupants of the flats in the complex. On a Saturday people would often be retrieving bikes and other items from the sheds, but at that time of night the area was quiet.

Rowe reached back inside and retrieved a dental floss dispenser, snapped off a short length and placed it half in and half out of the groove the window would sit in, near the hinge. Then he shut the window and locked it from the outside. The alley was a dead end to his left but in the other direction it gave pedestrian access to a recently constructed neighbouring housing estate, and that was the way Rowe headed.

He weaved his way through the streets of the estate at a fast walk to appear as if he were out solely for exercise. It was a chilly night in any case, so the pace helped him stay warm. There were other people around, but they were mostly teenagers or people on their way into town – nobody he was overly concerned about. He kept his speed up as he left the estate and navigated a long residential road that looped around the outside of the town centre and eventually came out on Grounds Way, the road off which Fenwood police station sat. As he neared the main road, he took a moment to re-check his surroundings. He had not detected anyone tracing his movements since he had left the flat and that remained the case as he arrived on Grounds Way.

Rowe moved swiftly along the pavement, passing the public car park on his left and not crossing over to the station where he had done previously. He walked further up the road until he came to a pedestrian crossing and used it. Traffic was very light and only occasional taxis and fast-food delivery vehicles passed him on the road. Reaching the other side of the street, he came back on himself towards the police station.

He left the pavement just as he came alongside the St John's Ambulance depot that was positioned next door to the station and walked across the grass divider that separated both buildings from the foot traffic. Despite the ambulance depot being far smaller, the two structures were of virtually identical style, having been built concurrently. Both were in darkness, lit from the front only by streetlights. There was a gap between the two buildings of about five feet, which Rowe presumed had been included in the original plans to maximise footprint area for each and indicating that they were indeed constructed at the same time.

Rowe disappeared into the gap, keeping alert for anyone who might be watching his movements. There was a security camera mounted on the wall of the police station next to the gap, but Rowe knew that the camera – along with all the others on the outside of the building – had been a dummy for some years. It was another cost-saving measure where the smaller stations were concerned, the idea being that external CCTV coverage would instead be provided by council-owned cameras that overlooked the station. The problem was that the council's cameras only monitored the street rather than individual buildings, meaning large parts of the station were not covered. Rowe had also learned from Meredith when they had viewed the Lockscreen footage that the new programme did not extend to the outside of the station. He was confident he was not being watched.

Moving down between the buildings, Rowe was looking for a particular spot and found it with relative ease. Towards the far end of the gap – which had been fenced off at its inclusion to protect the respective parking security of both operations – there were two small, high windows built into the police station's back wall. Rowe calculated that the second window along was the one which looked out from the cell Burnell had been in. Not that there was much for an occupant of the cell to look out at.

Rowe stood beneath the second window and stared up at it. It was divided into three by vertical bars on the inside and he estimated it was roughly eighteen inches across and eight inches tall. Not much of a window at all, merely a break in the wall to meet the legal requirements of that type of building. It would allow some daylight into the cell in corresponding hours, although, as he had established, the vista on offer was unspectacular. At night though, the window and its neighbour would have been almost completely dark, except for the glow of a three-way security lamp behind the fence to the left of where Rowe was standing. That was what interested him.

Although Rowe knew that his chances of viewing the Lockscreen CCTV a second time were slim to non-existent, he had at least seen it once. His memory of the camera view that showed the inside of Burnell's cell was that the window had been completely dark. It was one of those things that had dimly registered in the back of his mind at the time but only surfaced later.

The security lamp was positioned centrally to the gap, on the station side of the dividing wall between the station and the ambulance depot. It was adjacent to an LPG gas heating tank and cast light into the depot's car park to the left, into the small bike shed courtyard that Rowe had stood in with Stanwell on Thursday morning to the right and straight ahead into the gap where Rowe was positioned. If his memory served correctly, there was a single security light at the nearest end of the station car park also.

Looking at the brightness of the security lamp and its proximity to the window – a few feet away but well within range – Rowe found it hard to imagine that a trace of its glow wouldn't be visible from inside the cell, even allowing for how the cell's own ceiling light may offset it. He considered that the fact it was a timed security lamp could possibly be a factor, then reasoned it was unlikely it would have been timed to switch off in the middle of the night. He also thought it was unlikely that the lamp had been broken or faulty in some way on the night in question, because that would mean that less than 72 hours later it had already been fixed, at a station which had not been significantly used in the last three days. Possible, but unlikely. Rowe reckoned that if he were to put money on it, he would bet the lamp had been working that night yet for some reason wasn't evident on the CCTV.

That was a loose end that he didn't like.

Twenty minutes later, Rowe arrived back at his flat. At that point he was pretty sure that no one had been following him. He had taken the same route back from the station that had brought him there and had seen nothing suspicious. Thinking back, he realised he hadn't seen anything even remotely like a car or person following him since he had left Rachel Worth's house that afternoon.

He let himself back in through the window, mostly to see if the strand of dental floss had moved or been broken, and as far as he could tell it hadn't been. Walking back through the flat, he flicked a table lamp on, and found no obvious sign of anything being disturbed or out of place. Rowe took out his phone in the hope there might be something from Ferry; he had periodically checked for a message while he was out but had tried to remind himself that a watched pot never boils and resolved to leave the phone in his pocket.

As it turned out, there were two messages waiting for him. The first was indeed from Jim Ferry and it was a voicemail. When Rowe pressed the button to listen to it, Ferry sounded sombre and not his normal self. He said he wouldn't be able to get the information Rowe wanted after all; he had gone into Oxford station that afternoon and started some preliminary searches, only to receive a call from someone at Scotland Yard telling him that his searches were forbidden. His supervisor would be contacted. At that point, Ferry was just hoping his pension would be safe.

The voicemail ended and Rowe exhaled with frustration and concern. He had not intended to compromise Ferry and felt guilty that he had pushed his friend into a corner. He also knew Ferry had been his last chance.

Distractedly, Rowe looked back at the phone and clicked open the second message, which was a text. It was from a withheld number and the way it was presented meant he almost deleted it immediately. The message read:

LOCAL WOMEN!
Want to talk to you. Ike!

Rowe stood in the middle of his flat and stared at the message. At first glance, it looked like pure spam. The word 'talk' was in blue and underlined suggesting it was an external web link, and his name was missing the first letter with the full stop preceding it appearing to be a typo. Only it wasn't his name, it was someone else's. A name he hadn't heard or seen written in a very long time.

He lifted his eyes from the screen and stared into space as he considered whether he might be imagining the connection. His gaze came to focus on something he had missed when checking the flat a few minutes earlier. There were a few outdated post-it notes attached to the fridge, which was about six feet in front of him, but in the middle of them appeared to be a Polaroid-style photograph, held in place by a fridge magnet.

Stepping closer, Rowe didn't touch the picture but could see what it was easily enough. The image showed a woman slouched on a sofa with her head lolling back and her eyes closed. The photographer looked to have been in a crouched or seated position on the floor in front of her. The woman could have been either asleep or unconscious were it not for the gashes in both of her wrists. They were facing upwards, and her arms lay limply by her sides. Blood covered most of the sofa cushions around her and much of the floor by her bare feet. Her mouth hung open. A folded piece of paper sat on top of the sofa, propped against the wall behind the woman's head.

Despite the volume of blood on the sofa and the grotesque repose of the clearly deceased subject, Rowe recognised both. The sofa was one that he himself had perched on a couple of days before, and the woman slumped dead on it wearing a white dressing gown was Rachel Worth.

He had no doubt about that.

Taking a kitchen towel from the counter next to the fridge, Rowe gently removed the photo from under the magnet and inspected it. On the back was a single word written in black marker pen:

STOP

21

ROWE SAT AT THE table in the middle of his flat. He had carried the photograph over from the fridge and it was laid in front of him next to his phone. The lamp on the table offered the only light in the room.

He believed the picture being placed in his home was not just a warning to him but also a statement of power and reach by whoever had done it. There was no sign of forced entry, and no one had climbed through the bathroom window. The perpetrator had simply walked through the front door.

The photo clearly depicted the scene of a suicide, although Rowe thought the very fact the image existed all but confirmed the death was being staged as such. He was also willing to bet that the folded piece of paper on top of the sofa was a suicide note of some kind – either typed by someone or written in Worth's own hand by coercion – and that it made a link with Steve Symonds' death as Worth's motivation for taking her own life. All of that was an assumption, but it was Rowe's best guess. He thought if the intention were to frame him for her death then the picture he was looking at would likely be different. He also accepted that nothing was impossible.

Rowe wondered if the Sergeant's clear devastation at Symonds' death had given whoever was watching the perfect excuse to carry out her murder and link the two. Symonds had apparently been disposed of very soon after the cell death incident, which suggested his death was more urgent somehow – either to ensure his silence or as a punishment, perhaps. Killing Worth so soon after Symonds – the only two regular staff members on duty at Fenwood that night – seemed to Rowe like a rash and conspicuous move unless the pair could be linked in some other way.

He thought the romantic connection between Symonds and Worth, however strong or otherwise it may have been, was a viable cover story for the entity responsible for their deaths to use. Maybe some kind of documentary evidence of their relationship existed. Or perhaps it was Rowe himself who had uncovered it on his two visits to Worth's house, and somehow the details of those two meetings were heard by a third party.

There wasn't much Rowe could be sure of simply from the photo alone, apart from one thing: Rachel Worth had died very soon after he had walked away from her door that afternoon. All the lighting in the picture appeared to be natural, coming, he guessed, from both the front window and from Worth's rear French doors. It being November, it suggested that the image couldn't have been taken much later than mid-afternoon. Rowe estimated that Rachel Worth had likely been dead within an hour of his visit, if not sooner.

Rowe sat back in his chair and forced his eyes away from the photograph. He didn't know yet what had happened at Fenwood a few nights earlier, but two of the main players were suddenly dead. His investigation had been cut short, he no longer had access to any police files or evidence and virtually everyone who could potentially gather information on his behalf had been shut down for various reasons. Even Nick Stanwell, in the gentlest possible way, had distanced himself from the situation. Rowe knew that all of that, including the brazen planting of the photograph, meant he should finally leave the cell death alone.

But someone had entered his flat and threatened him. Apart from anything else, that act wasn't something he was ready to ignore.

Rowe grabbed a room-temperature bottle of Hobgoblin beer from a box under the kitchen counter and sat back down at the table with it. To say he was unsure what to do next was an understatement. He had briefly considered reporting Worth's death to the police – possibly anonymously – but had decided against it. In the best-case scenario, the police would simply rule it a suicide, and in the worst case they would discover he had been at the house that afternoon and try to link him to it as a murder. In any case, someone would find her body eventually and things would take their course.

He drank from the bottle and thought about who else Worth's death might impact on. Laura, perhaps, but she had played no real part in the event at Fenwood. Rowe had an urge to contact her, but he knew their conversation earlier had probably been enough. He wouldn't drag her into the new development if he could help it. Then there was Jim Ferry, who he had failed. It was after 10pm, but Rowe felt the need to address Ferry's message. Or maybe he just wanted to talk to someone. Rowe called his friend's number, and it was eventually answered.

Ferry still sounded downbeat.

'Hello mate. Had to duck outside…the Angela-tron has ears everywhere.'

'Jim. I got your message. I'm sorry, I should've known this thing was getting too hot.'

'That's OK, Rower. I agreed to do it after all. Thought it'd be easy enough to make some early inroads without stirring up a wasp nest. Clearly I was wrong.'

'Who called you and what did they say?'

'Didn't get a name. I was looking at the database of open cases assigned to the Yard - no detail, just a list of surnames really. Then the phone went. Nearly jumped out of my size nines as the office was so quiet. Whoever it was said they were from the Yard and that I was accessing data I wasn't cleared for. I was to log out immediately, my supervisor would be contacted and presumably some concrete shoes prepared for a forthcoming boat trip...I tried to explain that I have access to the database for my job but apparently the fact I was able to access it doesn't mean I should have.'

Rowe exhaled in the same way he had when he'd heard Ferry's voicemail. 'Shit. Heard anything from Miller yet?'

Nigel Miller was Ferry's immediate boss.

'Not yet. But you know Miller. He's dropped enough hints over the years about how non-specific my role is...this will be the Christmas present he's been waiting for. Like I said in my message, if I come out of this with my pension intact it'll be a result.'

'Sorry, Jim,' Rowe said again.

'Needless to say, mate,' Ferry sighed, 'I won't be able to assist with your enquiries from now own. Marathon beer-tasting expeditions, yes. Swashbuckling vigilante crime-fighting, no.'

'Understood. As it happens, this thing just went up a few notches. You'll hear it through the grapevine soon enough, but let's just say my drifting off for a quiet sabbatical somewhere is no longer an option.'

'Hmm, well none of us needed to be Mystic Meg to know that was never happening anyway...you go careful though mate, whatever it is.'

'Thanks Jim, I will.'

Ferry seemed about to hang up, but then he spoke again.

'Not wanting to blow one's own trumpet, old fruit, but if this is still rolling on, who are you gonna get to do your dirty work with me out of the picture?'

'Well, I suppose I'm on my own for now,' Rowe said, but his voice tailed off as something else popped back into his head.

'Enigmatic as ever, Holmes.'

'Always. Talk to you soon, Jim. And sorry again.'

'Forget it. Just means it's your round next.'

After hanging up, Rowe sipped at his beer and opened the unusual text message again. The conversation with Ferry had reminded him of it after the bombshell of the Rachel Worth photo had pushed it to the back of his mind. He knew if the message was what he thought it was, it was something he couldn't ignore no matter what else was happening.

Ordinarily, Rowe would rank a web link in a spam message from a withheld number of unknown origins alongside an unsolicited email from a Nigerian prince in terms of likely credibility and urgency. But he had his reasons for believing the one he was looking at to be different.

If the web link under the word 'talk' led to an unscrupulous scam site of some kind, it wasn't exactly giving Rowe the hard sell in the message's wording. Anyone reading the message quickly enough might not even notice it was a link. He also thought the "LOCAL WOMEN!" introduction would be enough to put off 90% or more of potential recipients, particularly as that was the wording that would appear in the message preview. If anyone had been scrolling through Rowe's messages looking for suspicious communications, he guessed they would be unlikely to give a text like that a second look.

Even if someone did, he thought the very presence of a web link would be a key indicator that it was spam. In the more recent stages of the modern age, no one wanted to click on web links in spam texts. In addition, they would likely assume that "Ike" was a misspelling of "Mike", typical of the errors common in fraudulent messages. He was sure it wasn't a typo, but it concerned him that he might be looking too hard for something that wasn't there.

It was a risk of sorts, but Rowe knew he had no other option. He clicked on the link and waited for it to open.

THE LINK OPENED INTO a web browser page that was white with the words 'failed to load' in black lettering in the top left corner. No other words, letters, symbols or images were visible. Also, there were no pop-up ads, banners or invitations to subscribe to anything that came up, which Rowe viewed as a small mercy.

He chose to perceive the blank and unhelpful screen as something to put off unwanted prying eyes. Few things were more irritating or likely to spark impatience in the modern internet user than a blank screen that appeared not to have loaded correctly. However, as a test he closed the window and clicked the link again. Same blank white page, same message. He looked at it for a few seconds before trying something. He started highlighting small sections of the white screen with his fingers, working on the slim possibility that there could be hidden wording on the page – white lettering disguised against the white background. Soon enough, to his surprise, he found it.

Corner by Patrick's house. 11.

Rowe read it and re-read it. His instincts had been right. The hidden message was yet another layer of precaution, but the person who sent it had clearly trusted his ability to find it. On top of that, Rowe understood the message and knew exactly where the location it referred to was. He also knew there was a strong chance that it would not be understood by anyone else who might find it.

The original text had been sent at 9:50pm and the time on his watch was 10:46pm. Rowe considered what to do next, but not for long. His flat was not secure. He knew sitting around in it like a victim was not an option. Whether the message meant what he thought it did, or whether it was in any way linked to everything else that was going on was impossible to know unless he got moving. Still dressed in his dark jogging gear, he grabbed his keys and left via the front door.

Patrick's house was about ten minutes on foot.

Patrick Wynn had been a small kid that Rowe had known at primary school. The boy's parents had moved to Fenwood for his father's work and the family moved on again just over a year later. Rowe and Patrick had become fast friends in that year and Rowe had visited the Wynn house several times, mostly because it was bigger and – to him – more exciting than his own parents' house.

It was located in a more expensive area of town that was further out from the centre and in the opposite direction to the police station from Rowe's flat. The street boasted large gardens and driveways in front of generally tall and wide houses that were not uniform to each other. The house where the Wynns had lived was one of these and stood on a corner, with a cul-de-sac running down its right flank.

At the same fast walk he had used earlier, Rowe arrived on the corner at 10:58pm by his phone's clock.

He stood on the angle of the pavement where the adjoined streets met each other. He felt exposed. There was nowhere to conceal himself or hang back to wait for whatever was coming: and there was no way to know what that was. As far as he could tell no one had followed him there, but that felt almost meaningless in the circumstances.

A lot of the houses were in darkness at that time, probably owned by older people with earlier turning-in times. Patrick's old house was one of them. Rowe had no idea who had lived there since the Wynns had gone. Some other house lights were on though, and he wondered if anyone had seen him standing on the corner yet.

A phone rang. A muffled sound, relatively distant. A digital reproduction of the classic telephone trill. Rowe's first thought was that it was coming from inside one of the houses – maybe one neighbour ringing another to ask if they'd seen the shifty character loitering on the corner. Once he attuned his ears though, he realised the sound was outside, not close but not far away either. And it seemed directed at him.

He looked around, moving a few steps in each direction to gauge where the ringing was coming from. He quickly decided it was straight ahead, which was the opposite corner on the cul-de-sac. He trotted across to the pavement on that side and found the ringing was coming from a dry-stone wall in front of him. The wall bordered a house and a row of moderately tall fir trees stood immediately behind it, offering privacy to the domain from the road.

Not able to locate the source of the ringing by sight, Rowe started gripping some of the capstones on top of the wall until he finally found one that came loose. It was broken in two halves, and he pulled the nearest half away to reveal a mobile phone. It was a cheap, basic model that was around twenty years out of date, but its screen was lit up and it was still ringing. He picked the phone up, looked at it for a second, then pressed the button to answer. Rowe spoke quietly into it, conscious that the ringing may have attracted attention in the street.

'Hello?'

'Were you followed?'

The voice was steady but broken. Slightly hoarse. Rowe thought he recognised it but wasn't as certain as he'd have liked to be.

'Hard to be sure but I'm leaning towards no,' he said, not really knowing how best to answer.

'I'd lean towards yes if I were you.'

Rowe looked around, again not sure how he should play it. Or what was happening.

'Are you who I think you are?' he asked finally.

'Listen,' the voice said. 'M5, junction 27 services. 3am in the lorry park. Make sure you're followed.'

'Make sure I'm followed? I need to know who you are.'

'Patrick's house. Krang.'

Rowe knew what it meant. Patrick Wynn had always had the latest Teenage Mutant Ninja Turtles action figures thanks to his dad's business trips to America, and Rowe was especially jealous when he'd got one of the alien supervillain Krang. It was probably the memory he most associated with Patrick.

'This line is secure, but we shouldn't test it,' the voice continued. 'Be there and we'll talk.'

The call was ended before Rowe could speak again.

On the way back to his flat, Rowe dismantled the phone and disposed of the individual components at various stages on his route. He was moving quickly and trying to make sense of the evolving predicament as he went.

In his mind, there remained two real choices - three, if one considered the going away and hunkering down for a few weeks strategy to be a genuine option, which he didn't. Rowe knew it was either stick or twist. If he chose to stay put, he could watch the fallout from Rachel Worth's death, hope he wasn't a target himself and that it would eventually blow over. Whereas if he did what the voice on the phone was asking, he could learn something vital or at the very least confirm the caller's identity one way or the other. Both options had their elements of danger, but one was reactive and the other pro-active. It wasn't a hard decision.

Something that was clear was that the voice on the phone had known either that Rowe was being followed or had been followed. That suggested some knowledge of the situation he faced and that the hidden message hadn't been an unrelated bolt from the blue.

As he neared home, he turned onto a path that ran between two rows of 1960s-era blocks of flats. The sound of a scuffed shoe came from a long way behind, and Rowe stopped and turned. Saw no one. He was quite literally tired of looking over his shoulder; yet more reason to take the course of action he was about to.

When he got back to the flat, he changed clothes and threw a few things into a rucksack. He didn't yet know how long he'd be gone. The place looked generally untouched, but he didn't feel it was worth looking too hard. The photo of Rachel Worth still lay on the table. He brushed it into the rucksack using one of the envelopes to hand, thinking it was best not to leave it lying around.

He thought one last time about contacting Laura, telling her where he was going. But there was too much to explain. He couldn't involve her in something he himself wasn't able to quantify yet. If he wasn't going to be back before their planned meeting the following night, he'd call her then. If he could.

Rowe stepped out of the front door before closing and locking it, as redundant as that act felt in light of the photograph's appearance. A mildly ridiculous thought crossed his mind that it was the start of his new life – one where he had nothing to lose. He guessed that even if that were true, it didn't mean it was necessarily a good thing.

He unlocked the Vitesse and threw the rucksack into the footwell of the passenger seat. Then he got in, shut the door, and sat for a moment in the darkness. He was tired. Mentally and physically. Sleep would have to wait, however.

He turned the key and revved the engine. Then he reversed, turned, and left the old glove factory courtyard, heading out of town to the west.

THE ROADS THAT LED west out of Fenwood were long, single-laned and surrounded by fields and farmland that was bordered with hedgerows and Cotswold stone walls. In the hours of daylight these roads could be a picturesque nightmare, oversubscribed due to providing one of the only feasible routes to the M5 motorway and thus to the west, southwest and to Wales.

In the late night into the early hours, the vistas weren't as easy to admire but progress was more readily made. Rowe had changed the CD in the Vitesse's player and James McMurtry – son of one of his favourite authors, Larry – was singing about a couple named Ruby and Carlos. Various other albums cluttered the door pockets and glove box, and Rowe planned to revisit several of them on the journey. He was very conscious of the time, but he wasn't in a rush.

As he advanced through a hilly, tree-covered stretch of one long road that led out of the county into Gloucestershire, Rowe thought about what his approach to the rendezvous would be. It was still fair to say he had no idea what he was walking – or driving – into. The contact could be bogus. The rendezvous point could be a trap. Lorry parks at motorway service stations were generally dark and possibly insalubrious places at night, and the cover they provided could mask a multitude of sins. Rowe conceded that, as dubious meeting places went, service station lorry parks ranked pretty highly.

Another possibility he considered was that there was no rendezvous at all. It was a ruse to get him out of the way, possibly to plant something more damning in his flat to link him to Worth's death. Or in order to hurt someone close to him. Rowe put the thought out of his head; he reasoned that if he or anyone in his immediate orbit were under threat they would have been targeted already. The two people that had died so far were directly linked to Burnell's death at Fenwood, and he believed that fact was key.

Burnell. Rowe realised that the events of the previous 24 hours or so had distracted him from one of his original objectives, which had been to find out more about the dead man. Ferry had dug up some basics, but a lot more was still to be established. The fact that Burnell's parents had died in an identical fashion to his own was particularly troubling to Rowe. The train of thought brought another possibility to his mind of what awaited at the rendezvous; that being, exactly what he hoped it would be. And that it would bring answers with it.

James McMurtry was about to conclude his part of the soundtrack to the road trip. He sang, *you'd a' thought that I'd know better by now.*

The Vitesse descended a steep hill and transitioned onto the dual carriageway that acted as a feeder for the M5. Rowe left the carriageway at the M5 exit, circuited the roundabout, then exited to merge with the motorway. Other than the usual array of haulage lorries, the road was mostly quiet as the time approached 1am.

Guy Clark played on the car stereo. Rowe was still trying to formulate a plan. Cruising steadily on the M5, he was looking for signs of someone following him. He had believed that someone had probably been shadowing him before he reached the M5, but also knew it was much easier to tell when a car was hanging back on the motorway. That was something he would continue to monitor. His only real strategy at that point was to familiarise himself with his destination as best he could – and not to get blindsided when he arrived.

His phone, which was lying in the passenger seat, lit up in his peripheral vision. Not a call – a message. He glanced over at it for a moment, saw the message was from a withheld number again, and glimpsed the preview line:

REMINDER: LOCAL WOMEN!

Rowe was tempted to open the message right then, as thoughts of what it might contain went through his head. Instructions, a change of plan...an abandonment of it. But he left the phone where it was and looked out for indications of the next service station. He would park up and read the message properly, and in doing so perhaps draw out his follower. If indeed there was one.

As it turned out, there was a service station much closer than he expected, and he diverted into the slip road at a fair speed. He followed the road up and pulled into the large main car park of the facility, where other vehicles were spread out like birds on a wire. He positioned the Vitesse very deliberately in the centre of the car park, equidistant from the entrance and the main rest area building. He was a few spaces away from any other cars on all sides and could clearly see the car park entrance to his right. If his follower arrived, he would see them, but no other vehicle had entered behind him yet.

Over the next few minutes, a handful of other cars gradually came into the car park. None of the occupants looked remotely interested in him. Some simply got out and went into the building to use whatever amenities were open at that hour, and a couple didn't stop, just drove straight out of the exit – which was behind him – and toward the BP petrol station at the back of the complex. Rowe decided the follower was either playing it cool or didn't exist and picked up his phone to read the message fully.

REMINDER: LOCAL WOMEN!
Talk now

The word 'now' was another web link highlighted in blue. Rowe clicked on the link and the 'failed to load' message appeared again on an otherwise blank, white page. He began to highlight areas of the page to search for a hidden message as he had last time and eventually found one, which was more detailed than the first.

Draw tail to lorry park. Continue thru to hotel
- park in front. Check in. Leave phone in room.
Back door. Don't be early

Rowe read through the message several times. Clearly the contact was confident Rowe was en route, or even somehow knew that he was. The hotel used as cover – he could see that. He found himself slightly relieved that the rendezvous wasn't taking place in the lorry park, but he recognised the sense in using that as cover also. Anyone following would need to stay close when he disappeared among the HGVs in the dark, and they would therefore witness him entering the hotel. Rowe presumed the contact must have booked him a room at the hotel as a decoy move of some kind and the 'back door' referenced was where he would meet the person in question. It seemed like a lot of guesswork and a lot of faith for him to place in the contact. It also meant Rowe would not be able to get the lay of the land at the lorry park ahead of time as he had hoped to.

He had been looking up every few seconds as he read the message, keeping an eye out for anyone entering the car park. For whatever reason, the contact deemed the presence of a follower to be important to the plan, but Rowe had yet to see any evidence of one. It was 1:15am and he estimated it was around 45 minutes from here to the Junction 27 services he was headed to for the 3am rendezvous. Apparently, he couldn't be early. Which meant he had an hour to wait.

The time passed slowly, and Rowe was tired. There was still no tangible evidence of anyone watching him, so after three quarters of an hour, he decided to run a final test.

The car park had thinned out even more by that point. He started the Vitesse and moved out of the space he was in. Then he drove in the opposite direction that the arrows on the tarmac were pointing, until he reached the car park entrance, where a sign stated that strictly no exit was permitted. Rowe ignored the directive and drove out that way, looped around to the actual designated car park exit and entered through it. He didn't know if anyone ever actually got punished for that type of brazen anarchy, but he was willing to take the risk.

As he came in through the exit, he found what he was looking for. On his right-hand side, a black car was moving steadily towards him, as if preparing to exit. Rowe was in the process of turning left – to follow the arrows in their intended direction – but as he did, he caught a glimpse of the black car's driver. It wouldn't have been enough for a jury – dimly lit and seen through weary eyes as it was – but Rowe recognised the face. He wasn't surprised or fearful, in fact he almost enjoyed the continuity of it.

The face, Rowe was sure, belonged to the coroner's assistant.

23

DUE TO THE DESIGN of the car park, the supposed coroner's assistant had been left with little choice but to use the exit he had been headed for. Rowe looped around slowly and left the same way as the black car – identifiably a Mercedes – about thirty seconds later. At that point he was on a deadline and headed for the main services exit. On the way, he passed the BP petrol station at the edge of the services and saw the black Mercedes parked in a shadowy part of the forecourt. Rowe was sure the driver would know he had been made but nevertheless had a job to do. The man was salvaging the situation as best he could by returning to the spot that he had presumably been waiting in for the last hour or so.

Rowe re-joined the motorway and kept an eye on the time. He regulated his speed as best he could according to the clock and the distances given on the road signs he passed. Satellite navigation would have been an obvious help, but he didn't want to use his phone any more than was necessary. He had no idea whether that mattered or not. Behind him, what he presumed to be the black Mercedes was hanging behind the Vitesse, about a hundred yards back and two lanes over.

When the Junction 27 service station came into view, Rowe was a few minutes early. The contact would have to live with that, he decided. He slowed into the entry lane and weaved up the inclined road that circled the services, continuing past the main car park on his right and towards the lorry park which was signposted ahead. The service station was laid out almost identically to the one he had just come from, which was not unusual. The only difference was that there was a hotel towards the rear, close to the petrol station.

He reached the lorry park, turned down between the first row of HGVs and slowed almost to a complete stop. The lorry park was almost completely full at that time of night. The range of haulage lorries, car transporters and other huge vehicles created a wall of uncertainty on both sides and the area was as dark as Rowe had expected. He continued crawling forwards, constantly observing what was around him in case of the unexpected while he waited for the Mercedes to appear behind him again. After a few more seconds, it did.

The car's lights were off as it nosed around the corner, but Rowe caught a flash of its bodywork in his rear-view mirror, just before it came to an abrupt halt. The driver had clearly been surprised to see the Vitesse virtually stopped out in the open.

Rowe sped up slightly. At the far end of the lorry park the road snaked to the left and as the Vitesse edged forward he saw the corner of a brightly lit sign appear that belonged to a Days Inn hotel. The Mercedes had started moving behind him. It had occurred to Rowe that, if another car were to appear from the direction of the hotel, he would essentially be trapped. That remained a possibility, but he had determined that the trust he was putting in the contact included watching his back.

No other car appeared. He made it out of the lorry corridor, followed the road to the left and then turned a relatively sharp right into the Days Inn car park. He found a space directly up against the front of the two-storey, pale brick building and parked in it. In the mirror he saw the Mercedes drift past the car park and continue forward, presumably intending to lurk at the petrol station again – this one a Shell branch.

Rowe understood better why the location made sense. The hotel had both front and back car parks, but only the front was visible from the Shell station, which itself was the only realistic vantage point for anyone attempting to watch him. However, he thought it was possible, even likely, that the Mercedes driver would explore both car parks once Rowe went inside the hotel, which meant he had to be both vigilant and fast.

He grabbed the rucksack and got out of the Vitesse. Locking the car, he went into the hotel through its double front doors. A bored-looking young man behind the desk regard him both suspiciously and with the mild contempt of someone who didn't want to be disturbed.

'Hi, I'm checking in. Name of Rowe.'

Rowe said it as quickly as he could without sounding impatient. The young man began tapping at a computer lethargically.

'Two nights...one guest,' the receptionist said. 'All our rooms are non-smoking...continental breakfast is from 9-10.30 on a Sunday...parking is free for guests only...fill out this form.'

The speech was delivered in a punctuation-free monotone. Rowe thought it sounded like someone from a 90s comedy sketch show that he couldn't place, or some form of pretentious modern poetry. The boy was giving him a surly look as he placed the form on the counter.

Rowe filled out the form as quickly as was humanly possible and handed it back. The room had apparently already been paid for by the contact, which the young man confirmed before the key and room number were sluggishly handed over. The room was on the first floor. Rowe thanked him and walked past the left end of the desk to a door behind that led to the lift and stairs. He used the credit card-style key to swipe through the door, moved past the lift and ran up the single flight of stairs to his floor. As he did, he noticed another door which he hoped led to the back entrance, although through its window he could see that whatever was beyond was in darkness.

He found his room at the far end of the first-floor corridor. Opening the door and going in, he didn't turn on the lights but pulled the covers back on the bed and ruffled it to look as if it had been slept in and put his phone in the drawer of the bedside table. He then fished out his wallet and left a ten-pound note under a glass. His hope was that a maid would find it and remember the tip if anyone asked.

Rowe left the room again, ensuring the door was locked, and hastily tracked back down the hallway to the top of the stairs. There was a windowed door to his left that had 'Rear Car Parking' written above it and which he could see led to more stairs. He went through it and found a compact stairwell, lit only by the lights overlooking the car park which shone indirectly through what looked like the back entrance.

He descended the stairs to the door and swiped his key over the red light of the sensor, but nothing happened. He tried the door anyway and it was locked. The lights were still off in the stairwell too, which meant they weren't motion-activated as he had hoped.

He looked at the door behind him and was able to see through to the lift and stairs annex but also to reception and the front door. Directly facing the front door, parked in a space, was a black Mercedes. The silhouette of the driver could be seen behind the wheel, but a face wasn't clear. Rowe suspected it was the coroner's assistant, watching who came in and out. He hoped the man hadn't considered the back door yet.

Rowe was unsure what to do. As the stairwell was dark, he thought it was unlikely he could be seen, but his silhouette could nonetheless attract attention. At that moment he realised that a vehicle had appeared outside the back door, perched up on the kerb. It was a Land Rover Defender, and Rowe estimated it was either as old or older than his Vitesse. He thought it might have been blue although it was hard to tell in the sparse light, and the driver was in shadow.

The contact.

The Defender was enclosed by parked cars on both sides, and it seemed to Rowe that parking where it had was a feat in itself. Even so, if the contact was intending to drive him somewhere, it was a flaw in the plan. The rear car park was surrounded by the hotel itself, two steep, grassy banks – one opposite which descended to the motorway on its far side and one to his left which bordered a service road near the Shell station – and the route back to the front car park which was flanked by cars on both sides. Rowe realised they would have to leave that way, via the front of the hotel where the Mercedes was parked, which would negate all the preceding subterfuge.

The door remained locked. He guessed the contact knew he was there, hence making himself known in such a way. But it wasn't obvious what the plan was from that point on. There was no way Rowe could ask the kid on reception to unlock the back door without making it obvious to the Mercedes driver. And what exactly would his reason be for that request anyway?

He looked back at the Defender and saw that the driver seemed to be holding something to his face – a phone, possibly. Suddenly the lights came on in the stairwell. Rowe tried the key card against the sensor again, but it had no effect. He stepped to one side, against the wall so he was out of the vision of the Mercedes driver but knowing the movement would be conspicuous. He stole a glance back through the glass towards the front door and saw the lights of the Mercedes had come on. He had been seen. The coroner's assistant was likely heading for the rear car park. At that moment, the light by the door turned from red to green and the sound of a lock freeing itself was heard.

Rowe grabbed the doorhandle, yanked it open and ran out toward the Defender, rucksack in hand. The passenger door swung out and he leapt inside. A literal leap of faith.

The dilemma of leaving the car park still lingered; in a few seconds the Mercedes would appear from behind and effectively block their exit. There was no time to address it. The Defender roared away from the kerb, out from between the parked cars instantly, and, instead of turning, headed straight towards the grass bank ahead of them. The front tyres thumped into the kerb and threw Rowe up out of his seat. The tyres kept traction somehow and climbed the bank with ease. Rowe was again propelled upwards when the 4x4 flew over the top of the bank and landed heavily on the grass of the banks' other side, next to the service road. The wheels spun and the Defender surged forward just as powerfully as before, bringing them out of the service road and towards the main exit for the motorway.

Rowe didn't see the Mercedes in his wing mirror.

The Defender left the motorway as soon as it feasibly could, diving down what Rowe thought looked like a private road that was not signposted. They kept up a semi-treacherous speed on the rural roads they travelled as the contact took several turns without warning or much adherence to the vehicle's brakes. There was no lighting on the route and the contact was dressed in dark clothing with a hunter's cap that covered much of his head and neck. He had long, stringy hair and a bushy beard obscured the half of his face that wasn't adorned by steel-framed glasses. After a few miles he spoke for the only time that he would until they reached their destination.

'Sorry about that. I didn't think your tail would come into the car park and that back door is never usually locked. It's a fire exit. The kid on the desk must be new.'

'How did the door get opened?' Rowe asked, somewhat vacantly.

'I rang the desk and asked the kid. Told him I had luggage. He sulked but did it eventually. Just in time I guess.'

Rowe nodded in the darkness but didn't speak. The voice was broken, slightly hoarse. He thought he recognised it but wasn't as certain as he'd have liked to be.

PART TWO

24

DEVON ROWE DIDN'T LIVE anywhere. Even if his home were to be defined by the place of his residence at that time, his younger brother didn't think he could have specified or even reasonably estimated where that was had he been asked to do so at gunpoint.

The journey seemed long although Mike Rowe hadn't kept an eye on the time. It didn't seem important to do so, somehow. In the pitch black the roads all looked like imitations of each other, while the trees and foliage that rushed past may as well have been on a repeating loop. Most of the roads were single track or unmarked until the Defender eventually turned onto what Rowe took to be a service road which, although very much like those they had just traversed, was clearly attached to private land. The road connected to other similar ones as they went deeper into whatever property it was that surrounded them.

Abruptly, they turned off the last of these roads onto an overgrown track that appeared to Rowe to be little more than a break in the grass peppered with gravel and hardcore. The Defender veered off the track and into long grass almost as soon as they had joined it. They came to a stop in front of a rusted corrugated iron construction that appeared only just big enough to house the vehicle. Devon got out, walked around in front of the Defender, and unlocked a padlock at the front of the structure.

Rowe had known the contact was Devon from the beginning. However, in the context of the uncertainty that was engulfing him he had not allowed himself to jump to any conclusions until they had met. He hadn't been able to identify him by voice or even sight immediately but sitting next to the man in the Defender, seeing his brother's hands guide the steering wheel and the inscrutable eyes move between the road and the mirrors had been proof enough.

To the left of the shed-like iron structure and further back, the Defender's headlights gave peripheral exposure to an old house that may once have been picturesque bordering on grand. Like a rich person's house in a village created by Agatha Christie. It was clearly suffering from neglect and almost all the windows that Rowe could see appeared to have been broken. Any grass that was visible in front of it and around the Defender was absurdly long.

Devon got back into the drivers' seat and Rowe's eyes were drawn back to the iron construction. He blinked. With its doors open, he could see that the inside of the structure was not only larger than appeared possible from the outside, but also a complete departure from it in style. It was a solid, modern unit apparently designed specifically to house the vehicle they sat in. He realised also that Devon had opened a second set of doors behind the outer iron pair. The conclusion Rowe came to was that the crumbling exterior was intended to disabuse any interested parties of the notion that anything of value lay inside. He wondered if the same was true of the house.

The structure was lit by spotlights embedded in the unspecified robust black panels that made up the ceiling and walls. Two workbenches and a collection of tools and other motor-related equipment sat at the far end.

Devon drove the Defender in, parked and turned off the engine. They got out wordlessly, walked back outside the structure – which Rowe supposed was closer to a garage than anything else – and Devon locked the two sets of doors again, studiously and continuously checking his surroundings as he did so. Rowe believed they had lost the coroner's assistant back at the services and thought it extremely unlikely that anyone else would have followed them, but it was clear that Devon was a very cautious man. He had completely disappeared for ten years, after all.

Rowe followed Devon, who carried a torch he had brought from the Defender, up towards the house. They took a seemingly indirect path through the long grass instead of via the track, which Rowe realised was because they were entering the house through a side door instead of the front. When they reached it, the door was not locked but looked as if it could have been untouched for some years. Devon stepped inside and Rowe followed; he thought the house was as cold as it looked from the outside and felt damp, like a cave.

They were in a hallway that led through part of the house into rooms on the left and right. The house was completely dark except for Devon's torch and some moonlight that stole through the windows at the front of the building. Leaves and other detritus covered the tiled floor and Rowe found himself questioning how and why his presumed-dead brother had apparently set himself up there. In doing so, he acknowledged that he still had no real idea what was happening and that he was traipsing through an abandoned shell of a house in the middle of nowhere on blind faith.

Devon stopped just after they passed what appeared to have been the kitchen on their left and opened a slatted wooden door on their right. He shone the torch down some steep stone steps.

'Watch your feet,' Devon said in the silence.

They made their way down into a small, low room that was clearly once a cellar of some kind. Two ancient, waist-high wine racks sat haphazardly in the middle of the floor, surprisingly still containing a handful of unopened and dusty bottles.

'This was the wine cellar,' Devon noted, somewhat unnecessarily. 'It was two rooms, but I commandeered the other one.'

He shone the torch on a wooden door to their right which to Rowe looked similar to the one at the top of the stairs except possibly newer. Devon took a set of keys from his pocket and unlocked it. There was another, plain black door immediately behind. That one had a keypad above the lock, and Devon used a combination of a key and a code to open it. When the door did open, he flicked a switch just inside the it and more ceiling spotlights came on, like those in the garage.

Rowe estimated the room was around fifteen feet by twelve feet in size, but with the same low ceiling as the smaller room. Devon had apparently converted it into a home and workspace in one. The same black panelling used inside the garage covered the walls and ceiling in the room and the floor was almost entirely covered with stiff, grey industrial carpeting. Against the far wall, from left to right as Rowe looked at them, was a small generator humming in the corner, a folding bed, a makeshift shower cubicle and another curtained section in the corner which he guessed covered a toilet.

Against the wall to their right was a table which held a wash bowl with cleaning products and accessories and bottled water stocked deep and high beneath it. Further along and next to where Rowe stood was another table which held a microwave, a hot plate, a portable coffee machine and neat piles of plastic crockery and cutlery.

Against the left wall was a desk that had at least two computer units sitting underneath it plus a laptop and two large monitors on top. Several other unspecified devices took up the remaining space. A comfortable looking but worn leather swivel chair was positioned in front of the desk.

The near wall to Rowe's immediate left was piled high with clear plastic storage boxes that appeared to hold clothes and other items he couldn't make out. The room was like a storage container itself. And it appeared to hold his brother's entire life.

Devon pulled a drummer-style stool out from next to the storage boxes into the uncluttered middle of the room and gestured to Rowe to sit on it. Rowe was grateful to sit down: the renovations to the room had made an already low ceiling even lower to the point where he was wary of standing up completely straight. The older brother seemed oblivious to it.

'Coffee?' the host asked his guest.

'Please. Black.'

Devon half-smiled as if he already knew the preference and stepped over to the coffee machine. He had taken off the hunter's cap and Rowe could see his hair was almost at his shoulders, although it was thinning on top. His brother's frame was skinny, almost malnourished, but he had the demeanour of someone who had stopped noticing or caring about it some time ago.

Rowe was still in a kind of dream-state, as he had been since he got into the Defender in the hotel car park. His missing brother was apparently alive, but he found the fact he still had no idea what that meant placed any emotion he might otherwise attach to it on hold.

When the coffee was brewed, Devon handed Rowe a mug before settling down with his own in the leather swivel chair. He faced Rowe with his back to the computer desk, crossing one skinny cargo-trousered leg over the other. In doing so, something metallic revealed itself between the bottom of the trouser leg and his boot.

A prosthetic leg below the knee. Rowe looked at it briefly then met his brother's eyes, but Devon gave no indication that he had noticed or that he was about to expand on the subject. Instead, he picked up where he had left off when he had first spoken back at their meeting point.

'I've stayed at that hotel myself in the past,' he said, sipping his coffee. 'That's how I knew about the back door. Maybe they've started locking it at night.'

'There was a guy in a Mercedes following me,' Rowe said. 'It's likely he saw us leave.'

Devon shrugged.

'Maybe. He didn't see us leave the motorway though. And the number plate of the Defender will be a dead end. You left your phone in the room?'

'Yes.'

'Thought so,' Devon nodded. 'You'd have been fiddling with it on the way here otherwise. Those things have a hold over people.'

Rowe didn't reply. After a few seconds he asked what seemed to be the obvious question.

'So...can I ask what we're doing here?'

'Yes, I should explain,' Devon sat up as if he had been neglecting his duties as host. 'This estate has been under an ownership dispute for over a decade. Neither of the parties who claim rightful ownership can set foot on it legally until a resolution can be found which, for various reasons, doesn't look like happening soon. There is a groundskeeper assigned to the property, but they are only contracted to attend to the main house and its immediate grounds. This is one of the secondary houses on the estate and they have no interest in it in any case. When the land title is eventually awarded this will be demolished and probably rebuilt. And I'll be long gone by then anyway.'

Rowe raised an eyebrow.

'In one way or another,' Devon continued, with the briefest of smiles. 'I've been here eight months now which is longer than I've stayed anywhere in the last decade. I'll probably move on soon, simply because I don't like to stay in one place too long but being here does have its advantages. Not only is it very safe – the windows of this place were broken long before I arrived

– but it's peaceful and the woods provide useful resources.'

'I bet they do,' Rowe said politely. 'Look, Devon...'

The older brother's eyes seemed to flash at the first mention of his name. Rowe thought it might have been a long time since he had heard it.

'...I don't exactly know why I'm here. Things had turned serious when I got your message. If you know who's following me or anything about what's going on I'd be grateful for your help. I don't know why you're living like this or where you've been for the last ten years. Forgive me if it's a lot to take in – it's hard to know where to start.'

Shortly after Devon's disappearance, Rowe had received a message from an unknown source saying that his brother was alive and well, but that Rowe was to tell no one. After some thought, and as time passed with no further contact, Rowe had dismissed the message as a dark prank. By whom, he didn't know. Nonetheless, he had thought about his brother a lot as the years went on. As far as he knew, Devon wasn't wanted by the authorities. He was merely missing and presumed deceased by the Army. Rowe had no idea what path had brought him to the present point in his life.

'Of course.' Devon held up a hand. 'I'll start from the beginning.'

'AS YOU KNOW, THE first explosion in Afghan put me out of commission for a while. And as you also know, I went back. Unfinished business and all that. Probably just pride. They stuck me out of the way as a Cyber Engineer with the Royal Signals at Camp Souter. It wasn't what I had in mind, but it was probably where my skills were best used. In fact, it was quite dull for the most part. The "war" was finished by then – so we were told, at least.'

Devon had brewed up more coffee and was back in the leather chair, which Rowe had begun to envy from his unforgiving stool. He doubted that his brother received many visitors. Nonetheless, he concentrated on the story being told.

'One day we had word that a soldier based at Souter had been killed in a roadside mine explosion. News like that was unfortunately common – we were losing at least one or two per month – so we had protocols for reporting the details to various "stakeholders", as they were termed. My team processed everything as normal and soon enough it became a story in the wider media. This wasn't unusual, only I noticed that this soldier's death was getting more attention than we would typically expect. His widow and parents were doing TV interviews, every news outlet was sharing his story and a fundraising page for the family had been set up online. The money being donated was incredible: over £100,000 in the first week. All from constant coverage on TV, online and in print.'

Devon drank more coffee and sucked at his teeth, as if a bad taste had entered his mouth.

'The problem was that I didn't know this soldier. I'd never seen or heard his name despite dealing with personnel lists every day. His details were present in the system, but I felt something wasn't right. Everyone in camp was expectedly sombre and regretful that another of our number had been taken, but no one seemed to know him. I wasn't able to confirm who had been out on patrol with this soldier at the time. When I asked around informally, I was met with a mixture of bemused confusion and defiant anger that I was even bringing it up, so I kept it to myself after that. I started to research the background of the soldier as best I could, including his Army history using the databases I could access. To cut a long story short, after digging as far as possible I came to the conclusion that this person didn't exist and neither did his family. Yet someone was raising a huge amount of money in their name.'

Rowe's eyes widened and he nodded slightly.

'Quite the conclusion to reach,' he said.

'I know what you're thinking,' Devon said with a wry smile. 'That it's only moments until I have us both sitting here in tinfoil hats. Well, I'm just warming up. I didn't come to that way of thinking lightly. It took many hours of quiet research. And after that, I started looking into other high profile soldier deaths where fundraising pages had been started. I concluded that at least half of those I researched were not real people. You have to understand, I knew the people in the Army that were officially reporting these deaths. In some cases, they were speaking publicly about the soldiers in question. I knew who they answered to, within the Army and otherwise. I knew that they knew the truth.

'Then I looked beyond soldiers into the other armed services, then into generally high-profile deaths covered in the media where crowdfunding money was being raised, which is nearly all of them these days. The story was the same: at least half were bogus. My view of the world changed completely.'

Rowe was still sitting quietly and listening. He was trying to keep an open mind, to fully understand his estranged brother's experience, but he was aware that his face was betraying him.

'That's OK, Mike,' Devon said. 'These are not things I expect anyone to just accept or agree with straight away. Quite the opposite in fact. That's why I knew I had to go it alone if I were going to change anything. I had lost all faith in my employers along with the establishment and the country they represented, and I felt there was nothing I could do about that either as service personnel or as a private citizen. So, I chose to be neither. The fact was I had committed myself to fighting back against the people responsible for this apparently universal fraud and others. I wanted to expose them. I planned my route out and disappeared.'

Rowe nodded. He was pleased to hear Devon use his name, but he also wasn't sure he knew what the story he was being presented with ultimately meant.

'Where did you go?' Rowe asked. 'Have you lived like this the entire time?'

'I've built up to this,' Devon half-smiled. 'I left camp with just a laptop and a doctored passport essentially. I'm sure you heard the details, but I faked an exercise accident as cover. An explosion in an isolated part of the base. I did my best to make it as real as possible – too real, as it turned out.'

He briefly glanced down at the prosthetic leg, acknowledging it for the only time that he would in Rowe's presence.

'A contact in the medical corps owed me a favour. Officially my body wasn't found, just some identifying items as a distraction. I went AWOL. My genuine injury made things more difficult, but it aided my disguise in other ways. Eventually amputation was necessary. Could've been worse, I guess. I've lived in several countries, stayed on the move. Obviously, I found my way back here eventually.'

Rowe drained the last of his coffee.

'So, after ten years,' he said, 'how much more have you learned about this…fraud stuff?'

'Obviously I started out completely on my own. But over the years I gradually came into contact – electronically, at least – with other like-minded individuals who were researching the same things that I was. As time went on, we discovered some of the sources and systems that are used to create things such as these false personas and their backgrounds. We're not talking about a back office at GCHQ that is responsible. It is a significant number of operators, in many places, using several largely opaque systems. The people I research alongside all live off the grid, like me. None of us have met in person.'

'And who are the people you're trying to expose exactly?'

'They don't have a name, at least not one that's known to us. They are employees of someone, certainly, but not the government. That would be too obvious and precarious. It's someone separate. With more power.'

'Why are they doing it?'

'Money would seem an obvious motive, but the manipulation of public sympathy cannot be ignored. Fake news stories are a propaganda as old as the printed word.'

Rowe said nothing to that. He wasn't sure if his brother was being deliberately vague or not.

'We started to focus in on some of their systems,' Devon went on. 'The ones we could find, that is. I'm not bad with computers but some of the others are at a different level. They can break any encryption. Eventually, about five years ago, we got to a point where we could see these systems and the evidence contained therein of what we already knew was happening. That was when we began using tactics to try and sabotage or at least slow them down as best we could. To let them know we were there.'

'Wait, so you've seen actual evidence of this fraud being carried out? Have any of you reported it?'

'Oh, we've seen huge amounts of it...but reporting it isn't going to work. Even lower-level ranks of the armed services and police are involved in these deceptions – although most probably have no idea how or why. Do you know how often false news stories appear in the media in this country? Every week, at least. Murders, kidnappings, gas explosions...and each time an officer will be wheeled out to talk about them as if they are genuine. These officers will be specially selected. They are told it is important for national security and for training and research purposes. And for their careers. The officers in question probably think it means they are highly thought of by their superiors, that they are being entrusted with a great secret.'

Rowe found the idea hard to swallow.

'Doesn't that seem like a risk to involve so many people? It wouldn't take much for one of these officers to go to the papers.'

'Put it this way,' Devon said quickly, as if he had expected the question. 'Let's say a guy who is now a pensioner but who worked in the NASA control room in 1969 comes out tomorrow and says the moon landings were staged. If the story made the news at all, the guy wouldn't be taken seriously. But even if some did believe him, there are systems in place that could immediately discredit the person by branding him senile or bitter in some way. The story would be forgotten immediately. This is exactly why it doesn't work to go through the established channels and why we had to find another way to fight the people responsible. Head on, and with aggression.'

Rowe nodded. 'I can understand that.'

And he could, in a way.

Devon finally downed the last of his coffee before continuing.

'Anyway. Since we began our attacks on their systems, our lives have become far more dangerous, unsurprisingly. When we started targeting them five years ago there were around twenty of us working on it.

196

Roughly one of our number has disappeared each year since then. We think they are picking us off one by one.'

Rowe's ears pricked up. He sensed that whatever was about to be said was the reason he had been brought there.

'The most recent is a member we knew as Sputka,' Devon said. 'He hasn't been online since Wednesday and as far as is ascertainable his last location was Fenwood. That's why I contacted you.'

'Ah, OK. You didn't just feel like catching up after ten years then?'

'It's not safe for me to contact anyone.' Devon's expression was unreadable. 'I saw the reports online about the cell death at Fenwood police station. James Burnell. The name didn't mean anything to me, but it was probably false in any case.'

Devon set his mug down on the desk behind him before turning back to face Rowe.

'Each time we have lost a member in the last five years, there has been a police cell death in or near each member's last known location. We believe James Burnell was Sputka.'

'How did you know this Sputka was in Fenwood?' Rowe asked. 'Considering where we're currently sitting, I'd have thought your colleagues would be reluctant to share their locations.'

There was more coffee in Rowe's mug, while Devon was abstaining for the time being.

'After the first member, Cojin, disappeared, we collectively agreed on a signal we would use if any of us were ever in danger. It's a simple button press hooked up to a GPS tracker so that it wouldn't rely on the person accessing a computer or phone. Most members apparently sew them into the lining of a jacket or similar. With Cojin we made the link to the cell death without much else to go on but after that the GPS's were used on each occasion. Obviously, we can never be sure that the locations we get are final – and there's not much we can do in the way of practical help at the time – but it gives us a starting point to work from.'

Rowe shifted on his stool and rubbed his head. He exhaled slowly.

'Alright. Maybe if I fill you in on what's been happening it'll help us both to make some sense of this. Hopefully.'

He told Devon the story from the beginning. He started with the Hannah Crockett death and how that had ultimately led to his presence at the cell death scene. He described the issues he had had with the scene along with his interactions with Grantley and what he had seen in the cell. Devon's mention of the GPS tracker sewn into a jacket reminded him of the coat he had seen confiscated from Burnell when he was brought in on the CCTV.

'Black with green and red diamonds on the back?' Devon asked.

'Yeah. How did you know?'

'Sputka had described it to us. It was another identifying signal.'

Rowe nodded and thought maybe that could be why it had been confiscated. He talked more about the Lockscreen CCTV, then outlined his later conversations with Stanwell and his various encounters with Vickers.

He said he was no longer a police officer. Then he mentioned the deaths of Symonds and Worth and how the latter had seemingly been used as a warning to him.

He also told Devon about Laura and how the cell death had in some way allowed them to reconnect. It somehow felt right to give his brother some personal news, if only to remind himself that they were indeed brothers. And maybe in the hope that Devon might share something more personal of his own.

By the time Rowe had finished the story, it was approaching 6am. He knew they needed to talk more, but he was feeling the effects of the previous day's events and saw that Devon recognised his tiredness.

'Let me chew on this for a while, Mike'. Devon said. 'You're welcome to crash on the camp bed there. I need to check on a few things on the computer.' He nodded to the desk behind him. 'I don't sleep much these days anyway.'

Rowe agreed. He took off his shoes and laid down on the bed, which appeared freshly made. Despite his recent intake of coffee, he was asleep in seconds.

25

IT WAS APPROACHING NOON when Rowe opened his eyes, momentarily wondering where he was. The hum of the generator and whirring of the computer base units soon stirred him and served as a reminder of his location.

He turned over and sat up. Devon was not in the room and the twin doors that led outside the self-contained space stood slightly open. Rowe glanced over at the table to his left and saw a note propped up against the washbowl. It said CLEAN WATER, written in capital letters. He made use of the chemical toilet then washed his hands in the bowl. It wasn't clear to him how the shower worked if it wasn't connected to a water supply, but he decided he would address that issue later. After making himself a cup of coffee, he ventured out to find Devon.

Rowe navigated the wine cellar stairs with the light from the converted room and emerged through the door into the ground floor of the house. By daylight it was just as derelict as he had perceived it to be in the dark, but more of its former charm was evident too. The place was beyond repair but still held a glimmer of the idyllic country house it had probably once been. Tempting as it might have been for Devon to fix some of the more glaring issues – boarding up the downstairs windows and perhaps putting locks on the doors – Rowe could see how it made sense to leave the above-ground section of the house untouched.

He walked out of the side door, off an overgrown side path and into the long grass. It was a bright, chilly morning and in the daylight he could see the house was surrounded by very tall fir trees, some of which encroached onto what once might have been the garden.

Devon was at the rear of the house, sitting on a rusted metal bench up against the building's back wall and looking out on the dense grass and weeds. There were remnants of the back garden's intended landscaping still visible, beyond which was another group of tall firs that appeared to extend back into a deeper wood.

A bowl of apples sat on the bench next to Devon and he was holding his own cup of coffee.

'Breakfast,' he said, nodding to the apples.

'Thanks.' Rowe took one and sat down, studying it momentarily before joining his brother on surveying the greenery. 'Surely not even you can get firs to grow apples...especially in November.'

Devon smiled very briefly.

'Sainsbury's. I'm not a complete caveman.'

Rowe nodded.

'You're not worried about sitting out here for too long?'

'No. Like I said, no one comes here now. Besides, I have sensors around the perimeter and beyond. I'll know if anyone gets within half a mile – and considerably further in some areas.'

Rowe looked at his brother then glanced over and noticed a professional-looking rifle leaning against the wall next to where Devon sat. It had a large scope mounted on it and appeared, to Rowe's semi-educated eye, to be military issue.

'Old habits die hard,' the war veteran said without moving his gaze. 'Thought it was best to have one to hand. And this is as good a place to practise as any. No one bats an eyelid at gunshots in the country, and that's if they even hear them to begin with.'

Before his initial injury had sent him home and he had been impelled to retrain as a cyber engineer, Devon had been an exemplary sniper in the British Army. Rowe had heard it said that he was the best. He knew it had been difficult for his brother to give it up. Rowe wanted to ask where the rifle had come from but decided against it.

'At least you're not letting your talent go to waste,' he remarked before changing the subject. 'What do you do for money now?'

Devon laughed for the first time since they had been reunited.

'The beauty of the internet, Mike. It's quite easy to make a steady living, or better, these days using a few pre-programmed systems and relevant algorithms. Completely legal too. It's true what they say – there's an app for everything now.'

'No trail?'

'Not one that anyone would bother to follow.'

They sat looking at the natural panorama in front of them on what Rowe was discovering to be a colder day than he had first thought. Nonetheless, he sat still. He suspected that Devon would have come to some conclusions following their conversation the previous night and was allowing him to get to it in his own time. Eventually, he did.

'It seems things are more serious than I thought,' Devon said out of the silence.

'Oh?' It wasn't the opening Rowe had hoped for.

'You've had two warnings now, not one.'

Rowe turned to looked at Devon again, and in the stark daylight his brother's face was gaunt, almost haggard, and his body appeared frail. He looked far older than he was. His eyes had the hollowness of someone who hadn't slept in a long time. Maybe years. Rowe waited for him to expand on the statement.

'You mentioned your girlfriend, Laura, was attacked while you were investigating the Hannah Crockett death. If you don't mind me asking, what was the nature of the attack?'

Devon had asked the question clinically, as if it were part of a scientific study. Rowe leaned back against the bench.

'Laura was coming home in the early hours after a late shift. Apparently, she was hit from behind in the car park of her block of flats. The attacker tried to drag her into a vehicle, but she managed to fight him off. Eventually whoever it was gave up and drove away. The person was dressed in black with a balaclava. The vehicle had no distinguishing marks and a false registration. There were no witnesses and nothing on camera. I heard all this second hand – Laura hasn't talked to me about it.'

Devon was quiet and seemed to be thinking.

'The timing of it is too coincidental,' he said at last. 'As soon as you began to look at Crockett's death as something other than a suicide, Laura was attacked. That was warning one. When you did the same with

Burnell, you were followed with the intention to intimidate. And when that didn't work, you were sent a clear second warning with the photo of Rachel Worth. Of course, this means that Crockett's death was the starting point of this series of events and is directly linked to everything else.'

Rowe said nothing. Devon went on.

'Steve Symonds' death looks like something different: a punishment of some kind perhaps. Worth's death was used as a warning but doesn't mean she wasn't killed for similar reasons, given the link between her and Symonds. But the attack on Laura was the first shot across the bow, and that's because you were getting too close on Crockett.'

'But what does that mean?' Rowe asked, confused. 'Are you saying I was right about Vickers? That everything that's happened up to now is because I linked him to Hannah Crockett? Help me out here Devon, because I don't see how any of this relates to your friend Sputka – or the conspiracy stuff for that matter.'

Rowe could feel frustration and anger building inside him. Apart from anything else, Devon had managed to plant the idea in his head that Vickers could have been responsible for the attack on Laura.

'OK.' Devon set his mug down on the stone paving and clasped his hands over his crossed legs. 'It's tempting for you to look at this Vickers and his boss as the major players because of the Crockett case and their general dislike for you. But I'm seeing it from the perspective that it is part of a wider project to eliminate people like Sputka and the others we've lost. It's conceivable that someone like Vickers could be employed in that as a useful idiot of sorts, but he probably wouldn't be entrusted with anything as serious as we have discussed. The person you should be focusing on, and far more concerned about, is Commander Grantley.'

Rowe eyed his brother. 'What about Grantley exactly?'

'We believe he is the person who is heading the investigation into our work. And therefore, ultimately responsible for the deaths of our colleagues. So far, we have not been able to evade him despite efforts to tighten our own defensive measures. Maybe he can't be evaded.'

Devon paused for a second, as if contemplating that last rumination, before continuing.

'We know a certain amount about Grantley, but not much. He holds great power. There are stories about his history and past associations. He certainly did not reach his current position by accident. What we do know is that he has been untouchable to us thus far, in every sense.'

Rowe sat forward, looking out at the long-deceased garden while he considered what was being said.

'The kind of people we are talking about here,' Devon said, 'are as professional as they come. Excuse my bluntness, Mike, but if they wanted to kill you, they would have done it by now.'

'So why haven't they?'

'I think it's obvious.'

Devon's eyes met Rowe's, for what felt to him like the first time.

'They need you to help them find me.'

Rowe studied his brother's eyes, and Devon seemed to read his thoughts.

'Don't worry, they don't know where we are. I've been doing this for a long time. Although I'm sure they suspect we're in contact. Bringing you here was a risk in some ways I admit, but it was necessary. I had to know what we were dealing with.'

'How much did you already know?'

'Some. Not all. It didn't take much to piece things together from the news reports on the deaths of Burnell and Symonds. Not long before I picked you up, I heard the radio chatter about Worth's body too. I knew her name from the Burnell reports. But you've filled in some gaps for me – I didn't know about Hannah Crockett before, or about Laura. At a guess, I would say Crockett died because she knew something – probably about the Burnell plan. You ruffled some feathers, so Laura was targeted. Then Burnell dies in his cell. You are hand-picked to work it. Symonds dies. You zero in on Worth. She dies. All of these things happen in the sleepy town of Fenwood – my hometown. They wanted to attract my attention, using you as a conduit. Which, of course, means they now know who I am too.'

A cold wind was blowing through the trees and swirling around the garden. Or at least it felt that way to Rowe.

'So, what happens now?' he said after a while. 'I'm guessing you have a plan.'

'Not a plan exactly. A starting point maybe.'

Devon turned his body and rested his right elbow on top of the bench.

'Find out exactly what this Vickers knows once and for all. About Hannah Crockett and everything…whatever it takes. He needs to be ruled out or in. Then we'll talk about how to handle Grantley and his team. They are ultimately the ones to be concerned with. They're the operatives on the ground.'

'That's not going to be easy, to put it mildly.' Rowe said it with a touch of exasperation.

'But you can do it. Look, Mike, I know you didn't expect any of this. But everything I've told you here is true. It's real. Eventually they will find me, I have no doubt about that. All I want is for a small part of their world to be exposed or damaged in some way. To show that someone is fighting back. I know you have your own motivations, but I'm asking for your help too.'

Rowe said nothing.

'I'll get you back to the hotel later,' Devon said. 'Your friend in the Mercedes won't be going anywhere. But first, I think we should take a drive out to the country.'

26

DEVON RETRIEVED THE DEFENDER from the iron garage-shed and he and Rowe steadily made their way out of the maze of roads that connected the various parts of the nameless country estate. In the light, Rowe could see the vehicle was at least thirty years old and was indeed a faded pale blue colour. It certainly didn't look out of place in the countryside.

When they emerged back onto public roads, Rowe observed that it wasn't significantly easier to keep track of their progress or changes in direction in daylight than it had been in darkness. After a while he gave up and simply allowed Devon to navigate them to their still undisclosed location. His rucksack sat on the floor between his legs – the change of socks and underwear he had brought had come in handy before they left, although the mystery of the shower remained unsolved.

Instead of concerning himself with his exact location, Rowe sat in the rattling, utilitarian machine and thought about Laura Cross. He had spoken to her the previous afternoon, and he hoped to see her again that night, but a lot had happened since then. He debated whether he should have called her again after Worth's picture was planted in his flat. To warn her.

Despite their important reunion a few nights earlier and Laura filling in some blanks from the previous months, Rowe realised he felt guilty that he still understood so little of what had troubled her in the time. Didn't he have a duty to protect her? Or was that, like so many aspects of his worldview, painfully old-fashioned and part of the reason they had drifted apart to begin with? He had no idea, and that fact in itself felt like a dreadful failing.

What he did know was that if Devon was right about the attack on Laura being intended as a warning, then there was no guarantee she was safe. She wasn't the neutral bystander he had hoped she was. He needed to talk to her soon, but he also needed more answers before he did so.

Devon had been driving in his quiet and studious way and Rowe broke the silence when he spoke.

'When you say Grantley's team are the operatives on the ground, what do you mean? Surely they have to report everything through the Yard?'

Devon looked at him out of the corner of his eye before replying.

'Their movements are probably sanctioned by someone senior at the Yard, yes. But I would wager that Grantley and his team aren't based there and probably barely set foot in the place. Grantley started out in the Met but would've been recruited by one of the shadow agencies early. From what my colleagues and I have learned over the years, it's not unusual for young officers who show promise to be recruited in that way. This often coincides with a somewhat meteoric rise through the ranks.'

As Rowe opened his mouth, Devon cut him off.

'If you're thinking that Vickers could be one of these officers, I'd say it's possible but also doubtful. The examples we have come across are almost all from the Met or their feeder academies. A few officers were recruited from other regions in the past, but at some point that seemed to stop for reasons unknown. Maybe it was easier to monitor recruits in one place. Even so, if this Vickers is the pushy, glorified errand boy you say he is, he doesn't sound like their sort of material. The people we've identified tend to be good at staying outside the light.'

'What about Grantley's sidekicks, are they recruits from the Met too?'

'Possibly. They might also be straight up henchmen, born into certain families and trained for their roles from a young age. Grantley is very senior now; you said there were two with him, but I think we can count at least three, with more in reserve.'

'Three?'

'This "coroner's assistant". He has to be their man. Which reminds me - when you were at the scene, did you recognise the coroner himself?

'Yeah, he's the Oxford guy.'

'Right. That means he's in their pocket too. That's not unusual.'

Rowe scratched his head and exhaled, still not sure what to make of Devon's narrative. He decided to change tack slightly.

'So, if we're now sure this was an "operation" and that James Burnell was actually Sputka, how did it happen? I had some theories about foul play, but I can't get past the Lockscreen CCTV. Everything was on camera from the moment he was brought in. He didn't leave the cell, and no one went in until he was unresponsive. If someone got to him, it's a locked room mystery. This Lockscreen stuff apparently can't be tampered with. It seems like a tough system to beat.'

Devon made a noise that might have been a chuckle.

'Tough system, yes,' he said, 'but it's their system. It was developed for and in partnership with the Met. These people would know exactly how it could be circumvented and exploited.'

'Do you?'

'I'd need to have witnessed the particular scene to know what was and wasn't possible. You saw it, what do you think?'

'Well…' Rowe rubbed his chin and stared out at the road. 'The CCTV footage itself looked genuine and I couldn't fault it. There was one thing though. The camera showing the inside of Burnell's cell gave the impression that it was completely dark outside the window. Thing is, there's a bright external security lamp right next to that window. I think the glow should have been visible in the footage.'

'Interesting. Could have been a trick of the light from within the cell maybe.'

'Maybe. While I was still assigned to the case I tried to get hold of the council's external CCTV footage to check that the light was on. I also asked for the bodycam footage from the two PCs to see exactly how Burnell…Sputka was apprehended.'

'Worth a try. But chances are, even in the unlikely event you had been allowed to obtain that footage, it wouldn't have shown anything that would've helped you. These people don't leave anything to chance.'

'Everybody makes mistakes.'

Devon didn't respond.

27

NOT SURPRISINGLY, DEVON HAD been keeping to the back roads for the duration of the journey, which to that point had lasted about half an hour by Rowe's watch. He was intrigued then when the Defender paused at a junction next to something resembling a main road that had relatively steady traffic passing on it. They turned left out of the junction and Rowe saw a sign for Rapton Airfield, which was marked as being a mile further on.

The name rang a bell with Rowe for some reason, but he couldn't think why. Devon jogged his memory.

'Up the road here is what used to be RAF Rapton. It was closed about a decade ago and the personnel based here were absorbed into other bases in the region. It was out of use for a while but is now a public airfield, as you have probably worked out.'

Rowe remembered the base closing. It had been national news at the time as, up to that point, RAF Rapton in Somerset was one of the major transport hubs for moving troops to and from Afghanistan and Iraq.

'Gotcha,' he said. 'Is that where we're headed?'

'No.' Devon checked his mirrors. 'We're headed to James Burnell's house.'

Rowe looked at his brother for a long moment before slowly turning his head back to the road. He had come to accept that Devon was explaining things in his own way and time. Jim Ferry had given Rowe the supposed home address for Burnell in Somerset, but he hadn't managed to focus on it before now.

Devon turned a sharp left into a housing estate which immediately looked to Rowe to be large and winding. It seemed to be filled with two and three bedroom-size houses that had uniformly white doors and window frames, each with their own gardens (front and presumably back), driveways and garages. A main thoroughfare ran through the middle of the estate with identical-looking cul-de-sacs branching off it on both sides at regular intervals.

The first few cul-de-sacs they cruised past showed evidence that a number of the houses were occupied with cars, bicycles and even the occasional person visible. As Devon took the Defender further into the estate however, it became obvious that most of the side roads were not heavily populated and, as they went deeper still, that some were possibly not inhabited at all.

They turned right onto one of the last cul-de-sacs and Devon turned the wheel abruptly, stopping the Defender in the middle of the road and effectively blocking it.

'Nice parking,' Rowe remarked. 'Learn that in the Army?'

'Just making a point. Come on.'

They got out and Rowe looked up and down the street, which held about six very similar houses on each side of the road. There were no signs of life in any of them, and nothing to suggest any were about to present themselves.

'That there is James Burnell's house.'

Devon was pointing to a house next to where they were standing on the left side of the street. Rowe looked at it before walking across the unkempt lawn – which contained various fragments of litter that looked long-entrenched – and peered in through the front window. The living room was completely unfurnished. The carpet looked old and stained, as did the walls. Everything was off-white in colour although Rowe got the impression it may not have started out like that. The room looked as if it may have been left open to the elements at some point.

He then stepped past the front door and looked through the kitchen window where he found a similar story. There were no appliances or furniture and there was a generally abandoned feel to it. After a brief investigation he ascertained that there was no route to the back of the house without breaking a lock, so he gave up and walked back to where Devon was standing near the Defender. They stood and gazed back at the house as if it were an exhibit of some kind.

'There are housing estates like this next to military bases all over the country,' Devon said. 'Even those attached to active bases have their fair share of empty units, but nothing on this scale. The current owners of the airfield may have access to some of them. Not many. The MoD still owns all of this and occasionally tries to sell it off with varying degrees of success. Most of these things have been empty for a decade. A caretaker might come round and check the locks once a month at best – more likely it's just a drive-by visual check. Beyond that there just aren't the resources to maintain them.'

'So did Sputka give himself a false address?' asked Rowe. 'Or did someone else do it for him?'

'The latter: Sputka wouldn't have been able to falsify his address in official records, and I don't see why he'd want to. Like me, he didn't officially exist. This was assigned as the family home address that James Burnell inherited when his parents supposedly died. Which is clearly not true and not possible. But no one was officially ever going to be allowed to get far enough down the road with this to find that out.'

Rowe glanced around at the other houses on the street. It was a ghost town. Like houses built on a film set, made just believable enough to look real on camera but little more. There were no sounds from living things to be heard.

He turned back to his brother.

'I suppose you know the official story of how Burnell's parents died?'

Devon looked at him. 'Yes.'

'Same way as our parents. Exactly ten years after – to the date.'

'Mm. I found that when I started researching Burnell off the back of the media reports. They knew the date would catch my attention even if nothing else did.'

'So that's when you knew they'd identified you.'

Rowe said it as a statement rather than a question.

Devon nodded.

'Yes. And that Sputka was dead.'

28

THE DEFENDER WAS BACK on the smaller rural roads. Heading in the general direction of Junction 27 services, Rowe presumed, although he didn't ask. He was still allowing Devon to take the lead, to dictate their path both literally and in terms of the story that was emerging. He seemed to know a lot more about the situation than Rowe did, that was clear. Questions and loose ends still swirled in Rowe's head as a light rain patted the Defender's windscreen.

'What about Shehzad and McMurray, the officers who picked up Burnell – sorry, Sputka? Are they players or not?'

He asked the question as Devon guided them through a picturesque village that exhibited a lack of modernity which Rowe found endearing.

'Very likely not. I guess they weren't based out of Fenwood?'

'No, they were rostered late on.'

'Makes sense. They turn up, they're told to respond to a call, they go through the motions. Just the usual mindless robots. Even if they did think anything was off, they wouldn't say so.'

'That's what I thought.'

Rowe gazed through the passenger side window as the Defender increased its speed coming out of the village and fields began to dominate the scenery.

'Something else you should keep in mind.' Devon's voice was quiet but earnest enough to snap Rowe out of his mental gymnastics. 'Grantley was likely in charge of the operation, and people like Worth and Symonds may have done most of the legwork at the scene. But there would also be a local contact. Someone who could be trusted to orchestrate the details in advance and who had proved his or her competency in the past. One of the "sleeper" foot soldiers that these people have everywhere.'

'Right…but I'm guessing you don't know who that is?'

'No, I don't. That's a job for you, brother.'

Rowe looked back out of the window and scratched his head.

'I know you think I'm barking up the wrong tree,' he said, 'but I'm telling you, Vickers fits the profile of the person you just described. He appeared at the scene for no apparent reason and stuck close to Grantley's team. And after everyone else had gone it was just him and Symonds left in the building. He's been acting like he didn't want me anywhere near the case but maybe that was because he knew I'd do the opposite of whatever he wanted. And don't forget he even admitted to putting a tracker on my car. If he's not their man he's certainly acting like it.'

'Who are you trying to convince?' Devon half-smiled. 'Listen – never rule anything out. Anyway, you can ask him nicely later.'

Rowe raised an eyebrow but didn't reply.

Eventually, signs for the motorway started to appear. Rowe guessed they were somewhere near the maze of roads they had joined when leaving the M5 around 12 hours earlier but were approaching them from a different direction.

Shortly thereafter, Devon slowed and pulled the Defender into a muddy passing place, then turned off the engine. Rowe could hear the sound of traffic hurtling past but was not able to physically see the motorway from where they were positioned. Both sides of the road they were on were lined with tall firs that reminded him of the ones surrounding the derelict house on the nameless estate.

'The hotel is on the other side of that field. Give me your room key.'

Devon was pointing to their right, past the line of firs and at a field that sloped upwards to an invisible summit. Rowe gazed fruitlessly in that direction for a moment before taking out the key and handing it over. Then he reached for the ageing door latch on the passenger door before realising that his brother was already out of the vehicle.

'Wait here,' Devon said as he slammed the drivers' door. Rowe saw him walk quickly across the road and disappear into the trees on the other side. Devon was wearing a black waterproof jacket from which he'd pulled the hood up over his hunter's cap in the rain. Rowe noticed the keys were still in the Defender's ignition and wondered momentarily – and paranoically – whether his brother would actually return.

Five minutes later, Devon came back the way he had gone, wearing sunglasses on a grey November day. With those, his coat hood, hat and thick beard combined virtually none of his face was visible. He opened the drivers' door again but stayed standing on the road in the drizzle.

'Guy in the black Mercedes is still there,' he said. 'I went in the back door. Even if he saw me, I doubt he could have made a positive ID. Here's your phone.'

Devon took it out of his coat pocket and handed the mobile to Rowe.

'Don't turn it on unless it's safe or necessary to do so. Preferably both. Now, give me the keys to the Vitesse.'

'What for?'

'I'll distract our friend and retrieve it. It may have a more sophisticated tracker on it now – if it has, I'll need to deal with that. Until then, you're driving the beast.'

Devon cast a hand over the driver's seat as if he were a salesman in a Land Rover showroom. Rowe regarded his brother blank-facedly for a moment.

'Get in for a second, Devon.'

The older brother glanced up and down the road before climbing in and shutting the door. Rowe waited for the clanging of metal on metal to fade before he spoke.

'This has been a crazy few hours for me, brother. My head's spinning.' Rowe had been looking at Devon, but his gaze had moved to the road ahead of the parked Defender. 'I'm grateful for you helping me out and I'll do everything I can to get to the bottom of this. But first I need to know one thing.'

'OK,' Devon said quietly. 'And what's that?'

'Why did you really desert in Afghan?'

Devon didn't seem surprised or unsettled by the question. He answered with a level voice.

'It's as I said. I found the institution I was working for was involved in a high-level fraud which ultimately extended much further. I couldn't take their money anymore and I couldn't combat it by any legal means. Plus, I had no home or life to speak of to return to. So, I just went.'

'I can see that – to a point. Maybe I'm just not that type of person but faking your own death and committing yourself to a life off the grid and on the run seems like an awfully big step to take just because your employer turned out to be crooked.'

Rowe turned to face his brother again. It was a few seconds before Devon responded.

'Maybe. All I can say is things got personal.'

Rowe nodded. It wasn't the full story, but he hadn't expected much more. He felt it was enough to be going on with.

The younger brother extended his hand, and the elder brother shook it briefly but firmly.

'Remember – I'll make contact,' Devon said. 'Talk to Vickers.'

Devon then removed the keys from the Defender's ignition and handed them over, which Rowe thought was odd if he was supposed to drive it from there anyway.

'Good to see you again, Devon,' he said.

Rowe watched him climb back out of the Defender and shut the door firmly. Then Devon set back off through the trees again. When he was out of sight, Rowe got out of the passenger door, walked round, and took his place in the drivers' seat.

When he started the engine something about it, that he couldn't put his finger on, felt good. Like a fire that had gone out a long time ago had sparked again.

29

IT WAS DARK WHEN the Defender reached the outskirts of Oxford, and the roads were still damp from the light but incessant rain that fell. The area Rowe had arrived in, like many parts of Oxford, was prohibitively expensive to most on the housing ladder, but he knew that Neil Vickers lived in a flat there that the DCI's parents had paid the deposit on.

Bizarre as it seemed to him in light of recent circumstances, Rowe had once attended a party at the flat during his early days with the police. It was at a time when Vickers himself was relatively new to the service and wanted to appear popular, so had invited half of Oxford station round one Friday night. Rowe recalled retreating to the nearest pub as early as possible that night, but he still remembered the location of the flat.

The street was typical of the part of Oxford it was in, stylistically at least. It contained large and grandiose houses that were mostly split up into student accommodation with the odd private residence scattered among them, typically inhabited by academics or people linked to the university in some other way. The building where Vickers lived was unusual in that it contained private flats rather than anything connected to the university, although Rowe assumed its landlord either was or had been somehow connected in the past. Most things in Oxford were.

He parked the Defender in a darker area of the street, under the shadow of an overhanging tree. He didn't bother to pay for parking using the necessary app or phone number, reasoning that any attempt to levy a parking fine against the vehicle was likely to be unsuccessful. There was also the fact that he had enough experience of the notoriously inadequate parking provision in Oxford to ensure he had stopped caring about such things a long time ago.

Rowe made his way carefully up the street towards Vickers' building. He hadn't been aware of being followed since taking charge of the Defender and hadn't expected to be. He guessed that was part of Devon's plan, such as it was. Either way, he was sure Vickers would have no idea he was coming.

The street was quiet on a Sunday evening and only a single cyclist passed him as he neared the wide, gravel forecourt of the building. Vickers' silver Mercedes was sitting in a space in the forecourt. Rowe walked steadily across the gravel, glancing up at the street-facing windows and checking whether any residents happened to be looking out. He didn't see anyone, but he noticed a light was on in Vickers' flat as well as in that of his neighbour, both of which were on the first floor.

He stepped into the alcove in front of the door and pressed the buzzer for Vickers' flat. There was a security camera inside the alcove, but Rowe was gambling that his presence would not be scrutinised after he had chatted with Vickers.

After a few seconds a voice answered, and Rowe recognised it as the impatient, uppity tone of the flat's resident.

'Yes?'

'Hi, got a food delivery for number 6 but they're not responding.' Rowe said it in a high, anxious register that he imagined a teenage delivery person might possess. 'Their light is on, man. I've been here before. Can you buzz me in?'

Vickers murmured with irritation in response but after a few seconds the door audibly unlocked. Rowe went in and headed straight up the stairs that were opposite the door. He reached the first-floor landing and quietly navigated his way back on himself and down a corridor to the right where he found the door numbered 6. He knocked discreetly but loud enough to be heard from within.

There was a thud and a rustling of paper from inside the flat, followed by footsteps that seemed to become more impatient as they came nearer. The door didn't open at first, which Rowe had expected hence he was standing to one side of it with his back to the wall. He envisioned Vickers looking through the fisheye confusedly. As he hoped, the door eventually opened when either Vickers' curiosity or annoyance got the better of him.

The DCI poked his head out of the doorway, slightly over the threshold. He was just starting to speak when Rowe pointed the gun at his head.

It had seemed odd to Rowe that Devon had placed the Defender's keys in his hand before he left. When Rowe had stopped on the motorway for coffee, he had inspected them out of curiosity.

One of the items on the keyring was clear plastic and made to hold a small photograph or picture of some kind. Instead, there was a piece of paper inside that simply read 'GLOVE BOX' in black ink. He leaned over to the passenger side and opened the compartment. There was a handgun inside, wrapped in an old piece of cloth. Rowe recognised it as a Glock 17, standard issue for the British Army. He took it out carefully and saw that the serial number had been filed off and the gun was far from new. Strangely he didn't feel any great surprise either at seeing it there or in the knowledge that his brother possessed it. Rowe surmised that it had probably come from the same source as Devon's rifle had – possibly even the same source that had assisted him in his desertion from Afghanistan, although it was impossible to know.

At least he knew finally what his brother had meant about asking Vickers "nicely".

Rowe had passed a police firearm course a few years earlier and generally knew how to handle a gun, but he was certainly no expert and had never had a reason to carry one in the course of his police duty. But in the context of things as they stood, he could see the sense in having one to hand.

The instant that Vickers registered the gun in his peripheral vision, he tried to slam the door shut. However, Rowe was already moving forward and got a booted foot in the way to prevent it closing. He managed to push the door wider and stepped inside, at which point Vickers tried to grab the gun. Rowe still had forward momentum and used it to punt Vickers in the stomach with his right foot, which doubled him over, and followed up by clumping him in the head with the hand that held the gun.

Vickers fell to the floor and Rowe followed his descent, pinning the DCI's left arm to the carpet with his right foot while his left knee nestled in the crook of Vickers' right elbow. Rowe kept the gun aimed at his head.

It was a large apartment and Rowe could see they were in a spacious living room that held two sofas and opened into a kitchen space on his right with a dining table next to it that had six chairs. He vaguely remembered the layout from his previous visit but thought the colour of the walls may have changed. It had been a while after all.

Vickers was barefoot, wearing jogging bottoms and a t-shirt and had an enraged look on his face. Blood trickled from the new injury on his left temple.

'What the fuck is this Rowe?!' he spluttered. 'You've lost your fucking mind!'

'Shut up.'

'Let's not pretend you've got the balls to use that, Rowe,' said Vickers, gesturing with his head at the gun in a display of patently false bravado.

'Best you assume I have, Neil,' Rowe said. 'Now…I'm gonna let you up and you're gonna sit on the sofa over there. Any deviation to that plan and sitting down won't be fun anymore.'

Rowe had no actual intention of firing the gun if he could help it – especially not in a quiet residential building where the security camera had just captured him arriving. In fact, the Glock wasn't even loaded. He had left the cartridge back in the Defender's glovebox. But it was important that Vickers retained the possibility in his mind.

He kept the gun trained on Vickers' head and slowly released the man's arms. Then he stepped back and shut the door behind them. Vickers stood up warily before petulantly shuffling over to the nearest of the two sofas. Rowe stepped past him at a safe distance and sat down on the one opposite. Vickers felt for his head wound and tried to burn a hole in Rowe with his eyes as he did.

'Now,' Rowe said as he rested his right elbow on his knee to keep the gun steady. 'Tell me everything you know about Hannah Crockett's death.'

30

VICKERS WAS NOT FORTHCOMING to begin with. He aimed several threats in Rowe's direction and described in detail what Rowe's future – or lack thereof – was likely to look like once the intrusion had been reported to DCS Judith Carne. Rowe eventually decided to move the conversation along and interrupted the diatribe.

'Information has come to light that suggests Hannah Crockett's death wasn't a suicide' he said.

'What information?!' Vickers demanded. His tone was derisory, but Rowe sensed a genuine curiosity behind it.

'Why was she trying to call you that night?'

Vickers' face changed.

'Hannah…PC Crockett and I had worked together,' he said. 'Maybe it was about work, how should I know?'

'Maybe? She didn't leave a message?'

'No.'

'So, Crockett phoned you about work and then when you didn't answer she hung herself. That right?'

Something resembling hatred flickered across Vickers' features, but he didn't speak.

'OK, Neil. Here's the thing. At first, I thought you got me pulled from the Crockett case because you were somehow involved in her death. But now I realise you just panicked. She and you were an item, weren't you?'

Vickers snorted dismissively. Rowe continued.

'And when she apparently committed suicide for no reason and left missed calls on your phone you shit yourself. Thinking you might get the blame somehow.'

The DCI's eyelids twitched.

'The attack on Laura Cross came as a welcome distraction for you,' Rowe continued. 'I now know that was meant as a warning to me – but not from you. You see, since our last conversation, I'm still being followed. Threatened too. I don't think you're behind it because you haven't got the balls or the influence. But three officers are dead – Steve Symonds, Rachel Worth and Hannah Crockett – and I think all three are connected to the cell death. Deep down, you know that Crockett didn't commit suicide. But I think your friend Grantley and his crew know what did happen to her.'

Vickers looked angry and slightly ill. His eyes narrowed.

'How did you know about Rachel Worth? That has been kept internal so far.'

'Like I said, information has come to light. I think Crockett, Symonds and Worth were all murdered. I don't think you did any of it. But I know you care about what happened to Hannah Crockett.'

Vickers stared at Rowe for a moment, then slowly sat back, his demeanour still agitated but becoming slightly more passive.

'Look…' he began, then stopped and exhaled. 'Hannah and I were seeing each other.'

Rowe held the gun steady but stayed silent.

'We had tried to keep it quiet,' Vickers said. 'Things had got quite serious, but I was worried it would impact on Hannah's career if people knew. Maybe I was worried about myself too. That created tension between us, and we were having some problems. When I saw the missed calls from her that morning and then heard she had been found dead, I thought it was something to do with our relationship. Maybe that was stupid, I don't know.'

Rowe was tempted to make a dark crack about Vickers flattering himself but decided against it. The DCI was still talking.

'When you turned the investigation towards me, I was obviously worried about all this coming out and me being dragged into it somehow, so I recommended to Carne that we shut it down. I used the angle of negative publicity related to an officer suicide, but she didn't need much convincing anyway. I've wondered about Hannah ever since. She did leave me a message – she said she was worried about something, but it was garbled, and I couldn't make it out. The idea she would kill herself didn't make sense. It still doesn't.'

A tear fell from Vickers' eye, and he wiped it away instantly.

'I think Crockett saw something she shouldn't have,' Rowe said. 'Was she working at Fenwood at any time close to her death?'

'Actually yes.' Vickers focused on Rowe again as if he'd forgotten he was there. 'She'd been helping out, wading through old files there on the upper floors. That was only a couple of days before she died. Do you think that's important?'

'I'm not sure yet. But it might be.'

Rowe stood up, keeping the gun trained on Vickers.

'I want you to know, Neil, that I intend to find out what happened to Crockett and the others. If I can do anything about it, I will. And if I find that you're part of it I'm coming back, and I won't knock. In the meantime, don't even think about crying to anyone about this little chat. As far as I'm concerned, you denied justice to Hannah Crockett. If you make trouble for me, I'll make trouble for you.'

Rowe moved towards the door as Vickers eyed him balefully. As he reached back for the doorknob, Vickers spoke up in what seemed like a last-second decision.

'There's something else you should know.'

Rowe stopped and drew his hand back again. Vickers was standing up.

'New evidence means Steve Symonds' death is now being treated as suspicious. You're officially a suspect due to the incident at Fenwood and the connection with Laura Cross.'

Rowe didn't offer a reaction, verbally or otherwise.

'There's also uncertainty around Rachel Worth's death,' Vickers went on, 'which is one of the reasons it hasn't been made public yet. The theory is that her suicide may have been coerced. And you were the last person known to see her alive.'

Rowe looked at Vickers for a long moment. He put the Glock back in his coat pocket.

'Keep your head down, Neil. You might not want to be in range when this hits the fan.'

He opened the door and left the flat.

31

AS HE WAS IN OXFORD, it wasn't too difficult for Rowe to join the ring road and head northeast, even though his home in Fenwood was further over to the northwest.

He took the Defender past the industrial estates on the edge of the city and towards the M40, which he then merged onto in a northbound direction. After ten miles or so he left the motorway, took the first exit from the roundabout, and drove another mile or so out into unspecified countryside. As he reached the edge of a village he didn't know, Rowe pulled the Defender into a layby, killing the engine and lights.

Rowe knew it had been necessary that his first stop was to see Vickers. He hadn't wanted the DCI to know he was coming, and he needed to know that his latest hunch had been right. After considering what Devon said, it was far more likely that Vickers was simply insecure and untrustworthy rather than anyone involved with – or relied upon by – a major operation. Rowe didn't like the man, but he was prepared to rule him out of the equation for the time being. He resolved to tell Devon that when his brother next made contact.

His priority at that point was to get in touch with Laura. She would be wondering why he hadn't made contact; they were due to meet tonight, and time was pressing on. He felt bad about it, but Devon had mentioned the possibility that his phone was being tracked and that Rowe should only switch it on when it was safe – hence his driving out to a place far enough away from, and not related to, his home. Or hers.

Rowe took out his phone and turned it on for the first time since he had left it in the Days Inn room in the early hours of Saturday morning. He was hoping in one sense that there were no new messages or missed calls to be picked up, but in another he wanted to find that Laura had been in touch.

There were two messages – a text and a voicemail. The text message was from Jim Ferry, sent on the Saturday. It was giving Rowe the heads up that he was both a suspect in the Steve Symonds case and being discussed in relation to Rachel Worth's death. That was accompanied by his friend's obligatory warning to "go careful", while Ferry also mentioned that he had first left a voicemail. It wasn't lost on Rowe that Ferry was still trying to be helpful, even if he couldn't be directly involved anymore.

Rowe wasn't remotely surprised that his name was being linked with the two deaths. If anything, he was surprised it hadn't happened sooner. He knew the run-in with Symonds at Fenwood was never likely to be brushed under the rug as Carne had suggested it would be. And as soon as Ferry had told him that Symonds had died in a car accident, Rowe could see the potential set-up coming. The death could be presented by those responsible for it as either a tragic accident or a sinister murder, depending on whether Rowe remained an issue to them or not. The "new evidence" had apparently seen to the latter.

Linking him to Worth's death was much easier of course, given he had visited her just prior to her death.

Fingerprints – whether genuine or subsequently planted – could be used. It wouldn't take much to initiate an investigation that would make Rowe's life very difficult.

While he was briefly considering the potential ramifications, a thought occurred to Rowe that struck him as important to act on before he did anything else. He opened a search browser and began looking for a particular piece of information, using details he had filed away in the back of his mind earlier. It took a couple of minutes and a methodical process of elimination, but eventually he found what he was looking for. He committed it to memory.

Rowe then clicked to play the voicemail from Ferry with the intention of then deleting it. As he did so, the automated voice on the answerphone informed him there were in fact two new voice messages stored. The second was from Laura Cross's number.

He knew it wasn't something she typically did – preferring to speak to a person rather than a robotic void – and that a text message would usually be more her style. He pressed the corresponding number and waited for it to play, intending to call her straight back once he'd heard it.

There were no words in the voicemail. At least, none that could be deciphered in the message's standard form. To begin with, it sounded like an accidental call; the muffled sounds of a phone shifting in a pocket or under a leg. The noises were intermittent and had no clear pattern. A voice could be heard speaking, but there was no way for Rowe to determine whose it was or what they were saying. It sounded to him like a male voice, but it was distorted and distant. He tried turning his phone's volume all the way up but even then, it remained impossible to discern anything useful.

He knew that when someone uses a recording device in the movies, every sound in the room is heard perfectly clearly no matter where or how the device is concealed. In real life, trying to surreptitiously record something with a mobile phone was not easy, especially if the phone was at a distance or obstructed by something, or both. Rowe thought it might be possible to isolate and enhance the sound on the voicemail using specialist equipment and expertise, but neither of those were available to him at that moment.

The message cut off after 60 seconds of similar sounds, which he guessed was the standard limit for a voicemail. Rowe immediately tried calling Laura's number. No answer. He waited until her own voicemail kicked in but did not leave a message, then he tried ringing the phone two more times just in case. No answer.

Rowe played the message again. Instinct told him it wasn't an accident. Laura had called him deliberately, he was sure, because she wanted him to hear what was being said and who was saying it. But, for some reason, she hadn't been able to move the phone any closer to the voice than it was.

The second listen was no more fruitful than the first, although he was careful to take note of the exact time that the message was left.

The time of the voicemail was 7:08pm. The time on his phone clock was 8:35pm.

Rowe almost tipped the Defender over on the roundabout as he tore back towards the motorway.

32

THE DEFENDER CAREERED TO a halt outside the building that Laura Cross lived in around thirty minutes later. The Sunday night traffic had been light and consequently Rowe had pushed the bulky vehicle to its limits, cutting the journey time to almost half of what might have been expected.

Despite it being past 9pm on a November night, there didn't appear to be any lights on in Laura's flat that he could see. The building was a kind of inverted U-shape with five flats on each one of three floors. The flats at the ends of each floor faced each other in the arms of the U-shape. Laura's flat was one of these, on the left end of the first floor above the ground level as viewed from the road.

The block shared a cul-de-sac with two other blocks of flats, one of which was similar to Laura's and one which was used as sheltered accommodation for elderly residents. It was the opposite side of Fenwood from where Rowe lived and further from the centre of town. The area was known to be generally quiet and at that time on a Sunday was virtually silent.

On his breakneck drive to the flat, Rowe had tried to call Laura's phone repeatedly. There was still no answer, and eventually he switched the phone back off. The voicemail had become more disturbing to him with each second that passed.

He slammed the door of the Defender and sprinted towards the closest set of concrete steps to the first floor of the building. Dim, circular lighting affixed to the walls between each flat lit the walkway, which he needed to follow all the way round from right to left in the U-shape to reach Laura's door. As he rounded the second bend of the U, he could just make out in the sparse light that her front door was ajar.

Rowe reached the door and stopped. The lock wasn't obviously broken or forced, the outdated metal door with its top half window made of frosted glass was simply standing open a few inches. Rowe looked in through the kitchen window, but the room was dark and offered little insight except for the fact that no one was in there. There was a light, however, casting the edge of its glow across the entrance to the living room, which was about ten feet away, dead ahead of the front door and marginally visible through the gap between the door and its frame.

There was movement to his right and Rowe turned his head, glimpsing a person moving back from a window in one of the other flats. A neighbour keeping an eye out he supposed, one that had probably seen him arrive there many times in the past and would be able to place him at that spot if ever they were asked.

With that in mind, Rowe chose to step inside the flat before making any noise. He used his forearm to push open the door enough to get past it fully and stand on the mat, which laid on top of the hallway's cream-coloured carpet. He pushed the door back to its frame but didn't close it fully. For some reason, doing that felt claustrophobic to him. Or dangerous.

There was a silence in the hallway that suddenly made the idea of calling out or announcing his arrival in any way seem almost improper. To his right was the doorless entry to the kitchen and on his left was a closed door which he knew led into a small second bedroom that Laura mostly used for storage. Next to that was the flat's compact bathroom, opposite the door to the main bedroom which stood slightly open, as it often did. No illumination came from there. Straight ahead was the living room from which the only light came.

Rowe didn't move. Instead, he stood still and forced himself to feel the energy of the place. He did his best, and there was almost none. It was like everything had been drained from the flat purely because the front door had been left standing open.

The outer edge of the light – the glow from a table lamp – was not far in front of him but he was momentarily paralysed where he stood. It felt somehow unnatural to move forwards. There was no sound, no disturbance in the flow of the air. Rowe tried to breathe and as he exhaled his hands shook and his legs felt hopelessly fragile. He had driven with fierce abandon to get there but was unable to take another step.

'Laura.'

The syllables came out so uncertainly that if anyone had been able to hear them, they may not have recognised it as a name. There was no response – no evidence that anyone or anything was in earshot. Had he actually said it out loud? He wasn't even sure of that.

He stepped forward at last, with some effort. Directly ahead, on the far side of the living room, was a large window, which in daylight looked out onto the tree-lined patch of grass that belonged to the block of flats. It was dark, and all Rowe could see in the window was his own haunted reflection.

The reflection was possible because of the lamp, sitting on a table in front of the window, next to a lounge chair that Laura had found in a charity shop several years earlier. Rowe liked the chair a lot, unofficially claiming it as his by sitting in it every time he came to the flat. Seeing it just reminded him that it had been an awfully long time since he had been there.

Laura had never minded him claiming the chair because she preferred the two-seat brown leather sofa that sat against the wall to the left of the door. Which was where she was sitting right then.

Rowe had moved forward far enough that he could see where the lamp threw light on her socked feet. They were crossed in a relaxed fashion on the carpet. For a split second he felt a distant relief; the notion that the foreboding that hung in the air might be lifting, until he saw the stillness of her limbs. He recognised instantly that they were far too still.

Gliding in a disabling fog, he entered the room and looked down at Laura Cross. The woman he loved and for whom his feelings were so great that they sometimes threatened to suffocate him when they were together, let alone when they were apart. It hurt him to think about her. She was beautiful, even at that moment. Like he had seen her so many times, before things had changed between them. Peaceful and asleep in her corner of the world.

Her head rested on the back of the brown sofa, her eyes were closed, and her arms folded restfully. She was in jeans, with her hips forward and her legs out in front of her. Rowe couldn't help the thought that if it hadn't been for the two neat, closely spaced bullet holes in the centre of her chest, she could have died in her sleep.

Because she was undeniably dead, however it had come to be.

Rowe stared at Laura for an incalculable amount of time. He couldn't move. His emotions had all but ceased to function. The last thing he registered was the edge of a mobile phone, which was protruding from the gap between the small of her back and the sofa cushion behind, which itself was darker than he remembered as it was soaked in blood.

He was standing in the flat of a woman who had been shot dead, whilst carrying a gun in his jacket pocket. The woman was the love of his life. But at that moment the situation, his destiny, his life didn't matter. His body finally gave way and he fell to the floor, sobbing uncontrollably with no concept of time or consequence.

At some point he found himself in the lounge chair, numb and hollow and still sobbing. Laura was still dead.

Outside the window the night had grown grotesquely dark.

PART THREE

33

THE FLUORESCENT LIGHT IN the long, high-ceilinged room was bright and the walls were white and severe looking. Rowe blinked expressionlessly, barely aware of his surroundings. The man facing him was saying something, possibly asking a question but Rowe couldn't hear it. Eventually he held out some money and the man took it.

Rowe was standing at the counter in the Shell garage at the Junction 27 services on the M5. Despite his all-consuming numbness, he recognised the absurd mundanity of the situation. The Defender needed fuel and had barely made it that far on fumes. It would not have lasted to his intended destination if he hadn't stopped to fill up.

In doing so, he was also aware enough to buy a bottle of the first available whiskey. There was no question in his mind that he would need it.

The Vitesse was gone from the Days Inn car park across from the Shell garage. As was the black Mercedes driven by the coroner's assistant. It was almost possible for Rowe to believe that they had never been there at all.

With as much analytical thinking as he had been able to muster at the time, Rowe had realised there was nowhere else he could go. There was no way he could return to his own home. Looking for sanctuary with a friend or ally – Jim Ferry and Nick Stanwell came to mind – was out of the question. There was also no way he could be found at Laura's flat, even if leaving there had felt virtually impossible for him to do. In these most extreme of circumstances, there was suddenly only one place he could go and one person who could possibly help him.

He was grateful at least that he had taken the time to identify the location just before he had heard Laura's voicemail. He knew the name of the estate his brother was covertly residing on. Devon had given him enough information about the land dispute and the rough geography to allow Rowe to narrow it down. It struck him that that might have been deliberate on Devon's part, given Rowe had no other means of contacting his brother directly.

Rowe climbed back into the Defender in a zombie-like trance. It was past midnight, and he couldn't recall much if any of the two-hour journey leading there. He knew any sane person would not have been attempting to leave home, let alone drive any significant distance in the wake of the trauma he had encountered. But he knew he had no other choice.

He had decided not to use any technology to guide him to his destination, thinking the risk of using his phone was higher than ever. As he moved to exit the services and re-join the motorway, it struck him that he could have bought a map to help his progress, but he didn't have the energy to finish the thought. It felt horribly irrelevant to his fractured brain – as did the idea of consuming food or sustenance.

Once he was on the motorway, he took the same sharp turn down the unmarked road that Devon had taken less than 24 hours earlier. From there the route would be tricky, especially in the dark, but there were certain road signs that he would look out for that he hoped would lead him roughly in the right direction.

It took about 45 minutes of traversing the indistinguishable back roads that he remembered – collectively, if not individually – from the previous night, but eventually Rowe found the estate. It wasn't signposted specifically, but the villages that bordered it were and they had been his guide.

He entered the grounds via a different route to that which Devon had done, although Rowe had no reference point for it. In entering there, he saw bright lights from what he supposed was the main house, which appeared before the building itself did. It was a grand stately home, long and wide with two deep floors and an endless number of windows. The illumination came not from the house itself but from ground-level security lights that sat externally in the garden and shone on the outside of the building. Something about the darkened windows of the abandoned home reminded Rowe of the houses on the street where James Burnell's registered home stood. It felt false and disquieting to him somehow.

He travelled the winding roads of the property, past smaller, lone houses that were hard to distinguish in the dark. Driving essentially blind, he tried a few minor dead ends before coming to another, longer road that seemingly led nowhere. Remembering what Devon had said about the location of the house and its low priority, Rowe tried the lane, looking blearily for signs of the dilapidated building or things that were close to it.

What he hoped was that Devon would be waiting to greet him. His brother had mentioned sensors that he had placed around the grounds which would alert him to any approaching vehicles. When Rowe finally spotted the house and its iron garage-shed near the end of the otherwise unpromising road however, there was no welcome party visible.

He turned onto the break in the grass that led towards the garage and stopped short of it. He turned off the engine but left the Defender's headlights on and waited. He hoped Devon would either appear or signal him somehow. What he didn't want to do was anything sudden which might peg him as an intruder or result in a misunderstanding.

Rowe waited for a full five minutes, but nothing happened. The house was dark and silent as he would have expected, but the lack of any response to his arrival didn't feel right to him. With his mind blank and an increasing confusion added to his numbness, he managed to recall the fact there was a torch in the Defender. Devon had used it the night before to light their path to the house. Feeling with his right hand down into the door pocket next to him, he located the item with relative ease and pulled it out. It was a Maglite, solid and durable, which had clearly seen some use. It was heavy in his hand.

Despite having the torch, Rowe left the headlights on in the Defender and got out. He used the Maglite to illuminate his path through the unkempt grass. He could see that the same rusted padlock was in place on the outer doors of the iron garage-shed as he approached. Shaking it, he found it secure, but was then distracted by something else. The garage looked different in some way.

The light from the Maglite couldn't reveal much through the narrow gap in the rusted doors but, at the very least, it seemed to Rowe that the black second set of doors within the shed were gone. Rowe moved around the garage to his right to find a better vantage point from which to see inside. He found a small hole in the corrugated exterior and shone the light through that allowed him to see a section of the floor and opposite wall of the structure.

It was empty. The floor appeared to be the same concrete slab he had stood on the previous night, but the entire inner structure was gone. Where the tools and workbenches had hung and stood against the substantial black material walls was simply more corrugated iron. He turned the torch upwards as best he could, and the spotlights and black ceiling were also missing. It wasn't just that these things were no longer there, it was that it looked like they never had been. The shed was simply old and rusted and might even have collapsed given a hard enough shove.

Rowe's brain was struggling to process what he was seeing, already full to bursting as it was. With little or none of the caution he had exercised thus far, he trudged through the long, wet grass towards the house. Pushing through the side door he made his way inside the abandoned shell purposefully, without stopping to scan any of the rooms. He already knew what he would find.

Rowe kicked open the door to the wine cellar and started down the stairs. The first room was just as it had been before, with the two surviving wine racks and scattered bottles. The twin doors to the second room were gone completely, along with the keypad lock system. Rowe shone the torch on the archway the doors had rested in and saw only minor drill holes and indentations where hinges had been attached. He stepped into the room beyond.

It was bare apart from a dusty floor. No black walls or ceiling. No carpet. No computers. No bed, no toilet unit, no coffee machine. It looked to Rowe as if no one had stepped inside it in years.

'FUCK YOU, DEVON!!!'

The sound of his voice echoing in the cellar room surprised even him with its desperation. He felt weak and hopeless. He was incredibly tired. Through the fog of his mind, two ludicrous thoughts occurred to him at that moment.

First, the notion that it was the wrong house, and that Devon was sitting in an identical one on the other side of the estate. Maybe his brother would come and find him soon.

Insane, he knew.

Second, the idea that the entire meeting with Devon had been an invention of his mind, brought on by a psychotic episode due to the stress he had been under. The covert hideout had never existed.

Insane also, but maybe slightly less so.

If both of those conceptions were crazed, he wondered how on earth Devon had transported all of his equipment out of there. It was impossible by any reasonable measure. Suddenly Rowe was incredibly tired of thinking.

He found himself back at the Defender. He got in and turned off the headlights. Put the Maglite back where he had found it. His world was completely destroyed, and his brain had not even begun to process that fact, let alone how things would pan out beyond that night.

Rowe picked up the whiskey bottle from the passenger seat. He thought it might be his only chance of sleep, if he was ever going to find any.

34

SLEEP HAD COME SURPRISINGLY soon. Rowe had drunk a good portion of the whiskey bottle's contents quickly, but his exhaustion was so acute that his body craved rest even despite his damaged mind.

He woke up in the Defender's driver's seat, blinking and groggy. The paralysing numbness remained. He peered through the windscreen and found that, in daylight, it was much clearer that the iron shed before him was hollow. It was an empty shell that had ceased to be useful in its intended function some time ago. Similarly, the house somehow looked more dilapidated than it had the previous day. With the knowledge that its secret underground bunker had been spirited away, much of its mystery had gone also.

Rowe got out and stretched wearily in the bright, chilly morning. He remembered his rucksack, which was still with him, contained some clean clothes he hadn't yet used so he reached back into the Defender and retrieved it. He then wandered slowly up past the house and found the bench that he and Devon had sat on the previous day.

The bowl of apples sat in the middle of the bench. It appeared to have been replenished. Underneath the bowl was a note inside a clear plastic wallet – to protect it from the elements, Rowe presumed – written in black marker and bold letters. Rowe pulled it out from under the bowl and read it.

HAD TO RAMBLE.
GOOD LUCK.

IKE

Rowe looked at the note for a long time. Devon had again used his childhood nickname to confirm to Rowe that the note was indeed from him, as he had done with the coded text messages. Their father had often called the brothers Mike and Ike when they were younger, after the American brand of sweets with the same name. It had stuck until the boys got too old for it.

Clearly Devon had anticipated the eventuality that Rowe might return there, and Rowe found that that didn't surprise him. His brother was a planner.

He recalled Devon saying that he wouldn't be staying at the house for much longer and admitting that bringing Rowe there was a risk. The implication being that his life was in danger. Devon clearly wasn't someone who kept still for very long anyway, but Rowe thought perhaps the risk had ultimately been deemed too great and his older brother had decided not to take any chances. Even so, to have disappeared with the speed he had, it seemed undeniable to Rowe that Devon had planned his exit even before his visit.

That, in turn, suggested that Devon had another plan, alongside the one they had discussed. He was a secret operator, Rowe supposed, but it didn't sit well that he might be conducting covert business while expecting information to be shared in the other direction. Perhaps that was simply how Devon's new life worked, Rowe wondered.

He looked up from the note and out at the overgrown former gardens of the house. He realised he had gone there for his brother's help, yes, but also his comfort. There was none waiting, but it was still likely that the place was safe.

The thought came to him that Laura had been killed to draw him – and, perhaps, Devon – out of their hiding place when the news eventually filtered through. But instead, he had returned to Fenwood early and discovered her body before anyone else. The plan hadn't worked. Whoever had been trying to lure him would likely know by that point that he had been at her flat, but that didn't mean they knew where he was subsequently.

Rowe pushed the bowl across the metal bench and sat down next to it. Then he absentmindedly picked up an apple and bit into it. His body needed fuel even if it were the last thing he cared about. Sleep had helped to some degree. He wasn't thinking clearly, but some rest had allowed him to piece a few things together. For one, he had no doubt that he would be a suspect in Laura's murder.

He tried in vain not to think about her. The things he had never told her. The excruciating regret of their still partly unexplained and unresolved separation. He found his mind subconsciously trying to console his heart with half-remembered and probably confused proverbs and cliches.

Mostly a huge weight hung over him that he desperately wanted not to acknowledge, and which was the likely source of his numbness. It was something that told him that this was how love ended: without answers. With untold pain. It was a monster too vast and immoveable to disappear when it died, so it simply crushed those caught underneath.

He picked up the rucksack again and a bottle of water, which had been sitting next to the bench where Devon's rifle had been, and started walking. He wanted to be among the trees beyond the long grass and not think about anything at all. *"Live in the present and appreciate the nature around you"*, a therapist had said to him after his parents died.

"It's time I grew accustomed to being on my own", Robert Earl Keen had said.

As he walked among the tall firs, the movement keeping his body occupied if not his mind, Rowe couldn't help but think about his parents.

Brian and Aoife Rowe had died fifteen years earlier in a car accident whilst on holiday in northern France. Their car had hit a tree at 50mph killing them both instantly. It was recorded as accidental death. Due to the available physical evidence, it was determined that Rowe's father had fallen asleep at the wheel after several hours of travelling and that Aoife was already asleep in the passenger seat.

Rowe had been 23 at the time and a young police recruit, while Devon was in the Army and had already undertaken his first deployment in Afghanistan. The news of the accident had stunned them and brought the brothers closer together for a brief time, after years of drifting apart. Rowe didn't think Devon had ever had a strained relationship with their parents exactly, but he had always been distant, preferring to live away from home as soon as he was old enough and only communicating when necessary. The older brother was driven and focused but undoubtedly aloof.

Meanwhile, Rowe had been torn about his career choice and the direction his life was taking. He knew he wanted to write creatively somehow but was hindered by self-doubt. Mostly he blamed that on existing in his father's shadow. It was the same thing that had compelled him to join the police – proving to both himself and Brian Rowe that he was capable of doing the job. As so often with such intentions, his campaign to win his father's respect ultimately hadn't mattered.

Aoife Rowe had been a self-employed upholsterer and a seemingly boundless creative force. The younger son had admired her very much. She had an intelligence and strength of character equal to that of her husband, but that shone through more readily to Rowe due to the dynamic of their relationship. He and his mother had been very close, even if he resembled his father in significantly more of his characteristics.

Never having said goodbye to either of them was a wound that wouldn't heal. As he contemplated the path of his life to the point he had reached, he felt more sorrowful than ever about that fact. He wondered how they would have viewed his life if they could see it. Right at that moment, he needed them in a way he never had before.

Rowe felt he had learned in the years since his parents died that death is not final. That the people he loved lived on as long as he did, in his heart. He just couldn't see them or ask their advice. And that didn't help him.

He was still walking though the wooded area and came across some wet, softer ground and surface water that he deduced was coming from a natural spring. He crouched and put his hand in the water, then put it to his face. It was cold but refreshingly so, and Rowe realised his cheeks had been damp with tears. The water from the spring felt restorative, if only for a few seconds. He stared up at the sky for a while and then at the trees around him. He could see what the attraction had been to Devon in setting himself up there. Perhaps his brother had found somewhere equally as good, he wondered.

In the stillness of the wood and the estate generally – Devon had been right, there were no signs of life there – Rowe felt comfortable enough to change into his fresh clothes and use the spring water to wash himself at least rudimentarily. He drank deeply from the bottle of water and felt slightly more physically awake. Although his mind was a fog of grief, anger and confusion, a wall was still in place that kept them from crippling him – like he was watching them from behind soundproof glass. For the time being. It meant that he could think lucidly enough to realise that staying there any longer was not an option. Not for him and not for Laura.

Rowe looked back in the direction of the house. He had the idea that Brian Rowe would have known what had to be done. And what was that exactly? Rowe thought he knew, but his father and mother were long dead. His brother was in the wind, possibly for good. And Laura Cross was also dead, a fact it was impossible for him to accept. He would not be able to reconcile these things in his mind for a long time.

But there was also a newly recurring notion in his mind that his parents' death had been the start of the present chain of events somehow. Leading to where he stood. Whether that was true or not, the plain fact was that he was still alive. And Rowe knew it would be a great disservice to everyone he loved not to use that one, slim advantage while it remained.

He took one last look skyward. One last look at the trees.

Rowe started back for the Defender.

35

THE BUCCANEER WAS A hostelry that most locals knew of but only a select few had considered entering due to it being a pagan-owned bikers pub with a somewhat diverse clientele. It sat on a hidden back road between two villages outside of Fenwood, a road which had become almost obsolete when the main road into Fenwood from the northwest had been created. The only reasons one might travel the road latterly would be either to visit the pub or to avoid the attentions of some authority or other elsewhere, two things that Rowe didn't think were mutually exclusive.

He snaked down the narrow road in the Defender at just before 7pm and saw the lights from the pub coming up on his right-hand side. On the other side of the road from the Buccaneer's old-fashioned front gate, which led to the uninviting and battered front door, was a makeshift car park. It was essentially loose gravel on a large area of disused ground and at that time played host to a handful of well-used motorcycles and a red, US-style pickup truck. Beyond these was a large and long heap of gravel about five feet high which shielded the rest of the parking area from view of the road. The shielded area was where Rowe went to search for Jim Ferry's car.

He pulled the Defender round behind the gravel pile and was straight away confronted with Ferry's scuffed and ageing VW estate sitting on its own. It had once been Azur Blue, Ferry had told him, but had since turned a colour that Rowe deemed uncategorisable. He parked next to it, killed the Defender's engine, and waited.

Five minutes later he heard hurried footsteps approaching from behind the gravel pile, followed a few seconds after by Ferry emerging around the side of it, walking quickly and wearing a huge fleece jacket which was pulled up over his mouth.

'Jim.'

Rowe said it discreetly but loud enough to be heard from his open driver's window. Ferry stopped in his tracks and his expression went from surprise to confusion to concern in the space of a second or two.

'Rower,' Ferry said finally, gathering himself. 'Been wondering where you'd got to mate. I'm...so sorry about Laura.'

Rowe nodded vacantly to acknowledge the last sentence.

'Get in.'

Ferry took a furtive glance over his shoulder before quickly moving around to the Defender's passenger side and climbing in. He shut the door behind him carefully and glanced around the interior.

'Very rustic,' Ferry said. 'How did you know I'd be here?'

'Angela told me.' Ferry's face momentarily took on a look of mild panic before Rowe continued. 'About six months ago when she said you were going to the gym after work on Mondays. And I knew you weren't stupid enough to go anywhere you'd be spotted.'

The older man relaxed slightly.

'Ah. Well, they're a decent bunch in the Bucc, mate. I like to keep up appearances as it were.'

Ferry half-smiled as he said it, then immediately became serious again.

'I don't know what's going on Rower,' he said quietly, 'but you're top of the shit list right now. They've got you in the frame for Symonds, Laura and maybe Worth too. It hasn't gone public yet, but Carne is on the warpath. She thinks I'm protecting you. They've had uniform driving past the house – I think Ange is getting ready to ceremonially burn the shed down with me in it.'

'Sorry, Jim,' Rowe said. 'I never knew any of this would happen. I've spent the last few days trying to understand it.'

Rowe then told Ferry about his reunion with Devon and what was discussed, his subsequent return to the deserted house, the encounter at Vickers' flat and his discovery of Laura's body. The last story was painful to relay but Rowe found it somehow therapeutic to tell it to a friendly ear.

All parts of the narrative came as news to Ferry.

'Jesus, Rower, this is heavy stuff. It's hard to know where to start. Where do you think Devon went to?

'No idea. He's gone. I guess he knows what he's doing.'

'I can't believe they killed Laura.'

Rowe didn't speak.

'So, what can you do?' Ferry said after a pause.

'There's only one thing really. Prove the cell death at Fenwood was murder and expose Grantley's local contact who facilitated it.'

Ferry paused a moment.

'Do you know who the contact is?'

'Yes.'

'Well, who is it?'

'Joanne Meredith.'

Ferry's eyes widened and he sat back in his seat, staring out at the gravel pile and the just-visible glow from the Buccaneer's windows beyond it.

'Young DC Meredith? How would she get involved in a caper like that?'

'Devon said the local contact would have to be someone reliable on the inside. He didn't specify age or gender. Meredith fits the profile – trained by the Met, even though she moved out here shortly after. Trusted with responsibility and knows how to keep under the radar. Plus, she worked at Fenwood when it was a busier place. She would be an ideal candidate for Grantley.'

'Wasn't she working the case with you though?'

Ferry still sounded bemused by the thought of Meredith's involvement.

'Not *with* me, in hindsight,' Rowe said. 'She was pushing back all the way. I blamed that on Vickers at the time but now I'm not so sure.'

'What about Vickers though? Isn't he a more obvious figure?'

'He's dodgy for sure. Incompetent, brown-nosing and a disgrace to his job, absolutely. Not involved here. I'm sure of that now.'

Ferry exhaled.

'So, what's the mo- er…what's your move? How do you prove any of it?'

'I need a favour.'

Ferry closed his eyes and said nothing, as if awaiting an unavoidable impact.

'This is Meredith's number,' Rowe said. He handed Ferry a piece of paper with Meredith's name and mobile number on it.

'I need you to send her a message asking her to meet you at Fenwood tomorrow at 10am. Do it from your personal mobile. Tell her it's for inventory work that Carne has demanded and you've both been picked at random. You're still technically more senior than her so she shouldn't question it.'

'Won't that sound a tad suspicious? Anyway, Fenwood's shut until further notice. Staffing issues…'

'I want her to be suspicious. I'm trying to draw her…*them* out. As for the station, I know a nice lady who has some keys.'

Ferry passed a hand over his face and sighed one of the high-pitched, exasperated sighs that Rowe recognised as being reserved for his more enterprising schemes. It was usually good-humoured.

'And how do I explain this one when the shit hits the fan?' Ferry protested. 'Oh, "I was just trying to get an impressionable young woman alone in a deserted building for the good of Queen and country?" That'll play well.'

Rowe looked at him. 'When this thing is over, I get the feeling no one will want to ask any questions. Whichever way it goes down.'

Ferry didn't respond. Rowe thought his friend had probably picked up on the grave tone in his voice and realised what was being implied.

'Mary Drinkwater is the civilian who works the front desk at Fenwood,' Rowe continued. 'I've written her number on the back of Meredith's there.' Rowe nodded to the slip of paper in Ferry's hand. 'Give her the same story as Meredith and make sure she only talks to you. Get her to open up at 8am – two hours before Meredith is due. If you can, collect the keys from her. If she insists on opening up herself, let her, but then find a way to get her out of there.'

'And where should I ask the chorus girls to set up?'

'Look Jim, I know this seems like a lot. I know it's a risk. But you're the only one I can rely on right now, and this is the only chance I've got.'

'I get it mate,' Ferry smiled empathetically. 'Consider it done.'

'Thanks Jim.'

'Have you got somewhere to stay tonight? I could set up the air mattress in the shed if Ange hasn't razed it to the ground yet.'

'That's a risk too far…but I appreciate it. I need to keep off the grid tonight.'

'OK mate – was sort of hoping you'd say that. My life wouldn't be worth living if Ange found you out there, let alone if some murky types from the Yard came calling. But if keeping off the grid's your thing, you've come to the right place.'

Ferry nodded in the direction of the Buccaneer. Then he opened the passenger door and started to climb out.

'Once you've got the station open tomorrow and the coast is clear I'll take over,' Rowe said. 'Then you should make yourself scarce.'

'OK. Until when?'

'Until it's finished.'

'Go careful, Rower. I mean it.'

'Can't promise that.'

Ferry nodded and turned to unlock his own car without shutting the Defender's door. Rowe watched him struggle with something in the passenger footwell briefly before re-emerging. He turned back to the Defender again and dumped a cardboard carrier filled with six bottles of Hook Norton real ale on the seat.

'Something to help you sleep tonight mate,' he winked. 'Just so happens I stocked up on emergency supplies after work.'

Rowe smiled, for the first time in what felt like an age.

'Cheers Jim, I owe you one.'

Ferry reached over and they shook hands, then he shut the passenger door. He got into his car and started it up. Rowe watched him reverse out and drive off. He started the Defender and reversed it back towards the rear of the parking area before swinging it round to the left and coming to a stop with the back wheels next to a grass verge. That bit further out into the darkness. He turned the engine off again but put the radio on. A voice to keep him company for a while.

He picked a bottle out of Ferry's carrier and used a spare key on the Defender's keyring to open it. Rowe had resolved to leave the whiskey bottle alone for a while, but beer seemed like an acceptable compromise. He held the beer up, both to see it in the glow from The

Buccaneer's lights and, he supposed, as a tribute to Laura's memory.

Rowe drank from the bottle and thought about the small lie he had just told Jim Ferry. And how his unknowing friend had then presented him with beer. Something to be grateful for, he knew.

He turned the radio up and turned in his seat slightly with the bottle, so he could see the glow of the lights from the pub.

36

AT 6:30AM THE NEXT morning – Tuesday – Rowe was driving down a long, rural back road in the semi-darkness. A good-sized house came into view on his left. Beyond it in the distance were the distinctive outbuildings of a farm.

The Defender slowed and turned left up a track between two hedgerows. Rowe found the track far easier to negotiate in the Defender than he had in the Vitesse, despite the rain that had fallen since his last visit and the steady downpour that was in progress which was helping to churn up the mud under the tyres.

Rowe followed the track around and along the back of the neighbouring field until he reached the ageing green machinery shed and the quasi-parking space in front of it. He pulled the Defender to a stop there and surveyed his surroundings. All was expectedly quiet for the time of the morning. The only exception was a repeated metallic clanging sound that he thought was probably coming from one of the farm buildings in the distance. The machinery shed stood as reliably unimportantly as ever. Rowe supposed that the Defender looked far more at home parked in front of it than the Vitesse had.

He got out and started towards the gap in the hedge on the other side of the shed, while remaining aware of his surroundings. He went through the gap and took the same route around the left-hand edge of the field that he had a few days earlier. There was no way for him to be shielded from view on the walk, which was one of the reasons he was doing it at an early hour.

Coming up on Nick Stanwell's property, he again moved along the back of the fence and looked for the gate. When he found it, he saw it was secured with what appeared to be a brand-new bolt and padlock that hadn't been there a few days earlier. He scanned the rest of the fence briefly, in case there were some other entrance he had previously missed, but there was none. Tree branches and foliage meant that attempting to climb the high, vertically slatted fence was going to be next to impossible.

The sound of a car turning off the road onto the track interrupted his thoughts. In the wet gloom, only the lights were visible through the hedge as the vehicle made its way carefully up the track. Rowe couldn't see the specific colour of it – let alone the make – through the thickness of the hedge, but it was clearly not a farm vehicle or a 4x4. He stood still and tracked its progress as it reached the right turn at the top of the track and continued, finally coming to a stop a few feet behind the Defender. The hedges were more widely spaced there, and Rowe could see it was a dark-coloured car and almost certainly the same shape as the Mercedes that had followed him previously.

That was good news, Rowe thought. While it was possible they had started following him again at some point in the last 24 hours, he presumed that, if that were the case, they would have either intercepted him or made some other move before then. On the contrary, he believed they had not been expecting him, a thought that was illustrated by the fact that the person had driven up the track in his full view with no attempt at disguise. It didn't surprise him that somebody had been waiting at Stanwell's house. Whoever it was had simply seen the Defender sitting out there and gone to investigate.

The driver got out of the dark car as Rowe crouched in the long grass in front of Stanwell's fence. He couldn't be certain at all, but the general size of the person made him think it was the coroner's assistant. The driver seemed to approach the Defender cautiously, peering through the windows with his right hand across his torso – resting on the butt of a gun, Rowe presumed. He didn't think the coroner's assistant had been carrying a gun on their first encounter, but the stakes had been raised considerably since then. The man seemed to complete his assessment and move cautiously back towards his own vehicle.

Rowe abandoned the idea of trying to enter Stanwell's property, from the rear or otherwise. As the driver got back in his car, Rowe stood up and started walking back the way he had come, hands stuffed in his jacket pockets. He knew he was visible, even if not totally identifiable, to the man in the car. As he turned left up the long edge of the field, he saw the dark car's door open again and the man step out, clearly looking in his direction.

Rowe continued to walk without breaking stride – as if he were out for a brisk stroll. The rain was still falling steadily. The man was still looking at him and was using the car door as a kind of shield with his right hand across his torso in the way it had been moments before. The morning was slowly growing lighter, but Rowe knew visibility remained poor for them both.

What had been made abundantly clear – in Rowe's mind, at least – was that these people were not going to kill him. He thought they could have found or made the opportunity if they chose to. If they wanted to draw Devon out by using the younger brother as bait, they would still need him alive and talking. Rowe hadn't lost sight of the fact that that remained an advantage to him, however small.

He kept walking up the outer edge of the field and saw that the driver still hadn't moved. Which in Rowe's view was a mistake. He was about to turn left again at the top of the ploughed field, which would mean the line of tall hedges and the position of the shed would block him from the driver's view. He saw the driver's head move then, probably realising he was about to lose sight of his target.

Rowe made the left turn and immediately ducked through the hedge and out onto the track, in line with the shed which was about fifty feet away. The driver still couldn't see him. Rowe remembered from his childhood how easy it had been to move in and out of and hide among these hedges, especially once they had lost their leaves. He glimpsed the driver starting to creep around the open side of the shed and immediately ducked back into the field out of sight again. His hands were still in his pockets.

If the driver did have a gun – as he most likely did – Rowe didn't think he would try to fire it unless he was certain of the shot and was within a sensible range. There was too much risk involved otherwise.

Determined to use that as another advantage, Rowe walked on further then ducked into the hedge and crouched within it. After a few seconds he saw the driver, wearing black clothes, appear slowly around the corner of the shed and start moving cautiously towards the main gap in the hedgerow. He seemed to assume Rowe was still in the field.

By then he was close enough for Rowe to see that not only was it indeed the coroner's assistant, but that he did have a gun. It was drawn, and the man raised it up in front of himself, knees slightly bent. Before he reached the gap, Rowe darted out of his hiding place into the field, ran about twenty feet forwards along the line of hedges then ducked back into it again.

That movement brought the coroner's assistant scurrying forward through the gap, gun ready, and as he did Rowe emerged back on to the track behind him.

In that moment there were only about ten feet between them. The man seemed to register Rowe's movement in his peripheral vision and swung around to face him.

But he was late. As he turned, Rowe shot him in the chest.

The force of the bullet sent the man thumping down onto his back and his gun spilling onto the grass. Rowe moved quickly forward and picked it up, keeping his own weapon trained on the man.

It looked to Rowe like he was dead. Blood spilled out of the wound and his mouth, and his eyes were glassy and unseeing. Rowe noticed the man was not wearing body armour; had clearly not been expecting a gunfight.

It was also clear he was not in a position to give any of the answers that Rowe might have been hoping for.

Certain the man had expired, Rowe stepped away, back towards the Defender. He checked the area for signs of any other person but could see none. A knot of guilt thudded in his stomach, and he realised his hands were shaking. There had been no other option, had there? He reasoned that the man, whoever he was, had surely been a trained killer – or an accessory to such – and had at the very least been complicit in the scheme to kill Rowe's own brother. He may even have pulled the trigger that killed Laura Cross, although Rowe had his reasons to doubt that.

The argument came into his head that, ultimately, the situation had become a war. Before that day, five people had been killed, if Hannah Crockett were included. One could say that the death of the supposed coroner's assistant was the first blow struck by the opposing side.

Still, the man was the first person that Rowe had ever killed. And he had done it calculatedly, in cold blood. For one despairing moment, he wondered if Laura would have been ashamed of him.

As he climbed back into the Defender and placed the man's gun safely into the glove compartment – his own stowed back in his jacket pocket – he decided that she wouldn't have been. The rules did not apply anymore. Suddenly, he had a duty to carry out. And he had started, so there was no way he could stop.

Rowe started the Defender's engine, fighting out from his internal struggle and becoming aware of the fact that the gunshot may have drawn attention. Devon had been right that people generally didn't notice gunshots in the country, but in the present spot they might. The only person in the vicinity likely to be firing a gun was the farmer who owned the fields, and as he wasn't the source of the discharge it seemed likely he would be keen to find out what was.

Rowe swung the Defender around in a hurried three-point turn and headed back along the track, past the Mercedes which sat impotent with its drivers' door still hanging open in the rain. It was approaching full daylight although the gloom from the dark skies remained.

As he turned the sharp left that led down the narrow track to the road, Rowe saw another vehicle appear at the opposite end. He didn't think it was a black Mercedes, but it might have been a Typhoon Grey Audi. Like the one he'd seen parked outside Fenwood on the morning of the cell death. The driver's face was indiscernible from the distance of roughly 100 yards, but Rowe presumed the farmer wasn't given to driving expensive saloons around his fields in November. It was back-up.

The grey car seemed to halt briefly when its driver registered the Defender's presence ahead, then suddenly continued forward, negotiating the mud with surprising ease. Rowe guessed whoever was driving it probably didn't know for sure who was in the Defender, just that they intended to cut off its exit.

Rowe's options were limited. He could reverse back but that would mean retreating to the machinery shed and ultimately a dead end. The field that he had just been walking around and the ones beyond it were all ploughed, and while the Defender could probably handle that terrain, each one was bordered by thick hedges and gates. He could get out and leave the Defender blocking the track, gambling that he could win another game of cat and mouse on foot with a second trained professional, but that seemed a huge and unnecessary risk. Only one real possibility remained.

He stamped on the accelerator and the Defender chewed up the patchy grass beneath its tyres and sprang forward. The grey car was still coming at a steady speed, but the Defender was gathering momentum along the slim track. As they came within about fifty feet of each other, Rowe saw that the car was indeed an Audi and that the rugby player-type who had been one of Grantley's minions at Fenwood was at the wheel. The man's face, while as thuggish and lacking humour as before, had an air of concern about it as the two vehicles proceeded straight for a head-on collision.

Rowe didn't brake or slow at all, reliant that the Defender's brute strength and his own complete commitment to the impact would be enough for him to prevail. Sure enough, as the gap closed to less than twenty feet, the Audi driver braked and swerved into the hedge on his left in the realisation that the Defender wasn't stopping. Just as it came to a stop, the Defender roared into the driver's side of the Audi in a cacophony of metallic rending that only a car crash could create. Rowe saw the man throw himself as far towards the passenger seat of the Audi as he could at the same moment.

The force of the collision pushed the Defender's right-side tyres up onto the side of the Audi and along it, smashing and shattering the windows and bending the body work, while the Land Rover's left side clattered and scraped along the hedgerow. Finally, the 4x4's tyres came crashing back down – the weight of the vehicle having barely been supported by the stiffness of the hedge – and continued its path.

As Rowe regained control of the Defender, he checked the rear-view mirror to see the battered Audi stuffed into the hedge, heavily damaged and with the driver's wing mirror squashed into the mud. He then glanced over and realised his own left-side wing mirror was gone also. The Defender was still moving though, and possibly still legal, although Rowe wasn't about to stop and survey any damage to the front end. He himself was in one piece, however, and he was breathing.

The Defender emerged from the track and turned right onto the rural road. There were no other cars – Mercedes, Audi or otherwise – in view. Rowe would have been surprised if any more had appeared considering the unannounced nature of his arrival.

His intention had been simply to talk to Nick Stanwell. There were things Rowe wanted to ask him, and he didn't think they could wait. He had even hoped the meeting might be enough to end things and remove the necessity for the task he had set Jim Ferry. But he also knew it had been an optimistic long shot, and one that had decisively failed.

That meant his plan B was all that remained.

37

ROWE DIDN'T SEE ANOTHER Mercedes or Audi on the relatively short journey to Fenwood. He wasn't surprised by that, as by then he had estimated that there was only one of each in the immediate vicinity that was interested in him, and he had just encountered them both at Nick Stanwell's place.

He stopped briefly at a food trailer on a back road outside of Fenwood. It was owned by a retired lorry driver named Billy and was squirrelled away on a little-used link road, not unlike the one The Buccaneer resided on. Rowe knew the location was not one Billy had initially been impressed with, but the high standard of fare on offer had soon made the place an open secret among those with driving jobs – as well as those like Rowe, who simply spent a lot of time in their cars.

The events that had occurred just minutes earlier meant Rowe wasn't interested in food, but he bought a bacon roll and a coffee because he knew he would need it. He barely spoke to the trailer's proprietor during their transaction. Billy was an old-school type with a radar for knowing when to engage in chit-chat and not and made no remark on the battered Land Rover that had appeared at his trailer.

Mostly Rowe had stopped just so he could be somewhere other than on the run or in direct conflict, which it seemed had been his only two settings lately. His nerves were frayed, his brain was still processing his shooting of the coroner's assistant, and the numb maelstrom from Laura's death still raged behind it all. But time was short.

He got back in the Defender and headed into Fenwood, eventually joining Grounds Way and turning into the public car park that sat diagonally opposite the police building. Driving to the very back of the car park, Rowe brought the Defender to rest a couple of spaces along from the old, decrepit caravan that still sat in the far-left corner. He speculated that a 'Police Aware' sticker might appear on it in a few weeks and its removal might occur several months after that. For the time being though, he felt the battered and damaged Defender would look relatively at home parked near it. The rest of the car park was starting to fill up at what was approaching 8am and he thought that might help to make the 4x4 less visible from the road.

Rowe took what he needed from the vehicle, which at that moment meant the coroner's assistant's gun – which he placed in his other jacket pocket – and the remains of his coffee and made his way out of the car park as inconspicuously as possible.

As he reached the low front wall of the car park, he looked across the road and saw Jim Ferry talking to Mary Drinkwater outside the main entrance to the station. He couldn't hear what was being said but Mary's posture suggested an unimpressed air: hands on hips and head tilted to one side as Ferry used hand gestures to animatedly get some point across. Eventually, Mary seemed to reluctantly hand him something before turning on her heel in annoyance and stalking away.

Once she was gone, Rowe threw his empty coffee cup in a bin and crossed over, catching up with Ferry as he was going in through the recently unlocked front entrance.

'All OK?' Rowe asked.

'Just about,' Ferry said, starting slightly as he turned and realised who had spoken. 'I used the famous baffle-them-with-bullshit technique. Works every time, except when it doesn't.'

'It's appreciated.'

'Meredith is on for 10am. She didn't say much. If she really is tied up with this crowd like you say she is then you should have your wits about you.'

Rowe nodded. They walked through into the dim corridor beyond the reception area. The rotund veteran constantly checked behind them for anyone who might be following.

'Still a lot of talk going on, Rower,' he said as they came to a stop. 'Wanted man for two murders and a potential third. It's a risk you being anywhere at the minute.'

'That's why I need to be here.'

Ferry cocked his head in what Rowe presumed was acceptance. Rowe wasn't ready to elaborate on the events of the morning at that point.

'You sure you're gonna be okay?' Ferry asked. 'How exactly are you planning to confront Meredith?'

'We'll just talk. And then she's going to help me.'

Ferry frowned and adopted the look of someone who knew they were potentially facilitating a nuclear-grade fiasco.

'It's OK Jim, you can get out of here,' Rowe said. 'Get to the office and act like it's another day. Just keep your eyes and ears open for me. And thanks again.'

'Alright,' Ferry exhaled. 'Go careful, mate.'

As he said it, Ferry pressed a slim hip flask he had apparently been carrying into Rowe's hand. Rowe gave a brief smile – recognising the gesture as his friend's answer to all stressful situations – and pocketed the flask. He headed off down the corridor, in the direction of the door that led to the rear stairs, as Ferry turned back for the main entrance.

Rowe went through the door that led to the stairs – knowing from his last visit that it didn't require key card access. He climbed them relatively cautiously, aware of the possibility that someone could be lying in wait for him either on one of the floors or on the stairs themselves. He was confident that the people interested in his whereabouts, along with their associates, wouldn't know exactly where he was at that moment. They had been surprised by his presence at Stanwell's house, and they had a mess there to clean up first. But that didn't mean he wasn't expecting them at all.

Rowe reached the first floor and was grateful that the door's lock hadn't been repaired. Breaking it again without the aid of the chisel might have been tricky not to mention time-consuming. He hesitated a moment but decided to go through the door, despite the schedule he was trying to keep to. Resting one hand on the Glock that Devon had left him in his right pocket, Rowe entered the large room and quickly but comprehensively surveyed the space. It seemed

277

untouched since his last visit. He looked briefly in the individual offices and the second larger room behind but found nothing to cause alarm.

Returning to the stairs, Rowe ascended to the second floor and saw no signs of anyone else. Again, he was grateful that the door lock there had also not been repaired. It didn't surprise him that no one had bothered to fix the two locks, as the entire building was surely in its final throes.

Even more carefully than with the first, he opened the door and stepped in. Nothing seemed to have changed there either. He made his way through the floor in similar fashion to that which he had done on the first, until he reached the smaller offices and the final larger room. He pushed through into it from the copy room and looked again at the mountain of boxes in the corner.

It struck him again, as it had the first time, that they didn't look right. The boxes were piled very high in a certain area.

Rowe looked at his watch. It was almost 8:30am. Assuming no one else found him first, he estimated he had a maximum of ninety minutes before Meredith arrived. And he thought he might need all of them.

38

AT FIVE MINUTES BEFORE 10am, Rowe was perched on two old file boxes in the far corner of the second larger room on the second floor of Fenwood police station. He took a swig – his third – from Jim Ferry's hip flask. It was whiskey of an unidentifiable brand but also had a kick to it that Rowe found cleared the cobwebs somewhat. Whatever the concoction was, it had warmed him in the cold building and steadied his nerves to some extent. His mind was still stormy, but he had gained a measure of focus.

He heard a voice some distance away. Possibly the other end of the first large room, near the door from the rear stairs. Then he heard it again, slightly nearer.

'Mr. Ferry? It's DC Meredith.'

The voice wasn't overly high-pitched but was undeniably feminine, and as it carried through otherwise silent floor it almost felt comforting to Rowe. Maybe it was natural, he thought, that a voice of such a timbre would be welcome to his ears at that moment in his life. He was willing to accept that simply for what it was, regardless of the circumstances.

Rowe heard sharp, business-like footsteps approaching and getting louder, then the opening of the door into the copy room. As she came through the second door into the room he was in, he didn't make a move to get up.

Meredith was wearing a short, black jacket over a white blouse with black trousers. Her straight, auburn hair was hanging down rather than tied back as it had been on her last visit to Fenwood. She wore short-heeled shoes to subtly elevate her diminutive height without being impractical. As she stepped into the space, Rowe thought she seemed slightly confused and possibly irritated at having climbed two flights of stairs to reach an empty room, before she froze to the spot when her gaze fell on Rowe.

'Hello, Joanne,' he said. 'Thanks for coming.'

Meredith looked at him with her mouth open.

'What…where's Jim Ferry?'

Rowe started to answer but the Detective Constable had already reassessed her approach.

'Michael Rowe!' Meredith said in a loud voice. 'I am arresting you for the murders of Detective Sergeant Steven Symonds, Detective Sergeant Laura Cross and on suspicion of involvement in the death of Sergeant Rachel Worth. You do not have to say anything, but it may harm your defence-'

Meredith had been taking out her phone as she spoke but froze and stopped talking when she saw the Glock. Rowe was on his feet, holding the weapon close but pointing it directly at her.

'Best not to do that, Joanne,' he said.

She looked at him wide-eyed for a long moment before eventually responding in a voice that attempted to be calm.

'Rowe…think about what you're doing.'

'I need to show you something.'

Meredith was pale. Rowe thought her mind was probably racing, trying to think of a way out. He gestured with his head for her to join him in the corner.

Where there had previously been a mountain of boxes it was more like a sea as the ones that were previously piled high had been scattered across the floor.

Rowe had spent most of the previous hour and a half moving the boxes to find what he was looking for. Not long before Meredith arrived, he had. Deep into what he estimated was the fifth or sixth layer of boxes there was a door. It was a regular-sized door made of wood, but it was covered in the flattened edges of cardboard boxes that had been stuck on with adhesive of some kind, which Rowe took to be a kind of camouflage. The door was the entrance to a standalone unit, which itself was also camouflaged in a similar way, although he hadn't been able to clear all the boxes around it.

The unit extended about twenty feet across by Rowe's judgement, and maybe twelve feet deep, although it was hard to tell due to the number of surrounding boxes. The unit also backed on to the window which looked out on Grounds Way, which he supposed meant there may have been another layer of boxes behind it. He could see it extended all the way up to the wall on his right.

He had already been through the door and knew what lay behind it. And it was what he had expected to find.

Meredith stepped slowly towards Rowe until she was a few feet in front of him, then stopped and looked at him defiantly.

'Whatever you're doing, it's going to end very badly, Rowe. Things will be much simpler if you just give yourself up.'

She spoke with the same effortful calmness, but Rowe knew she was frightened, and he was sorry for it.

'I'm not going to hurt you,' he said. 'I need your help. And when you've seen this, I think you'll understand why.'

Rowe used the gun to usher Meredith past him and towards the camouflaged door, which was to his right. He kept the weapon on her as she moved to the door and then gestured that she should stand in front of it. She gazed at it with both suspicion and bewilderment.

'Open it,' Rowe said.

She looked at him but didn't make a move to do as he said.

'I'm not going to shut you in there, Joanne. Just open the door.'

Slowly she did as she was told and pulled the metal handle downwards. The door suckered open and revealed a dark, unlit space behind it.

'Hit the lights' Rowe said.

Meredith looked around and saw a light switch to the right of the door. She flicked it on, and the space was bathed in fluorescent light. Rowe watched as her head moved up, down and to both sides, absorbing what she was seeing.

What she was looking at was a full, life-size copy of the mini corridor of cells in the custody suite on the ground floor. The doorway was positioned as if one were walking through to the cells from the custody desk. There was a cell door directly in front of her, one to its right, and another facing that on the door side of the unit. All were painted and faux worn in a way that Rowe presumed matched their genuine counterparts.

282

The floor seemed to be an either identical or very similar hard-wearing surface to that which was present in the real custody suite. The ceiling and tube light-fitting was also accurate, which Rowe surmised was to replicate shadowing as closely as possible. It was almost identical to the real thing, with only minor differences visible on closer inspection with the naked eye.

It made no sense for the unit to have been created on the abandoned second floor of the station, and Rowe could see that Meredith was computing its existence in her brain. The cell door opposite Meredith and to her right stood open, just as the door in the custody suite had done on the morning they had arrived at the cell death scene.

Meredith had moved forward and was standing a couple of steps inside the unit. She turned back to face Rowe, showing signs of confusion and impatience rather than fear.

'What is this thing?' she exclaimed. 'What is it *for*?'

Rowe stepped into the space with her, the gun having been placed back in his pocket.

'This is how someone beat the Lockscreen system,' he said. 'And how they killed Sputka – otherwise known as James Burnell.'

Rowe walked ahead of Meredith to the open cell door and went in. She followed close behind, and he could tell she was somewhat agog at proceedings. Rowe didn't speak but stood to one side so the Detective Constable could see what he was showing her.

'This is the only cell with a door that opens and that has anything inside it,' he said. Meredith seemed to still be processing the fact it existed at all.

In front of them was a bench with a thin rubber mattress on top of it. Above the bench, near the top of the back wall was a window divided into three, with glass that was completely black – Rowe thought it was actually black Perspex or similar, which he guessed would explain how it appeared on camera. Below, lying on the mattress, was the shape of a man wrapped in an orange blanket. Sandy blonde hair was visible on the back of the figure's head but little else. To Rowe – and, he suspected, to Meredith – it looked identical to the body of James Burnell they had seen a few days earlier.

But at close quarters it quite clearly was not. It was a dummy of some kind.

Rowe looked at Meredith and could see she was trying to comprehend what exactly it all meant. He walked back out of the mocked-up cell and stood in the corridor.

'There's this too,' he said.

Meredith came out of the cell to see Rowe opening a door which stood at the head of the mini corridor. In the real custody suite, that door opened into a compact store cupboard around two feet deep that held spare blankets, basic toiletries and cleaning equipment. The door in front of them also led to a storage cupboard, only this one was larger and used for surplus materials: wood, cardboard, paint and similar items that had been deployed in the construction of the set. All these things were stacked and pushed into hollow spaces on each side of the door, to allow access to another door at the back of the cupboard.

Rowe pointed at that door, which was a metallic grey affair and plainly part of the building itself rather than the new unit.

'Did you know that door existed?' he asked Meredith.

She looked thoughtful before responding that she hadn't known.

'Neither did I. It leads to some old fire stairs that come out on the ground floor next to a fire exit. I'm guessing the stairs became obsolete at some point when the external fire escape was built.' Rowe nodded in the direction of the rear of the building where black metal steps led from fire exits on the second and first floors down to the car park. 'Since then, there have probably been filing cabinets or boxes against this door to stop anyone using it. Someone has rigged up temporary lighting in there but otherwise the stairs are still in place. The door that opens onto the ground floor was locked but I took the liberty of opening it with a fire extinguisher before you arrived.'

'Why did you do that?'

'Because we will most likely need to use it.' Rowe looked at her pointedly. 'Those stairs are the access point for this unit; wouldn't make sense for whoever built it to have to lug all those boxes around every time like I just did.'

Rowe thought Meredith might ask why they would need to use the stairs but instead she said nothing for a few seconds. Her expression was mostly the serious, neutral one Rowe tended to associate with her, but a hint of a darkening frown had merged into it.

'Why are you showing me this, Rowe?' she asked, glancing around the unit. 'How did you know about it?'

'I didn't know about it. But I worked out that it had to exist.'

Rowe stepped back along to the other end of the corridor. He pointed up to a camera set high on the wall, which was positioned to capture the doors of all three of the false cells.

'That camera is positioned in the same place as the one in the real cell corridor downstairs. Ditto with that one.' He gestured to a camera situated over the door of the third cell, which was pointing down at the one that housed the dummy in a blanket. 'The images from these cameras would look identical to that from their counterparts in the real custody suite. They would have to, of course, for this to work.'

'For what to work?'

'You told me about the Lockscreen system, right? It's completely live, cannot be altered in real time and the feeds are stored and secured as soon as they are captured on a constant rolling basis. So, they can't be messed with retrospectively either.'

'That's right. And?'

'The only aspect of the system that can be influenced manually is which cameras will be recording the feeds. They can be allocated every 12 hours and if no changes are made, the system defaults to whatever cameras were previously allocated, yes?'

'Yes...' Meredith seemed to be growing impatient.

'You also said the allocated cameras can be changed more often than that, but it's difficult so most people tend not to.'

Meredith just looked at him.

'Here's what I think,' Rowe went on. 'At the beginning of the 12-hour period when Burnell or Sputka was killed – let's say midnight on the Wednesday – someone allocated these two cameras to the Lockscreen system, in place of the two corresponding cameras downstairs, for a very specific period of time. Rachel Worth was checking on Burnell every fifteen minutes, so let's say that is the wide marker.

'When the two cameras downstairs were switched for these two – maybe by Worth herself, who knows – she had to appear in this unit to look as if she were checking on Burnell as normal. Then she would also have needed to get downstairs to his real cell in order to administer whatever it was that killed him before the time period finished and the cameras reverted back.'

Meredith appeared bewildered.

'Well…that sounds like a pretty wild assumption and also a majorly flawed plan if Worth had to be in two places at once,' she scoffed.

'Something went wrong. A few things, actually. Which is why so many people are now dead.'

'Rowe…' Meredith's hands went to her hips as she glared at him. 'What the hell are you talking about? This is insane. Who on earth would go to this sort of trouble and why?'

'OK look. The dead man had the online identity of Sputka. His real name isn't known, but he was assigned the name of James Burnell as part of all this. Sputka was a member of a group whose work could prove highly damaging to certain powerful people. It seems the SDU team from the Yard have been conducting operations like this one for some time to remove members of that group. And the reason it was done here at Fenwood was to use me as bait to get to another group member.'

'Who?'

'My brother, Devon.'

'Devon? I...I thought he died.'

'He didn't die.'

Meredith said nothing in response and Rowe could see her mind was ticking over. He thought she was probably waiting for him to incriminate himself somehow with his clearly unhinged narrative, or to at least breach the last vestiges of its credibility in her eyes. It seemed he might as well carry on.

'I think Hannah Crockett was killed because she found this thing.' He gestured to the unit around them. 'She was doing some work here not long before she died. Then you've got Steve Symonds and Rachel Worth. They were the grunt workers in the operation, and either were or had been romantically involved. Guess they came as a pair. But Symonds fucked up that night when he got distracted by Laura.'

The mention of Laura Cross's name caused Meredith to shift uneasily. Rowe thought perhaps she was afraid of where he might be going with the narrative.

'I think Symonds was prompted by the person who facilitated this whole thing to invite Laura along. That person clearly didn't realise that Symonds had a romantic interest in her. Maybe Laura was late or early getting here – either way Symonds missed his cue. So

Worth had to complete both tasks herself in a short space of time. Symonds paid the price for it later, of course. And I guess those in charge also decided it was safer to eliminate Worth once I'd started focusing on her.'

'And Laura?' Meredith said it in a small voice, as if afraid of the answer.

'Purely to punish me.' His gaze was steady. 'She didn't know anything.'

Meredith nodded.

'Alright,' she said eventually. 'Two questions. One: if that was the whole plan, why would they choose a building fitted with Lockscreen at all? It just makes things more difficult.'

'An insurance policy is my guess. Lockscreen is meant to be beyond reproach, as you said. If the CCTV can't be tampered with, in theory no one will suspect foul play. And soon these cameras will be gone anyway'. He pointed to the two above them in the unit.

'That leads on to my second question. Why is this unit still here? Wouldn't it have made sense to destroy it immediately after it was used?'

'Simple – they didn't expect anyone to find it. Symonds and Worth wouldn't have told a soul even if they were still alive. And they had eyes on me in the unlikely event that I figured it out. Besides, the building is on the verge of closing and probably demolition too. It wouldn't be hard to disassemble this in amongst that kind of work.'

'You keep saying "they". Who is it – just Commander Grantley and his team? How would they have the access?'

'There's a local contact. Someone who coordinated all of this. I thought it was Vickers at first, but it's not. I even considered you for a moment. But the answer was a lot more obvious.'

There was a noise from somewhere on the second floor, just barely audible from inside the enclosed unit. Rowe realised it was a voice, accompanied by footsteps. He turned back to Meredith.

'Turn your phone on to video.' He said it in a hushed tone. 'Make sure you get everything. I'm taking out my gun, but I'm not planning to use it. You have to trust me.'

Meredith looked conflicted but started to take out her phone anyway. The voice and footsteps were getting louder, and it sounded to Rowe as if the person had passed through the copy room and into the room where the unit sat.

'DC Meredith?'

The voice was clear then and distinctive. Rowe saw in Meredith's face that she had identified it. He turned and walked out of the unit's door and into the room, among the sea of scattered boxes. He held the gun out in front of him, at eye level.

'Mike? What...where on earth did you get that?'

Assistant Chief Constable Nicholas Stanwell stopped dead, halfway between Rowe and the copy room door.

39

ROWE HAD TOLD JIM Ferry that Meredith was the contact in order to protect him, in case his friend were to be questioned by Stanwell or another interested party. Stanwell had indeed learned of Rowe's presence at Fenwood somehow, but Rowe thought that may have been more closely related to the earlier trip he had taken to the old man's house.

That trip hadn't worked out as Rowe had hoped in any respect. Instead, he had to settle for it having the effect of drawing Stanwell out – and effectively revealing himself as the local contact in doing so.

Meredith stepped out of the unit behind Rowe, and he saw her spectating cautiously, phone in her up-turned palm.

'DC Meredith?' Stanwell – who was in full uniform, despite apparently being on leave – exclaimed. 'What's going on? I thought Jim Ferry was here.'

He was blustering with a perplexed expression on his face. Rowe knew the old man would try to keep up the act with Meredith there, which was exactly why Rowe had wanted her present; so she could see it for herself. And document it.

'Sit down, Nick,' Rowe said, gesturing with the gun to a swivel chair that stood island-like among the strewn boxes.

'Mike,' Stanwell spluttered, 'I don't know what you've got yourself into, old chap, but I'm sure we can work it out.'

'Now.' Rowe said it more loudly.

As Stanwell walked with a stilted gait over to the chair and sat down, he looked past Rowe's shoulder at the unit with the same dramatic confusedness still etched on his features.

'What the devil is that in there?'

'Shut up,' replied Rowe.

Stanwell's look of confusion turned to over-cooked surprise. Meredith was still hovering behind Rowe, but he wasn't concerned about her. He knew asking her to record proceedings afforded her as much protection as it did him.

'We all know what that is, Nick,' Rowe said. 'You probably had it built. What I want to know is why. Why are you helping these people? And why did you kill Laura when you knew she was innocent?'

Stanwell didn't respond, merely gawped as if Rowe were spouting gibberish.

'You know what gave it away, Nick?' Rowe continued. 'It was when we had coffee at your place that morning. You brought up Devon's name twice after not mentioning him in years. I know you always thought he was a deserter and probably hoped he was dead. You never said it, but I could tell. The very idea he might've run away offended your old school sensibilities. But then you were suddenly asking if I'd heard anything. That was an odd question. Looking back, I'm guessing you were being put under a lot of pressure right then. Starting to get desperate. That right?'

Rowe had the gun trained on Stanwell's head, from a distance of about five feet. Stanwell's eyes had moved to the floor as Rowe had been talking, but they came up with a grave expression in them.

'You have no idea what you're talking about,' the older man said softly.

'Laura was killed by a *friend!*' Rowe hissed. He wanted to shout but knew if he let his emotions run loose, he'd never wrest them back again. 'It was someone she invited in and trusted. Probably the same person who tried and failed to kidnap her. I thought that stunt was just a warning, but now I think it was a failed mission which the assailant later had to make amends for – by killing her. That assailant was you.'

Stanwell's countenance remained grim. Rowe kept talking.

'You were also the one who got her to come to Fenwood that night, to ensure I'd get involved in the cell death. Only you didn't realise there was already a connection between her and Symonds. That led to Symonds fucking up and him paying the price. Then Laura did too.'

Rowe stepped forward and brought the gun within two feet of Stanwell's forehead.

'Rowe!' Meredith called out in alarm.

He didn't move and the show of aggression had the effect of encouraging Stanwell to speak in the tense silence, his voice still uncharacteristically quiet.

'Allow me to explain, Mike. Your Dad...'

Rowe tilted the gun forward very slightly as if preparing to fire. Stanwell hesitated before continuing, his face suddenly appearing very tired and old to Rowe.

'Your Dad and I joined the police together back in the late seventies as you know.' The Assistant Chief

Constable leaned back slightly in the chair, service cap held at his knee, and looked Rowe in the eyes as he spoke. 'Training college recruits – we had no real idea what we were doing at that age. A man came to visit us at our digs in London and said we'd been chosen from several hundred recruits as being suitable for specialised work. We had no idea who this man was or what that meant, but evidently it had all been cleared through our superior. We were to perform some tasks that would be in addition to our everyday duties and training and be rewarded significantly for doing so. The only catch was that this work was completely classified. A secret from everyone including our families. Naturally we both thought it was all too good to be true and possibly a practical joke being played on the new fish. When our first detail came through a few days later we were convinced it was a wind-up: the man on the phone told us to be at a certain address at a certain time of night, apprehend someone there and bring them to a warehouse. We did as we were told and arrived at the address, expecting someone to spring out at any moment and put us through some ghastly initiation or other. We knew our contact was parked up the road, watching. But nothing like that happened and it soon became obvious we were to do exactly as instructed. A middle-aged man was sitting and eating his dinner alone in the house. We knocked on the door, dragged him out of there and stuffed him in the boot of the car. Took him to the warehouse. Then we were obliged to stay for the festivities…the man was tortured in various ways for some time and, when it was established that he didn't know anything, he was shot dead. A few days later, both Brian's name and mine appeared in the local paper: two hero recruits that had cornered a dangerous gunman at an abandoned warehouse who had eventually turned the gun on himself. From there on in there was no way out. Our careers progressed quickly. New tasks were assigned to us, and we were unable to refuse.'

Rowe said nothing. He remembered the story of the two brave young recruits being told to him and Devon when they were young, but by their mother – not their father. He reflexively wanted to disbelieve the version that Stanwell had just told, but at that moment he couldn't think of a good reason that the old man would lie about it.

'Our extra-curricular work was not particularly regular,' Stanwell continued. 'There was no way of knowing for sure, but Brian and I decided we must have been just two of many recruited in this way around the country. Our names would occasionally appear in the papers in association with cases we hadn't worked, cases we had never even heard about. Sometimes one or other of us would give a scripted statement to a newspaper or television reporter about a case that didn't exist. It became part of our lives. I suppose we became desensitised to it. It wasn't often that either of us was personally sent to injure or otherwise engage with a target, but I can't say that didn't happen.'

Stanwell gave a half-apologetic, half-resigned look. Rowe could think of a million questions at that moment, but he didn't want to lose Stanwell's thread and the picture it was uncovering. Nonetheless, something Devon had said had come to the front of Rowe's mind.

When Rowe had asked his brother why he disappeared from Afghanistan, Devon had said that "things got personal". Coupled with what Stanwell was revealing, he wondered if Devon had stumbled on evidence of their father's involvement in the mass fraud he was researching.

'What do you know about my parents' death?'

Stanwell eyed him, but not in surprise.

'It wasn't an accident, was it?' Rowe said, realising as he did so that he had never considered the possibility.

'I don't know for certain,' Stanwell said in the quiet voice. 'Brian and I had grown distant; the years of secrecy had taken their toll on our friendship. What once bound us as tightly as any two people had ultimately driven a wedge between us. He wanted to get out, to at least live some of his life without the burden of our duty. I tried to tell him it wasn't possible, but he wouldn't listen. Chose not to, perhaps. Brian told our handler that he was finished with that work, and he and Aoife left for France. The rest, I suppose, is history. I think Brian knew what was coming. He chose to be with the woman he loved at the end, which was as much as he could have hoped for. As any of us could hope for.'

Stanwell, the widower, briefly gave a sad smile.

'Who was responsible?' Rowe asked him.

'There's no way to be sure.'

'Who was…IS your handler?'

'I think you know.'

Rowe looked at him. He didn't doubt Stanwell's honesty. The man was confessing a lifetime worth of sin, and Rowe had a strong feeling as to why he had chosen to do so at that moment. However, Rowe was not about to afford his father's long-time friend even the remotest sympathy.

'You were right from the very start, Mike.' Stanwell was staring into space, apparently ruminating. 'None of us truly has the right to sanction or judge anyone for anything, even if our roles give us permission to do so. It's one of the great imponderables in life that is rarely acknowledged. I used to think your attitude rather new age – sixth-form politics, if you will – but I have come to see the wisdom in it. Your Dad and I sent people to their deaths, both directly and otherwise, merely because someone told us to. And we didn't challenge it in order to preserve our own skins. Brian wrestled with that for his entire life, as have I. It was what fuelled his drinking. He was terribly hurt by your attitude towards his profession because he knew what we'd done and that, when it came down to it, you were right.'

He focused on Rowe again with a thoughtful gaze.

'Then you surprised us all by joining up, Mike. I know I played my part in convincing you. Not only did I know you would make a fine officer, but I thought it would help Brian to live with things as they were. And for a while it did. He was very proud of you, Mike. You became the man he had wanted to be. In the end I suppose you joined for the same reason as he did: the hope of one day changing things. Using the power that the job affords to try and achieve something positive. Until you found, as we all do, that it's really not as simple as that.'

Rowe was still listening. He was aware they probably didn't have much longer, but he needed as much as possible out of Stanwell.

'I'm glad you got out,' the older man went on. 'I'm sorry it was in the midst of all this, but you got out, nonetheless. Brian and I didn't have that option.'

'I don't believe there was no way out,' Rowe said.

Stanwell smiled sadly again.

'After Brian and Aoife died, I thought about trying to get out myself. Day and night, for years. I wasn't being utilised much and thought I might be able to somehow…retire. Disappear into the sunset. So, I tentatively floated the idea to our handler eventually. The response was not immediate but when it came it was devastating.'

It took Rowe a few seconds before he realised what Stanwell was alluding to.

'Gloria,' he said.

Stanwell nodded slowly and looked at the floor.

'They took her from me as a reminder of my position. Not that it could ever be proven of course; I woke up one morning and she was cold next to me. Natural causes due to an undiagnosed heart murmur was the official word. But I knew these people. Perhaps they expected me to take my own life as a result, but I vowed that I wouldn't give them the pleasure. In light of things now, perhaps I was foolish to be so stubborn.'

'You still have your daughter, Sarah,' Rowe said. 'That was reason enough to stay alive…until now. You've destroyed any chance of redemption.'

'Mike…'

'You were told to kidnap Laura and failed. The Sputka operation got screwed up. Then you lost control of me in the aftermath. You weren't the best man for the job: too old, too vulnerable…but you were chosen because you could get to me, and I was their best route to Devon.'

Stanwell looked like he wanted to speak but couldn't.

'But what happened then?' Rowe asked rhetorically. 'Were you ordered to kill Laura as a punishment? A punishment to us both?'

At that moment the man whom Rowe had known all his life started to cry. Tears ran down his face and he emitted mournful sobs with his eyes cast down in what Rowe took to be shame. After a few moments, Stanwell tried to speak again.

'I...I never thought...'

His own sobs cut him off again in mid-sentence. Meredith then appeared at Rowe's side, still holding her phone in one hand while putting the other gently on Rowe's gun arm.

'Mike, that's enough now.'

She said it with what sounded to Rowe like workshop-taught calmness.

'He hasn't told me what I need to know yet,' Rowe said. 'Or-'

The next few seconds happened in slow motion for him. A dream-like period in which he was unable to comprehend or influence anything that was happening around him, as if he were merely an observer to his own physical being. His brain couldn't compute events quickly enough because they happened faster than his mind was able to work.

Assistant Chief Constable Nick Stanwell was dead. A bullet from the Glock that Rowe had been holding, but was no longer, had passed through his brain. Joanne Meredith was a few feet to his left; the rugby player minion he had earlier encountered in the Defender was gripping an arm behind her back and holding a gun to her head. One of Rowe's own arms was behind his back, held there by the minion who resembled a smaller version of Commander Grantley. Rowe realised the Glock he had seized from the coroner's assistant earlier was also gone from his jacket pocket. The Commander himself was standing next to Rowe, holding the gun he had just used to kill Stanwell.

'Suicide,' Grantley said. His voice resonated over the ringing in Rowe's ears caused by the sound of the gunshot in an otherwise silent space. The man then moved his gaze from the lifeless body to meet Rowe's eyes.

'He took the coward's way out. Just like your father.'

40

STANWELL'S BODY HAD BEEN unceremoniously shoved off the swivel chair and onto the floor courtesy of Grantley's boot, and Rowe was pushed down in its place. To his right, Meredith sounded as if she were struggling both to catch her breath and stifle her emotions after what they had witnessed seconds earlier. The rugby player minion had already confiscated her phone and handed it to Grantley. Rowe himself was silent.

Grantley held the gun on Rowe in a gloved hand as his shorter helper stood back, hands crossed in front of him like a nightclub bouncer with one clutching a gun and blocking the door to the unit from which their group had just emerged.

Rowe thought that the trio must have arrived shortly after Stanwell and had taken the old fire stairs to avoid detection. They had probably heard most if not all of what the Assistant Chief Constable had said. Rowe felt it was surely a risk for them to be seen at Fenwood at that point and had hoped that they wouldn't appear.

The bones of his plan had been to show Meredith the unit, have her witness and record whatever Stanwell had to say and then for them both to get out of there. But he'd also known that was best-case scenario, hence bringing the weapons. And on the subject of the guns, he noted that while Grantley and the rugby player were holding them, they still wore their own under their suit jackets.

He guessed Grantley had likely been summoned from London after the underlings were caught unawares in the fields that morning. They had clearly been based at Stanwell's house, so the fact they had been surprised was probably viewed by Grantley as another unacceptable failure on the part of the local contact.

What was certain in Rowe's mind was that Grantley was the 'handler' Stanwell had spoken of. The man who had directly issued orders to both Stanwell and Rowe's father Brian on behalf of some higher power. He didn't think the Commander had always been in that role – being younger than both the men he supervised – but he had clearly held it long enough to have been instrumental in Rowe's parents' deaths fifteen years earlier, going by what Stanwell had said. Rowe wondered if Devon was aware of that fact, and suspected he was.

Grantley eyed Rowe and Meredith in a business-like yet mildly amused fashion.

'Did we come at a difficult moment?' he enquired.

'Let her go, she's not involved in this,' Rowe nodded towards Meredith.

'On the contrary,' Grantley replied calmly, 'she's very much involved. Which is why she'll stay. And die by your gun' – he turned Devon's Glock sideways and upwards to make his meaning clear – 'if you don't provide us with the information we require on your brother.'

Rowe didn't respond. He examined the men in front of him and was in no doubt as to their seriousness. They had entered, waited within, and emerged from the unit with frightening stealth and silence. The rugby player

302

was holding Meredith very still and without ceremony, the unpredictability Rowe had sensed from him on their first meeting seemingly gone. The mini-Grantley emitted the same level of focus. It was evident they had complete confidence in their roles.

As if to underline the fact, Grantley dropped the gun to his side and began casually looking around the room for something. A chair. He wheeled one over from the centre of the room and sat down opposite Rowe, the gun still hanging loosely as if to encourage complacency on Rowe's part.

'I am not generally in the business of discussing our work, Rowe,' Grantley said, with a conversational tone. 'But I appreciate much of this is revelatory to you and, considering the importance of our operation, I am prepared to accept that you may benefit from some salient background information.'

Grantley's eyes were emotionless, as if they were behind some kind of filter. To Rowe, the look was malevolent. The man had very dark skin and the minimal natural light that was able to penetrate their corner of the floor made reading his features very difficult. Although Rowe suspected that would be the case in almost any light: Grantley was not leading a high-level, clandestine operation by accident.

'Your conversation with the late Assistant Chief Constable will have been enlightening I'm sure,' Grantley said. 'It would be unnecessary for me to comment further, even to correct or clarify any of his points. You will have formed your own conclusions in any case. He chose to speak in the manner that he did in the full knowledge that it would result in his death. Infer into that what you will – the point is that you are not in the same position. If you satisfactorily assist us in the matter of your brother, I can ensure that yourself and DC Meredith will leave this place unharmed and without pursuit by any agency.'

Grantley's face didn't change but his body language relaxed slightly, as if he were glad to have the formalities out of the way. Rowe still didn't speak.

'Devon Rowe is a person of great interest to us,' the Commander said. 'We know you have had contact with him recently.'

Rowe felt Meredith's gaze on him at the statement. She was calmer than before and listening rather than resisting the rugby player's grip, which Rowe thought was the smart move at that moment. Grantley continued.

'We are acutely aware of his activities. Some of which, I will freely admit, are extremely advanced. For a long time, we didn't even know that Devon was controlling the attacks on our systems, but as we gradually removed key members of the group it became clear that he was the driving force. I'm sure your brother has given you his version of events. It is obvious he imagines himself to be a renegade warrior fighting the evil, all-powerful overlords that ensnared his father. Your father. It may or may not surprise you to learn that he is nothing of the sort.'

Rowe watched the head of the supposed Special Deployment Unit in silence.

'Your brother Devon is a domestic terrorist, Rowe. Probably the most dangerous terrorist that this country has ever known. You see, it is true that he and his colleagues have infiltrated some of our systems at times and hindered our progress – from a technical perspective – in some areas. As these attacks were related to national security they are classed as both cybercrime and terrorism. But overall, they don't amount to much more than a high-tech version of a teenager in his bedroom stumbling into classified Pentagon files. Concerning, yes, and requiring immediate attention, absolutely, but routinely combatted and rebuffed by our in-house technicians in most cases. No, what my team and I are concerned with is far more serious, hence the measures we are compelled to employ in situations such as this.'

Grantley didn't gesture when he said it but the stark fluorescent light from the temporary unit behind him and the lifeless body of Nick Stanwell lying next to where they sat spoke for him sufficiently.

'Our erstwhile operative here' – Grantley did then give a slight nod in the direction of the body – 'rather over-simplified the duties we perform, I fear. We are not in the business of manipulating the public – not strictly anyway. Our task is to manage the narrative in whichever way our decision-makers see fit-'

'And who are your decision-makers?' Rowe broke in.

Grantley smiled narrowly.

'That is not for me to say. Although I would suggest that if you must ask the question then it is unlikely you will comprehend the answer.'

The smile, such as it had been, disappeared and Grantley continued his previous thread.

'We present the world, Rowe, in the way that is best to do so at any one time. Say, for example, there were a growing anti-military feeling in this country today. If it were deemed necessary, we might stimulate a story about a heroic soldier, or laud the bravery of one who died in action. This creates what is deemed an agreeable balance in the eyes of the public and it is vital for the ongoing stability and protection of society. Whether the soldier existed or not is immaterial. I'm sure you can understand. The police, the government, the NHS, the banks...all can be viewed as good and bad in their own ways. It is a case of illustrating that to people in the correct fashion and at the optimum moment. Obviously, the importance of this work is heightened in times of war, and particularly in the immediate run-up to war.'

Rowe saw Grantley's eyes shine. The man was enjoying expounding on his topic to a feeble outsider.

'Naturally, this kind of work carries significant monetary costs. Therefore, occasionally, an idyllically picture-postcard family will die in a tragic accident, or a brave disabled child will walk from Land's End to John o'Groats for charity. The convenience and ubiquity of online fundraising is a most useful tool, if you get my meaning.'

It was cold in the building, especially on the uninhabited floors, but the chill that Rowe felt wasn't exclusively due to the physical environment. He had felt the same chill before, when in the presence of those truly without conscience or remorse. He was also tiring of Grantley's narrative.

'Yes, I get it, Grantley,' he said. 'You're a sick bastard that works for other sick bastards who apparently like to make up the news and rip off the public. Why does that make Devon a terrorist?'

'Clearly, Rowe, you have the same view of our work as your brother. You fail to grasp the benefits of keeping the world at a natural ebb and flow. General maintenance of the peace...and only pitting sides against each other when absolutely necessary. It is a practice that is at least as old as the printed page: giving the people a compass for their gratitude and a gauge for their expectations. In Ancient Rome, the poet Juvenal described "bread and circuses" satirically. He didn't comprehend the importance of control.'

Grantley stared for a moment and then sat forward, apparently as tired of further discussion as Rowe was.

'Your brother Devon is not simply some righteous online activist, Rowe – some honourable saboteur. Do you remember the Derwin Heights fire from a few years ago? Only vaguely, I expect. It was rather overshadowed by Grenfell Tower and the ensuing fallout. Derwin was an accommodation block in Bristol that suffered a more damaging fire and significantly more casualties than Grenfell did. Only it was situated in a rather more desirable area and didn't contain quite so many immigrants...it's almost too easy to know what will fly in the media sometimes.'

Grantley let out a chuckle after he spoke these last few words.

'Grenfell was, of course, a horrible accident, although we did supply some useful witnesses after the fact to ensure things were...positioned correctly. Derwin, however, was very different. The building was GCHQ controlled – that is classified information, but it is key to the story – and its occupants were all operatives connected with our work and their families. The fire was reported as being similar to Grenfell in terms of its initial causes, but that was not the case. It was caused by concealed devices on ten of the twenty floors. Fifty people died including women and children. The devices in question were set by Devon and his group.'

'How do you know that?' asked Rowe.

Grantley answered without emotion.

'Because they claimed responsibility for it directly.'

Rowe said nothing as he processed what Grantley had said. He had no way of verifying the claim, but then he also didn't know that everything Devon had told him was true or what his ultimate motives were. His older brother had taken him to a location, given him a story – while gleaning information from Rowe himself – then set him a task to fulfil before disappearing completely. It was impossible to know what truth or fiction was, Rowe realised, even if he wanted to believe one side over the other.

Grantley was watching him, probably recognising and revelling in his dilemma, Rowe thought.

'There have been other incidents also,' the Commander said. 'I imagine Devon will have mentioned the address that was attached to James Burnell, perhaps even taken you there. It is true that we have the use of many such former and current military housing estates at different times, and that they serve as living accommodation for our operatives. Your brother knows this too. He and his group have bombed six of them.'

Rowe stared at Grantley with a deadpan expression, but his mind was racing, and he didn't know how to respond. In the periphery of his vision, he felt Meredith's eyes on him.

'We do not believe the bombings were indiscriminate,' Grantley said. 'Devon Rowe's level of knowledge, skill and his occasional access to our systems will have provided him and his team with more than enough information on each location. Derwin Heights and all the housing estates were specifically targeted to inflict maximum damage and loss of life. That, Rowe, is the definition of terrorism. Your brother's weakness is that, like many mass murderers, he wants recognition. He wants us to know that he and his group can damage us in some way. They will never achieve mainstream notoriety, of course, as none of our media outlets would be permitted to oblige them. But Devon wanted us to know they existed, and that very fact put us on the track to uncovering their identities. Which eventually led us to their ringleader.'

Rowe looked around at the faces in the vicinity. There was no emotion from the three SDU members. Meredith looked fearful. Her eyes weren't quite pleading but almost. The irony, of course, was that he had no information to provide Grantley with, even in the unlikely event that he'd wanted to. He had a feeling Grantley knew it. Once again, Rowe's only use to the man was as bait. And once that purpose had been served, he would be of no use to him at all.

'OK.' Rowe said it in a tone that suggested they were about to do business. 'I'll help you because I have no other choice. I just have one question.'

'Which is?'

'Before we get to that, let Meredith go. You know as well as I do she has no business here, and she's smart enough to keep her mouth shut. Too many people have died already.'

'What's the question?' said Grantley, ignoring the request for Meredith's release as if it hadn't been made. The tall, imposing Commander sat forward, his long right hand loosely gripping the Glock between his legs and his eyes boring into Rowe's.

'Why did you order Stanwell to kill Laura Cross?'

Grantley blinked but otherwise didn't reply.

'It made no sense,' Rowe said. 'My life was already under threat, and you knew I would be coming back to Fenwood. Enough people had already died to raise suspicion around what you were doing. Killing another was a dangerous risk; it was gratuitous, unprofessional. Clumsy. Why do it?'

Rowe had chosen words that he thought might hit home with a high-level operator like Grantley. But the man just stared at him. After a few seconds a ghost of a smile appeared on the Commander's lips. Then his eyes showed something which Rowe couldn't place but that he could have sworn was born of confusion.

Then Grantley started to laugh.

At first it was just an amused chuckle, like the one he had emitted earlier, but it soon become a full, deep laugh, throaty and unchecked. The sound of it filled the large, dead room. Rowe regarded the man with what he knew was a murderous stare.

Rowe had already concluded that he and his fellow captive were as good as dead. And with Laura's death being considered a joke, he no longer cared about the surrounding henchmen, or the gun being held to Joanne Meredith's head. Rowe was a fraction of a second from launching himself forwards at Grantley.

But before he had time to move, the building exploded.

41

IT WASN'T THE WHOLE building that had exploded, just several parts of it. There had been more than one explosion. At that moment, it was impossible for Rowe to identify what specific direction they had come from.

He only registered that fact in the few seconds after the noise had erupted and the floor they were situated on had undulated and shaken. It took him a moment to be sure he was unharmed once the thunderous reports had subsided. There was no obvious damage to the room around him, but he sensed that was not the case elsewhere in the building. A fire alarm was sounding from below.

He was still sitting on the swivel chair but had been propelled sideways to his left; possibly by the movement of the floor, he thought, and possibly by his own feet out of sheer surprise. Grantley's chair had tipped over backwards but the man had maintained his feet. The smaller of the two-minions seemed to have just regained his footing, and both he and Grantley were looking towards where the rugby player and Meredith had been standing, which drew Rowe's gaze in that direction also.

The pair were on the floor, and in the seconds that had elapsed since the barrage, Meredith had got on top of the heavy-set man. She had a hand on his gun and appeared very close to gaining control of it. The rugby player seemed momentarily stunned and was only just beginning to offer substantial resistance when another loud explosion rang out.

That time the sound came from the gun in Grantley's hand. The bullet entered the top of Meredith's left arm, and she screamed in pain before slipping off the man and onto her right side. Blood began running down her dark suit jacket and onto the floor as her opponent hustled to his feet and aimed his gun at the young DC's head.

'STOP!' barked Grantley. 'Get her up.'

The rugby player glared at Grantley for a brief moment before grudgingly complying. The expression on the Commander's face was contemptuous. He had already lost one man to someone he would consider an amateur that morning – Rowe – and had apparently been close to losing another. Grantley's posture remained composed under the circumstances, but Rowe wondered if he felt that events had already got out of control.

'Let's go,' Grantley said as Meredith was roughly hauled to her feet, still bleeding and clearly in huge pain. 'Brazier, check the exits. I don't want to get trapped on the fire stairs.'

Brazier – Rowe noted that that was apparently the smaller minion's name – scurried out through the copy room to look for a way out and presumably survey the damage. Grantley turned to Rowe as Brazier left.

'This will be the work of your righteous, crusading brother, of course. Do you see what he's capable of now?'

Rowe didn't speak. He could hear unsettling sounds emanating from other parts of the building. Creaks and groans interspersed by clattering of varying degrees. What looked like smoke and dust could be seen rising past the windows around them.

Brazier returned in what seemed like an impossibly short amount of time.

'There are no exits, sir,' he announced breathlessly.

'Come again?' Grantley retorted, disbelieving.

'The external fire escape has been blown out, sir. As have the back stairs and the front stairs. It's just rubble.'

The front stairs were close to the station's public entrance, on the right as one entered the building. Those stairs had been unusable on all Rowe's recent visits to the station as the door that gave access to them on the ground floor also led to an evidence room and was therefore secured by a keypad lock. The stairs had rarely been used in the station's more recent years.

Grantley briefly looked as if he were about to argue with Brazier's troubling update but instead swiftly decided on the only other course of action.

'Check the fire stairs. Quickly.'

Brazier did as he was told and hurried into the unit behind them, heading for the concealed stairs. Again, he returned surprisingly soon.

'The ground floor level of the stairs has been blown also, sir. We can't get out that way.'

The Commander appeared pensive.

'This should never have been allowed to happen,' he stated darkly. Rowe felt the two minions shrink away very slightly.

'The fire stairs are OK on this floor though, yes?' Grantley asked sharply, returning to more practical matters. Brazier confirmed they were. 'Open the roof hatch near the door. Even if the fire escape is gone, there must be another way down from the roof.'

Rowe was forcibly compelled to lead the way as Grantley put the gun in his face, grabbed him by the jacket and shoved him towards the unit. Brazier had gone ahead of them, hurrying through the end door and disappearing out to the fire stairs to open the hatch that led to the roof. Rowe made a final glance down toward Nick Stanwell's body, which was being left to decay in the same way as the piles of obsolete equipment in the building were.

Rowe's mind was working as quickly as the situation would allow. He considered the possibility of using the unit as a weapon somehow, perhaps diving into the cell with the Burnell dummy inside it or wrestling Grantley in there. He guessed a move like that would be far too dangerous, however. Grantley and the rugby player were both armed and highly trained; any small advantage Rowe might gain would be instantly nullified by one or both men. He decided the only real option was to head to the roof as directed.

Behind them the still nameless rugby player was escorting Meredith along as quickly as she would go, which was not very. She was crying mutely and holding her right hand to her injured arm, trying in vain to stop the flow of blood. Her face was pale, and Rowe knew she would need medical attention very soon. He was sure Grantley recognised that too as the Commander made frequent, troubled glances back in her direction.

'Sir, should we leave her?' It was the rugby player asking in a deep, cold voice that entered Rowe's head like a knife.

'No,' Grantley replied quickly. 'No loose ends.'

As they approached the end door of the unit, Rowe heard a noise that was presumably the roof hatch beyond it being opened followed by the metallic clonking of feet scaling a ladder or something similar. Grantley motioned them through the door using the gun, but Rowe didn't move.

'She'll die if that isn't attended to soon,' he said.

Grantley stepped forward and grabbed Rowe's jacket again.

'That would be a shame,' he said agitatedly, 'considering the bullet came from your gun. Now move it.'

Another shove from one of Grantley's large hands forced Rowe through the door, and he stepped from the makeshift cupboard through the concealed door and onto the steel platform at the top of the fire stairs. Smoke was coming up from below. Festoon lighting was strung down the handrail of the stairs to provide illumination, and Rowe could see a couple of small fires burning somewhere towards the bottom.

It occurred to Rowe that the route they were taking was the only available one for a reason. Bearing in mind the story Grantley had just told him, he had no way of knowing whether that was a good or a bad thing. Either way, it was apparent to him that they were being deliberately forced to the roof, and that Devon was the likely engineer.

Rowe felt it safe to assume that Grantley knew that too. The man wasn't used to being trapped and was noticeably more hassled and uncertain than he had appeared up to that point. The Commander was nonetheless attempting to exude an air of calm.

The roof hatch – which was to the left of the door as they had come through it – was open and Rowe momentarily wondered how Brazier had done it so quickly. He decided it had probably been considered as a planned escape route from the beginning of the operation, back when the external fire escape had still been in one piece. Brazier was nowhere to be seen, and Rowe guessed that he was investigating the area above the hatch to ensure the route was safe.

He felt Grantley's hand on his back again, hastening him towards the hatch. There were steel rungs built into the door-side wall underneath it, which Rowe duly grasped and started to climb.

'Faster,' Grantley said. He was keeping the gun within six inches of Rowe's back and holding the rungs below in preparation to climb himself. Rowe looked down and saw the rugby player still propping up the fading Meredith behind.

'Brazier!' Grantley bellowed upwards. 'Watch Rowe as he comes up.'

There was no response from above, and Brazier wasn't there when Rowe emerged onto the roof. Rowe didn't try anything – didn't see sense in doing so at that stage in the scenario – and Grantley came up cat-like behind him, ushering him away from the hatch with the gun.

The hatch came up adjacent to the lip of the roof that overlooked Grounds Way. The roof itself was expectedly flat and largely bare, except for four air vent units that were evenly spaced across it in a square formation. Rowe estimated the units were roughly five feet square, with the closest one being a few feet to their left. Billows of smoke could be seen coming from the points of the building that Brazier had mentioned and Rowe registered for the first time how much outside attention the explosions must have drawn.

'Johns, get up here.'

Grantley was calling to the rugby player, using his name at last. Johns – Rowe suspected the man had been called 'Little' behind his back more than once.

Meredith was a virtual dead weight at that point due to the blood she had lost. Even so, she emerged through the hatch, pulling herself up to some degree but it was clear that Johns had done most of the work. He came up huffing and puffing after pushing her bloodied weight away from the hatch.

'Fat bitch,' Johns muttered bitterly.

'Takes one to know one I suppose,' Rowe said to the bulky operative in response. Johns gave him a homicidal look.

'BRAZIER!' Grantley called again.

Smoke from whichever small or large fires were still burning continued to pour upwards into the gloomy November sky. Rowe couldn't be sure, but the smoke seemed to him to be increasing in its volume. A light wind was blowing a lot of it back away from the group slightly, meaning the front edge of the building they stood on was relatively clear. Rowe was thinking about

318

the implications of that as Grantley yelled for Brazier again and once more had no response.

'There must be another way down – a service ladder or something,' Grantley said, more as an assessment than in panic.

Rowe recalled that there was such a thing on the far corner of the station, near where the cell windows and the LPG gas tank were located. He had seen it on his reconnaissance mission a few nights earlier. It was a service ladder, exactly. But he stayed quiet on the subject.

Another explosion went off. Another thunderous bang. All three of Rowe, Grantley and Johns instinctively dropped to their haunches and Meredith curled up tighter on the floor in her weakened state. No one dived for cover however, as the explosion had been at the far opposite corner of the building from where they were.

Rowe estimated it was either the exact spot where the service ladder had been, or as close to it as made no difference.

When the latest explosion had subsided, Grantley quickly ushered Rowe, and Johns with Meredith, further away from the hatch and towards the front corner of the building, which overlooked Grounds Way and the road that turned down to the station's front entrance. Rowe guessed that Grantley thought the hatch itself might be next on the list of targets, seeing as it had suddenly become the only real way off the roof, albeit one that offered little sanctuary. That part of the roof was also one of the only areas that was not engulfed in smoke or hazardous on some other way.

As Rowe again considered the significance of their positioning, a yell interrupted his thoughts.

'SIR!'

It was Brazier's voice, coming from somewhere off to Rowe's right. Grantley kept the gun trained on Rowe but opened his stance so he could glance over to where the shout had come from, which seemed to be one of the air vent units. Sure enough, Brazier emerged a couple of seconds later from behind the closest unit with an arm behind his back and his own gun held to his head.

Holding the gun was Jim Ferry.

The pair advanced forward at an angle, ensuring that Ferry's considerable mass was as shielded as possible by Brazier's body. Ferry drew them both to a stop a few feet from the group.

'Rower, we're getting out of here,' he said.

It was evident that Ferry's grip on Brazier was rock solid. Rowe had heard stories of his friend's physical strength – legendary among Oxford officers of a certain age – but had never seen it in action before. Ferry's soft, bagpuss-like exterior was the product of many years of sedentary office work mixed with the consumption of various unhealthy forms of junk food, but it was clear that a robust core remained.

Even so, Rowe surmised that Ferry must have got the jump on Brazier to overpower him in such a way. He thought the smaller man would surely have had training way beyond anything that Jim Ferry could have received, experience notwithstanding.

'Fire brigade will be here any minute,' Ferry continued, still talking to Rowe. 'And when they put the ladder up, you, me and Meredith are going down it first. Before the Sweeney tribute act, that is.'

The five people were arranged in a kind of uneven diamond in front of Rowe. Ferry and Brazier were to his right, Grantley was slightly left of centre and Johns was standing over Meredith, right of centre in his line of vision. Johns had his gun pointed downward at Meredith's prone body and Grantley was still steadily holding the gun on Rowe whilst clearly processing how best to deal with the latest development.

A siren could be heard in the distance, and Rowe presumed it was coming from the fire station on the other side of Fenwood. Ferry had been right, but it had already crossed Rowe's mind – and probably Grantley's – that the building would soon be surrounded by the emergency services. Voices could be heard from below; the explosions having naturally brought bystanders running. If that was the intended result of a plan concocted by Devon, it seemed to Rowe to be an unnecessarily elaborate way to achieve it.

However, Rowe also thought the scenario had to be close to being Grantley's worst nightmare. Someone who operated exclusively – and thrived – outside the light, as Devon had put it. Suddenly exposed on an impromptu outdoor stage, possibly even captured by phone cameras in the process of conducting his covert business. Yes, there would be ready made cover stories and alternative narratives prepared for such situations. But Grantley had already overseen a bungled operation,

321

and as things got decidedly worse, Rowe thought the Commander was running out of people to blame.

Grantley scoffed humourlessly at Ferry's stated plan of escape, his face having become bitter.

'You won't make it,' he spat. 'Rowe's brother Devon is using us for sport, like the mentally ill savage he is. He has isolated us here for his own amusement. If we don't kill each other first, he'll blow us all to kingdom come.'

'I wouldn't bet on it,' Rowe said.

Grantley gave him a sharp look, as if he didn't fully understand. Rowe didn't elaborate, but suddenly he was sure he knew the reason they had been guided to the roof and to that spot.

The Commander turned back to Ferry and Brazier.

'Let him go, Ferry,' he said in a flat, almost bored tone. 'If you try anything you will be shot, and your death ruled necessary force. He is a member of the Scotland Yard SDU. If we all end up dead, the narrative will only be told in our favour.'

Ferry stood firm for a moment or two, assessing his options. As tough and experienced as his friend was, Rowe knew the situation was outside of Ferry's wheelhouse. The old hand had apprehended Brazier smoothly enough but hadn't had a concrete plan beyond that. Rowe was grateful for his help but unsure how much it ultimately changed things.

'Jim,' Rowe said. A couple of sirens could then be heard, and one was a lot closer than the other. Time was short no matter what. 'Bring him here. Next to me.'

Ferry looked uncertain but, keeping his knees bent and his eyes on Grantley and Johns, managed to shuffle sideways and backwards whilst manoeuvring Brazier until he was next to where Rowe stood, virtually on the corner of the roof. The gun was in his favoured left hand, and he maintained the iron grip on Brazier's arm with his right.

'Strength in numbers, Rowe?' Grantley said. 'It certainly makes for an easier story. Your bit on the side over there will die soon. By your gun. Another woman you will have sent to the grave.' A sick smile appeared. 'Women aren't safe around you, are they? Well, never mind. You've served your purpose. Some of our associates will be locating Devon as we speak. As I said before, his urge for the limelight would always be his undoing.'

Grantley aimed his gun at Rowe, who was able to envisage the story the Commander would want told. Grantley would be the hero of the rooftop scene; defeating the bent cop (Rowe) and his accomplice (Ferry), while Johns – set back from the roof's edge and thus out of range of any camera – tried in vain to save the life of the valiant Meredith, whom Rowe had shot in cold blood.

'Don't move.' Rowe whispered it to Ferry, glancing at the gun to silently communicate a message.

A fire engine screeched to a stop below them on Grounds Way, its siren wailing unignorably. Yet more smoke billowed up from various parts of the building. Rowe looked at Grantley again and spoke loudly over the noise.

'You didn't answer my question about Laura.'

Grantley smiled without humour.

'Look around you, Rowe. I think you already know the answer.'

323

A sound was heard above all others in the next instant. It was akin to a heavy item landing on concrete having been dropped from a high point. Full-blooded, bottom-heavy. Echoing off the building and others around it. In that moment it reminded Rowe of being in the fields behind Nick Stanwell's house as a child; never quite certain whether a distant report was a bird scarer from the farm or...

Grantley's head tipped suddenly to the left almost exactly as the sound reverberated. A fine mist instantly emerged from it. His gun arm dropped down and his body followed. The beginnings of a commotion could be heard from below.

'Gun,' Rowe said.

Ferry didn't have time to react, but Rowe was already grabbing the Glock from his friend's hand. He got it up and aimed just as Johns was bringing his own weapon up, suddenly comprehending what had happened. Rowe shot Johns in the centre of his torso and the man fell onto his back.

Rowe was still moving forwards and headed straight for Grantley's limp gun hand, a few feet ahead of him. He sensed then that Brazier was on the same course by his side, having broken free of Ferry's grasp in the confusion. Rowe lunged, planted his left foot and pivoted on it, as close as he could get to Grantley's gun hand.

Brazier lunged for Grantley's gun in the same instant and, as he did, Rowe – falling backwards – shot him through the sternum. The range was virtually point blank and the bullet passed through the man's body, finally embedding itself in the top of Jim Ferry's right shoulder as he moved to grab Brazier from behind.

Ferry stifled a yell and collapsed to one knee. Rowe landed back-first on Grantley's lifeless body as Brazier slumped in a similar state next to the Commander. Rowe had the idea that they resembled a grisly, foreshortened mirror image of each other. He twisted around sharply, gun still in hand, to look back at Johns and saw that the man hadn't moved. One of Johns' heavy feet was propped up on Meredith's legs, who still lay on her side, deathly pale and appearing unconscious.

The smoke had grown considerably around them, and visibility was poor. The sound of sirens combined with the urgent and terrified voices below overtook everything.

42

THE OPEN FIRE SIMMERED, and the lights were on a low setting which combined to create both a physical and visual warmth inside The Bear and Rifle against the greyness of a late November day.

Rowe was sitting in one of the casual seats for drinkers, on the other side of the fireplace and away from the bar. A pint of Old Hooky sat in front of him and none of the small groups scattered at nearby tables had paid him any particular attention. His eyes drifted regularly to the door as he awaited his companion.

Shortly, through a section of one of the pub's tall front windows, he saw a car pull up outside the front of the building. The familiar, bowling ball-like figure of Jim Ferry emerged tentatively from its passenger side, favouring his right arm which was supported by a sling. As he closed the car door and moved away, Rowe glimpsed the unsmiling face of Angela Ferry at the wheel. Then the car moved off and was gone.

Ferry breezed into the pub and strode instantly to the bar without acknowledging or even looking around for Rowe and proceeded to try a couple of samples of the real ale on offer. Eventually deciding on one, he bought a pint and brought it over to the table.

'Where you been hiding this boozer then, Rower?' Ferry said, glancing around conspiratorially as he sat down. He did so gently, so as not to test his shoulder. 'They've got some serious sherbet on offer.'

'Thought you'd appreciate the finer points,' Rowe said. 'It also means we're not in the middle of Fenwood. Angela didn't mind driving you then?'

'Wouldn't say that exactly. She's taking a nose at the garden centre down the road.'

Rowe nodded and smiled slightly. He knew Ferry's presence there probably wouldn't have been authorised purely on its own merits.

'How's the shoulder?' he asked.

'Been better. You're lucky I've got more than one drinking arm.'

With obvious difficulty, Ferry used his good arm to pull a crumpled newspaper from his coat pocket and spread it on the table. It was a copy of that day's Oxford Mail with a headline emblazoned across its front page:

COPS' COMBAT TRAINING SCARE
Local cops continue combat training despite gas explosions

Rowe skimmed through the accompanying article which was peppered with quotes from Detective Chief Superintendent Judith Carne. The story it told was of a training exercise that had been interrupted by gas explosions, although in the confusion the officers involved had thought the blasts were part of the exercise. The report stated that no one had been hurt and, due to the explosions, the building had been officially condemned and was due for demolition.

Ferry gave Rowe time to read the article and then wordlessly turned the pages to another story. The piece covered the untimely death of Assistant Chief Constable Nicholas Stanwell, who passed away in his sleep on the day of the training incident due to a suspected undiagnosed heart murmur. Rowe remembered that being the cause that Stanwell's wife Gloria's death had officially been attributed to also. DCS Carne was again quoted, paying special tribute to Stanwell's long and distinguished service.

Finally, Ferry turned a few more pages to a third story, one about a missing person. A man named Mark Felman who worked for the Oxford coroner's office had not been seen for two days. Police were apparently looking to speak to him in connection with the death of Detective Sergeant Laura Cross.

Rowe closed the paper and sat back in thought. 'About as neat and tidy as they could manage, I guess.' He took a sip of his pint and was quiet for a while before he spoke again. 'Any word on Laura's funeral yet?'

Ferry shook his head.

'Not yet, mate. Awaiting the outcome of an investigation I believe.' He drank from his glass to create a pause before continuing. 'Carne was bloody shell-shocked by all this I can tell you. Getting Meredith's phone back out of Grantley's pocket was a masterstroke my friend…you're off the hook for everything. Of course, the Yard are denying any knowledge of Grantley and his team being present. They cleaned up the scene from what I hear. Carne is just busy ensuring none of it gets out. And Vickers seems to be keeping his head down, strangely enough.'

'Your pension might be OK after all then?'

'We can but hope.' Ferry raised his eyebrows over his upturned glass.

'How's Meredith doing?' Rowe asked, realising he didn't know.

'On the mend. I took some flowers over to her yesterday, she asked after you too. They're going with a training accident to explain her injury…and probably making it worth her while to keep quiet.'

'I didn't want her to get hurt. She'd have every right to be angry with me.'

'I think she understands mate.'

They sat and drank their beers silently for a while, digesting the situation as it stood.

'What I wanna know,' Ferry chimed out of the meditative quiet, 'is how did you know Devon was gonna shoot Grantley? I didn't think you knew where he was.'

'I didn't,' Rowe said. 'But as soon as the explosions went off it was clear he was nearby. Then I remembered the caravan.'

'Caravan?'

'There was a beaten-up old caravan in the far corner of the public car park on Grounds Way. It appeared not long after the cell death – I parked next to it the other day because Devon's Defender seemed to blend in with it. Then I thought about it again when we were on the roof. Made sense that Devon would be somewhere in the vicinity so he would know when to detonate the charges he'd set.'

'That's a point: exactly when and how *did* he set them?'

'No way to know for sure. But if I had to guess I'd say they and he had been in place for at least 24 hours. Snipers are used to waiting. He must've planted them in strategic locations on the outside of the building, which wouldn't have been that hard seeing as the place was empty and the external cameras don't work.' Rowe took a drink. 'He gave me enough credit that I would figure out the fake cell unit existed, and that I would draw Grantley and co. to the station. So, he used the cover of the caravan until show time came.'

'Bloody hell. Well, I suppose I should thank you for dragging me out of the line of fire...briefly, at least.' Ferry nodded to his wounded shoulder sarcastically. 'I guess Devon just went up in a puff of smoke afterwards then?'

'He might've just walked away. Someone as efficient as him could break the rifle down in a few seconds and be on the move within a minute. Even if anyone figured out where the shot came from, the gunshots on the roof afterwards would've been a distraction. And I'd guess the caravan is gone now.'

Ferry shrugged in a kind of bemused agreement.

'So, where did you spring from?' Rowe asked. 'I told you to get to the office.'

'I waited in the car to make sure Meredith turned up as planned. Felt responsible, I suppose. Then when Stanwell bowled up, followed by the Yard gang, I started to get concerned. Thought one of the heavies had spotted me. So, I headed up the external steps to the roof. You see, in the old days we used to go up there for a fag in the summer, and back then it was easy enough to get up and down through the hatch onto the old fire stairs. Problem was, when I got up there it was locked. Then the fireworks started. And as I was wondering what to do for the best, suddenly the hatch opens. On

330

seeing it was one of the Yard lads, I decided to hit first and ask questions later.'

'How did you manage that? Those guys were basically trained assassins.'

'He had his back to me. Fair to say he wasn't expecting anyone to be up there. Nice little rabbit punch, nicked his gun and Robert's your mother's brother.'

'Nice work. At the very least it put Grantley on edge. He was getting desperate right then.'

Ferry drank more of his beer, clearly conscious of the time.

'You reckon they'll be back for you?' he asked. 'Grantley's bosses I mean. If they think you're still their best route to Devon.'

'Probably. Unless someone else gets to him first.'

'Like who?'

Rowe didn't respond.

'Did Grantley tell you why exactly he was so important to them?' Ferry asked, trying a different tack.

'He said Devon was a domestic terrorist. Responsible for possibly hundreds of deaths, including young families.'

'What? Really? Did he show you anything to back that up?'

'No.'

They fell silent again, as Rowe chose not to elaborate further. He could see Ferry had neared the end of his pint but was clinging to the last dregs like a man in the clutches of a drought.

'There's something more here isn't there, mate.'

Ferry said it with such softness that it caught Rowe by surprise.

'I don't know,' Rowe said after a moment.

'Is it about Laura? You and Grantley were talking about her just before he was shot.'

Rowe breathed in and let his head drop slightly, then spoke after a few seconds.

'I don't think Stanwell killed her. Grantley didn't say it exactly, but he implied it wasn't their move.'

Ferry looked perplexed.

'So…who was it then?'

Rowe didn't respond. His friend seemed to pick up his thoughts.

'You don't think…Devon? No.'

Rowe met Ferry's eyes.

'If Laura hadn't been murdered,' he said quietly, 'would I have pulled a gun on Nick Stanwell? Would I have killed a man I didn't know in cold blood? The answer is no, I wouldn't have.'

'So, you think it was Devon…just to make sure you did what he wanted you to do. You can't believe that can you, mate?'

'I don't know.'

A horn sounded out the front of the pub and several heads turned to look. Rowe could see Angela Ferry in the VW estate, staring straight ahead, as if the pub didn't exist. Ferry didn't turn around, just downed the last drops of his beer hastily and stood up. He extended his hand and Rowe shook it.

'Gotta go. I'll talk to you soon mate. Go careful.'

'See you, Jim. You too.'

43

A FEW HOURS LATER, Rowe emerged from The Bear and Rifle's front door into the darkness of the late evening and the generally silent locality. He walked left out of the car park and kept going for roughly two hundred yards, eventually turning onto a gravel track where his Vitesse sat trustily waiting.

The car had been in its customary spot outside his flat when he had woken up the previous morning – the day after the events at Fenwood police station. Rowe had never returned to the Defender in the car park and knew it would be long gone.

Rowe unlocked the car and climbed into the driver's seat. The jewel case for a Robert Earl Keen CD, *Walking Distance*, lay on the passenger seat and he briefly thought about listening to it for a while. But he wasn't ready for his favourite music yet. Wasn't ready for anything but silence.

He thought about Laura, who had been sitting silently the last time he saw her. Casually arranged on her sofa, as if talking to an old friend - yet with the presence of mind to secretly leave Rowe a voicemail, because she didn't trust the other person in the room. He was now sure that person had not been Nick Stanwell.

There was only one person it could have been.

He rolled the seat back about halfway and shifted his position to get comfortable. He hoped the beer he had consumed would send him to sleep.

He hoped he wouldn't dream of Laura, or that if he did, he wouldn't remember it in the morning. The numbness that had cloaked his soul since she had died was gradually dissipating, and a monstrous, inhuman grief was waiting to take its inevitable turn. Tomorrow felt like an unforgiving concept.

Mike Rowe closed his eyes.

ACKNOWLEDGEMENTS

This book is completely fictional, and any resemblance to real people, places or situations will be purely coincidental. The only exception being the music referenced, which is 100% real. All examples of procedure, protocol, ranks and roles were gleaned from the internet, therefore any gaps or errors in these merely reflect a lack of competence and/or thoroughness in my research.

I would first like to thank Lynne Jackson, who edited the first third of the book before she sadly passed away while dealing with cancer. Lynne's cousin and my friend Chris Smith (*Three Wives & The Truth*) had recommended her services, and I am extremely grateful for the time and effort she put in to working on my book whilst coping with her treatment. Her patience with my use of commas was, frankly, saintly. I completed the editing job myself with Lynne's clear foundations as a guide.

Thanks also to my mum Kay, who had already proofread the first draft of this book before the editing process began - which is about as stern a test of its grammatical and narrative robustness as would be possible to find. My brother Ed also cast an eye over the book and gave surprisingly positive (for an older brother) feedback.

Thanks to the literary agents who took the time to read part of *Outside The Light* before deciding it wasn't for them. I realise old school crime thrillers maybe aren't what's hot right now, and the free time afforded to some in the pandemic probably spawned a lot of them. The truth is, I am a musician moonlighting as a fiction writer – perhaps it shows.

Lastly, thank you to everyone who has made it far enough to read these notes. I always thought writing an entire book would be beyond me, so I'm not quite sure where this came from. Ultimately, I'm just grateful I was able to complete the long processes of first getting it all down, then ensuring it made sense, and then getting it out there for you to read.

I do have ideas for more writing, but not enough of the vast amount of time it requires currently. So, as fun as this has been, don't hold your breath for the next one.

Ags Connolly
2024

Printed in Great Britain
by Amazon

47322598R00188